BEH
WA

Georgina Andrewes was born in 1959 in Winchester, Hampshire. She read Natural Sciences and took a Postgraduate Certificate of Education at Cambridge University and then worked for two years with VSO in Kenya teaching Science and Maths in a community school. She now works as a producer for the African service of the BBC. This is her first novel.

BEHIND THE WATERFALL

Georgina Andrewes

PANDORA

LONDON SYDNEY WELLINGTON

First published in Great Britain by Pandora Press, an imprint of the Trade Division of Unwin Hyman Limited, in 1988.

First published in paperback by Pandora Press in 1989.

Pandora Press
Unwin Hyman Limited
15–17 Broadwick Street, London W1V 1FP

Allen and Unwin Australia Pty Ltd
8 Napier Street, North Sydney, NSW 2060, Australia

Allen and Unwin New Zealand Pty Ltd with the Port Nicholson Press
Compusales Building, 75 Ghuznee Street, Wellington, New Zealand

---

British Library Cataloguing in Publication Data

Andrewes, Georgina
Behind the Waterfall.
I. Title
823'.914 [F]

ISBN 0-04-440353-4

Set in 10 on 11 point Bembo by Computape (Pickering) Ltd, Pickering, North Yorkshire and printed in Finland by Werner Söderström Oy

For Danny
and in memory of Mike Blake

With thanks to
Sarah Baylis, Barney Bardsley,
Melissa Benn and Lesley Thomson
of my Writers Group

CHAPTER ONE

The sound of men outside a house at night is not unlike the sound of donkeys. Jo, alone in her home in the African bush, reading by the smoky light of a hurricane lamp, heard donkeys brushing through the thorn hedge. Lazily, knowing that she wouldn't, she thought she should get up from the bed, put something on and run out beating a saucepan to scare them away. They destroyed the vegetables and nibbled the small pink flowers that were the only colour in her garden. She propped herself up on her elbows to listen for their huffing but there was silence again; just the charged hum of cicadas and the distant tumble of the river. She closed her book and craned her head back until she could feel the soft mass of her hair brushing between her naked shoulder blades. It felt good to ease the ache in her neck that came from working all day. They'd been dragging sandbags into the river to divert a channel for the new water pump – it was to be put in the following day and then there would be piped water in the village. Jo looked down to the curve of her white breasts and her sun-darkened arms; then she flexed the muscles just to prove that she could force herself to move despite the aching exhaustion. The donkeys didn't really matter, when there was water she'd be able to grow more vegetables. She turned on her back, wound down the wick of the paraffin lamp and closed her eyes. Relaxed on the hard comfort of the rubber-thonged bed she slept for a second or two and then remembering that she hadn't heard the news, flicked on the radio and fell asleep to the broadcast from London.

Silently, when the light from the house went out, the three men levered the panes of glass from the louvred window. Two of them climbed in and the third remained on guard, crouching in the shadow of the doorway. There was a bright moon making the garden look cold although the air was warm. A he-goat tethered to a post watched the man on the doorstep. A small snake slipped through the sand and disappeared under the corrugated iron side of the latrine, but the man didn't see it. His eyes were fixed on the track above the house, glancing only from time to time towards the far corner of the compound where the night watchman slept, drunk on honey beer, his torch and bow and arrows taken from him. The man clenched his panga, a large knife with a curved end to the blade, and listened for sounds from within the house. He thought they should have got to the woman by now but there had been no cry, no voices, no noise of a scuffle – had Maluki slit her throat as he had sworn? The man began to sweat, a bird-call if anyone comes, he rubbed his groin and shifted his thick-nailed toes to the edge of the step.

The two armed men moved swiftly through the house, barefoot on the stone floor they made no noise. The door to the bedroom was closed but not locked. They were tense and sweating as they pushed it open and raising their knives, stepped towards the sleeping woman.

Jo opened her eyes to the blinding beam of a watchman's torch and thought she had only dozed for a second, that she had not been asleep at all but had been listening to the news.

'You make noise I will kill you.'

In the glare of the light she couldn't see the face of the man who spoke but she felt a hard blade pressing flat on her neckbone and knew at once he was to be believed.

They hauled her from the bed and as she tried to break away, just to get the cloth from the chair to cover her body, they started kicking her and pushed her into the corner of the room. The walls were cold, the geckoes shot across them and cockroaches scurried in the dirt. One of the men tried to turn off the radio but he flicked the wrong switch and the newsreader's calm voice was replaced by a high-pitched off-channel whining.

'Where's the money?'

'I haven't got any.'

'You are cheating me. Where is it?'

No words came. He put a hand to her throat and banged her head on the wall and punched her stomach so that she gasped with the sudden dull swell of pain and collapsed to the floor. The other man was pulling the bed apart; he ripped the pillow from its case and hurled it at her, he tugged back the sheets and turned over the mattress but there was nothing there. The rough man pulled her up by the hair and flung her again to the floor. It was dirty with the sandy earth of the hills. He heaved up the mattress and began to slash it with his panga and she heard a twang as the blade slipped and bounced off the rubber thongs of the frame.

Jo let them tie her up. It sounded pathetic when she told people afterwards, but she didn't say how they'd slashed the bed so that the rubber thongs hung like ribbons of flesh. She was calm when she described what had happened, not knowing that calmness would be taken for acceptance. She was outwardly calm when the magistrate suggested she'd wanted it and the doctor supposed she'd enjoyed it. If she'd shouted at them or burst into tears they would have smiled with kindly indulgence. She tried not to flinch as the man kicked her and pushed his hands hard across her breasts. A moment when anything could happen – she hated herself when she described it later, when she explained it as if there'd been a sequence, a logic to the actions, as if in some way it was right. But there was no knowing. No pattern in this. She trembled, she was alone and no one was going to come.

'I want to fuck a white woman.'

'I've got a husband.' She closed her eyes as she spoke, not wanting to look at the man before he hurt her in case it fuelled his violence. Pain borne in darkness is different, dissipated in a mind that has no limits – he kicked her again and again with the hard flat of his foot until she could no longer stand the torment and screamed out and turned.

I let them tie me up because I didn't want to get hurt, is what she said, ashamed of the sores on her wrists where the rope had rubbed away skin. She should have explained that she'd remained strong inside, that the wounds said nothing, they were just marks on the surface and inside she was still tough. No one seemed to realise that.

'Why didn't you scream?'

She couldn't explain how the touch of the blade had choked back her screams.

'Didn't you try to bite or scratch?'

It was hard to describe her fear, how it was dense and suffocating and stopped her from fighting.

'So they didn't hurt you?'

'No, I was lucky.'

'Sounds like you were very lucky.'

Lucky – to be beaten and raped and left alive? So many times she was forced to express this gratitude.

Moonlight was coming through the thin stained curtains but the man had turned off the torch and the room seemed dark and unfamiliar. The house had been taken and was no longer hers. Jo was forced into the corner again, with her neck stretched up against the knife. The open door was only a few feet away but the distance seemed impossibly far and she knelt motionless, willing the great outdoors to burst in and free her. No one knew what was being done to her, if she died no one would ever know of her terror.

'Where's the money?'

Only the knife touched her body now, it was money not sex they wanted.

'Over there. In the cupboard.'

He started rummaging through the small pile of clothes and coloured cloths, thrusting them to the back of the cupboard.

'Where? This?'

'No. The bottom shelf.'

He was rifling through her papers – the untidy heap of unanswered letters and the water-stained plans for the pump. He was nervous and paid no attention to her answers but went on throwing things out more frantically, becoming angry and ridiculous.

'Is this it?'

'Yes. There. In the envelope.'

He snatched up the small brown envelope that contained the money for the water pump and hurriedly the two men left the room.

Jo remained shaking in the corner. She couldn't hear sounds from the room next door but knew they were still in the house moving around looking for things to take. What was there worth stealing? A stool perhaps, the cooking pots or a few coloured pictures from the wall.

She didn't expect the man to suddenly reappear, and yet was not surprised that he did. He forced her onto the flayed bed and she did nothing to resist, she was beyond caring, beyond hoping for anything other than to be left alive. She lay on her back, motionless on her bound arms, and stared at him.

'I'm going to fuck you.'

The word 'fuck' sounded strange coming from him and for a moment she let herself believe he didn't mean it.

'Will you like that? Do you want me to fuck you? What will your husband say? Does he like you to be fucked by a black man?' He was excited by his words.

'Will he like me? To take his white woman?'

'He'll kill you if you do.' She chose the words with care and momentarily he was stunned.

'Where is he?'

'Not far.'

'How will he know me? You don't know me.'

'I do. I've seen you.'

'All black men look the same to you.'

He put the point of the knife to her stomach.

'Do you want me to fuck you? Do you?' he said again brutally.

She had to answer. 'No.'

Then, when he put down his knife on the stool beside the bed, she knew he'd heard the tremble in her voice and that it was going to happen. She lay as if dead, passive and limp, not resisting as he thrust up her legs, but in her head she fought and bit and slashed him with the knife. As his excitement mounted he pushed his tongue into her mouth and she tasted his slobber and smelt his sweat. She forced herself to stare at his straining face, to learn it, capture it.

He moved off her slowly, looking down as he did, and then picked up his knife and walked out of the room. His anger had gone. He'd gone, she was alone. But just as she was beginning to shake with relief he reappeared at the doorway drinking the boiled milk from the small handleless pan she'd left on the stove. He came towards her again.

'Shall I pour milk over you?' he asked, taunting.

Jo just stared, beaten.

'And then fuck you again?'

He tilted the pan above the hollow of her naked stomach and she gave up trying to keep the fear from her eyes. It didn't really matter now, what he did.

'Turn over.'

'No.' She loathed him.

'Do you want me to untie you?'

Jo hesitated, not knowing what to think, unsure if he'd had enough. She turned on her stomach and held her wrists high above her back.

As he cut through the rope that bound her hands the knife nicked her skin. Sharp without pain.

Then, just before he left he took a hundred shilling note out of the stolen money and put it on the stool.

'This is for you.'

As soon as he'd gone she struggled from the bed and stood for a moment in the middle of the room, listening, but was confused and didn't know what to do. She shut the bedroom door and tried to lock it but her hand was trembling and she couldn't get the key in the hole. She tried to steady herself but it got worse, the end of the key hitting either side of the slot. Then she realised that she couldn't stay there locked in her bedroom until daylight so she turned to the chair to pick up her cloth to cover her body. It was gone. Hurriedly she dragged on a t-shirt and wound the sheet from the bed around herself, too shaken to remember that there was another cloth she could have taken from the cupboard.

The main door was locked and the key had been taken, so she climbed through the window where the panes had been removed. Terrified of the space around her she looked only straight ahead at the far-away house as she sprinted through the scrub, cutting her bare feet on the sharp rocks and thorns, feeling that at any moment she was about to be jumped on, knocked down, beaten and raped again. When she reached the house at the top of the slope she flung herself against it, pounding on the door.

'Help. Wake up. Let me in.' She glanced over her shoulder and pressed herself closer to the wall. There were the slow sounds of people stirring within. Then Jerusa opened the door.

CHAPTER TWO

Jo woke in a single bed with two other people. They'd hardly shifted in the night; she was pressed against the rough mud wall, Jerusa lay curled close with her legs drawn up to her body and Museo was clasped tightly behind. For a fraction of a second, in the panic of waking in this unfamiliar place, Jo couldn't recall how she'd come to be there. Then it flashed back.

'I'll wake the men. Stay here.'

Jerusa had run out into the compound, past the kitchen hut to the square house with the iron roof where her mother and father and the younger children slept. Jo was left standing alone. She heard shouting and banging on the doors, one of the women cried out, a dog started barking. Then a man appeared with a torch. She backed away from the door to the shadows at the edge of the room as the light went by.

Silence outside. She looked around the room; it was a place she was familiar with; narrow with a mud floor and one small window that was tightly shuttered. She could just make out the shape of the radio under its crocheted cover, the patterned gourd hanging on the wall and a plate on the table. There was still the damp mealy smell of the maize 'ugali' that had been eaten for supper. Jo often came here to share a meal with Jerusa and her mother and the children. Now she stood shivering against the wall. She felt a sticky dribble of semen run between her legs and wanted to wash – in a white-tiled basin, with warm water and a soft flannel. To climb into smooth clean sheets and feel the hand of her mother on her forehead. To cut out the world beneath heavy blankets.

Jerusa hadn't returned. Jo heard a movement in the room closeby and thought she saw the shadow of a man in the doorway to the bedroom. She froze, her pulse began to race. Again she heard a noise but staring into the dark space of the doorway that led from the 'table' room to the narrow bedroom behind saw only blackness. Then she made out the small figure of a child pressed against the wall. It was Museo, Jerusa's daughter, a girl of about nine or ten.

'Museo? Habari?' She greeted her with relief.

'Nzuri,' the girl replied and came into the room.

She lit a small paraffin lamp made from an old margarine tin and put it on the table. It spluttered and sent up dirty twists of smoke as it began to burn.

'Sit,' the girl said.

She fetched a cloth from the bedroom and put it around Jo's shoulders.

'What has happened?'

'Nothing, it's alright.'

'Are you hurt?'

'No. No.'

Museo opened the door of the rickety food safe and took out a pan of milk and a small paper bag of sugar. She was a tall girl with long limbs. It seemed that her head was big, but only because her body was narrow and her hair shaved short.

Jo took the small tin cup of sweetened milk and held it on her lap between both hands – it was still slightly warm from the fire and smelt of the cow – she couldn't bear to raise the thick white liquid to her lips. They sat in silence on the broken sofa and stared at the wall, watching the shadows of smoke spiralling upwards.

She couldn't believe it had happened, couldn't believe it was over.

'Some men came to my house to steal.'

'Yes.'

Museo answered as if she knew she were meant to understand, struggling to reach beyond the bounds of her own experience, beyond a child's half-knowing.

'But they've gone now,' Jo said, 'It's alright.'

There was a sudden swell of sound in the compound outside; noises of exclamation, people moving quickly. Jo looked out through the open door. Ben Kyalo was standing beneath the mango tree, holding up a hurricane lamp and other men were gathering round. They had knives and sticks and pangas. Ben Kyalo spoke, there was mumbling and movement amongst the crowd, torches were raised. Then from a distant part of the compound a woman cried out – a long throbbing ululation. It was taken up by another and another, when one ceased the next seemed to catch the call and carry it on. The men moved off, led by those with torches, but the wail went on, echoing out and around, along the ridge top and down across the valley.

'What's happening?'

Jerusa had returned with some of the women. There was conversation in Kikamba that Jo didn't understand, more and more people seemed to be crowding into the room.

'Jerusa, what's happening?'

'The men have gone to chase the criminals.'

'What's the noise?'

'They're calling out to warn, for people to wake and look out.'

Jerusa pulled on a cardigan and picked up her panga.

'Where are you going?'

'Down to your house to make safe your things.'

'I'll come with you.'

'No. Stay here, you must rest.'

'You can't go alone.'

'It's fine. Mother will come with me.'

Jo sat on the edge of the sofa chipping bits of enamel off the mug as the women gathered around in the dim shadows at the edge of the room. No one spoke to her. What were they waiting for, for her to wail and cry? She didn't know. She longed for one of them to come close, to hug her in their arms so that she could lower her head against their bosom.

Oh mother, mother, hide me from the world.

The sob surged within her, just a hand on hers and she could have cried.

But the silence seemed heavy with suspicion. More people gathered in the shadows. Did they blame her for what had happened? For waking their children in the night, for bringing distress to their home? She felt a dull, empty ache – all the struggles and friendships shifting to another pattern, of unbelonging, of being an outsider again. And she knew then that true belonging is where there's no restraint, where understanding is without doubt, without question.

Jo sipped the milk and felt sick.

When the men returned to the compound the women rushed out to greet them, and the babies bundled on their mothers' backs began to cry with the disturbance. Jerusa had reappeared with a pile of blankets and saucepans. She was slightly out of breath and spoke in gasps as she unloaded the things and stacked them in the corner.

'The cooker was taken and the food, there was nothing left in the cupboards.'

Jo didn't care.

'But I found the teapot and the lamp.' Jerusa took the hurricane lamp and green enamel teapot out of one of the blankets and put them on the table. 'They tried to take the gas cylinder, but it must have been too heavy and they dropped it on the track. Mother has carried it here.'

A small collection of salvaged belongings.

'Thank you. I'm sorry about all the fuss – waking everyone up. Can you explain I'm sorry?' Jo looked around and smiled. 'Jerusa, I'm going to cry.'

Jerusa's father, Ben Kyalo, was fully dressed in the clothes he always wore; trousers that had been mended and re-mended with zig-zagged patches, the purple nylon shirt with a zip at the neck and the dark jacket that had once belonged to a suit. His hat was pulled low on his forehead, pushing down the old folded skin of his face. He came in and spoke to Jo.

'You must return back to your house to show what happened.'

She went blank.

'She can't go now,' Jerusa said, 'She's been hurt.'

'We must know what happened.'

'It can wait till tomorrow.'

'It's OK, I'll go.' Jo said.

She put the cup on the floor and stood up, but Jerusa grabbed her arm.

'You can't go back to that place. It's too much. You must sleep.' She turned to her father. 'She must sleep now. Send these people away and let us sleep. It can wait till the morning now.'

The old man ordered the women back to bed and as they left Ruth came close and touched Jo's hair. She was a shy and silent woman, often apart from the others, whom Jo had never felt at ease with. Ben Kyalo shouted at her and she hurried out.

Only the grandmother remained, she was standing by the door close to the hanging gourd, muttering to herself. Her cloth was knotted across one shoulder in the old-fashioned way, and one of her breasts hung loose. No one ever paid her much attention; she was old and the children said they couldn't understand her because she used the ancient Kikamba words that had long ago passed out of the language.

'What's she saying?' Jo asked.

'She's speaking nonsense.'

'Can you understand?'

'It's just nonsense. She says it's witchcraft!'

Jerusa turned to her grandmother and ushered her out of the room clapping her hands as she did with the chickens that strayed inside to scrat for maize. But the old woman turned as she left and lifted a hand as if the last ounce of energy were given to her assertion. Then she went away across the earthy compound still muttering and murmuring to herself.

Jerusa lit the hurricane lamp and gave the paraffin burner to Museo, 'Go and fetch water,' she ordered her. 'You can wash and sleep,' she said to Jo.

'But what's happening now?'

'Some men are still guarding your house, the others have gone home.'

'Did they find anyone?'

'No, some of the men crossed the river. There was an old man down there who'd seen people running past his compound with things in their arms. But they went into the forest and it's not safe to follow there.'

'What happened to the watchman?'

'They found him drunk.'

'He wasn't hurt?'

'No, just drunk, he should never have been given that job, that man is too lazy.'

'They took the keys to the house and said they'd be back again.'

'Don't worry, they won't come back tonight. Everyone's alert now, they've all heard.'

The crying in the hills had ceased, the last echo must have drifted down to the riverbed and softly disappeared. Jo was overwhelmed with a sense of shame – all privacy gone, her distress had been cried across the valleys and into the hills. And tomorrow, what of the talk that she wouldn't understand, the whispers in the market-place, the looks, the fear? This was what it was to be alone. The tears began to flood. The scenes repeated; she saw her pathetic submission as he tilted the pan of milk above her naked stomach. And she yearned for Rick, miles away in England, for the man who'd comforted her before in times of sadness, who didn't mind her eyes red and swollen, nor her body ugly and crumpled. She could have told him about the milk, the taunting and humiliation. He would have waited, soothing, until there was no more sadness in her, and then she could have slept curled into his kind warm arms.

'Don't cry. Don't cry.' Jerusa held her hand. 'Are you hurt?'

'No, I'm alright.'

'But there's blood.'

'I'm OK.' She clung to Jerusa's neck. 'I'm sorry, I can't stop crying.'

'It will be better when it's morning.'

Museo returned with an empty bucket.

'There's no water.'

'What about grandmother, she has plenty?'

'She refused me, she said the evil spirits would enter her water jar.'

'That woman is a fool, go there and take some – silently.'

In a corner of the room Jo took off her t-shirt and screwed it up to wipe between her legs, not caring that Jerusa might think it dirty that she did so, then she splashed herself over and over with handfuls of cold water.

'I think you can wear this.' Jerusa had pulled a garment out of a drawer in the dilapidated chest. Jo almost laughed; it was a red slip with black lace, short and sexy. For the husband in Mombasa, Museo's father, or someone else, a lover perhaps? Jo took it from her and slipped it over her head. It was made of nylon and coarse lace, and the frill was rough against her legs.

'Where shall I sleep?'

'There's only one bed.'

Of course, how foolish to have hoped to sleep alone, they would sleep three to the narrow bed; a mother, her child and a woman who'd been raped. She climbed in and moved to one side. She thought of Museo in her outgrown dresses with her long bony legs, how she carried the other children on her hips as if she were already a woman, the ease with which she swung a baby onto her back, the patience with which she sat on a sack in the sun shelling maize with the older women. It was only when Museo visited her house that Jo saw her as a child; picking up a coloured pen with excited grasp, waiting to be told she could try it, laughing when it worked. Now they were together in a bed, hard and uncomfortable, Jo moved closer to the edge so there was more room behind. It was a wooden bed like hers, strung with strips of rubber and sisal, but it didn't have a mattress and where Jo lay the rush matting had slipped so that her leg rested on a row of bent-over nails. She leant her head on her outstretched arm and smelt the sweat of the man on her skin. Behind her Jerusa was murmuring to Museo, answering her questions, telling her to sleep. Jo listened to the gentle words and, longing to be part of their closeness, began to cry again. She cried gently without noise, letting the tears run down between her cheek and arm until she felt Jerusa stroking the palm of her hand over and over her shoulder, rocking her gently backwards and forwards. Then she'd put up her hand and held her friend's fingers tight.

Now in the early hours of the morning as animals began to sound across the valley and the first women made their way to the river, a crack of light came through the wall. Jerusa, her body warm and soft and eased by deep sleep, shifted dreamily against her, pushing Jo closer to the jutting sticks in the wall and burying her head close so that the hard oiled plaits rubbed against Jo's back.

Jo opened her eyes to the dark mud wall and listened to the noises outside. She thought of Isaiah, the mornings they spent together, his hard-muscled body stirring and pulling her onto him. That was what she loved; to push back the sheet and look at him, sprawled out on its whiteness, the dusty sunlight playing on him. Hot. Trickling water on her back, blowing, licking it up. Licking deeper. And outside the sound of children on their way to school. She could get to Nairobi in a day, find him, tell him.

The wind had brought a chill to the room and Jerusa drew the blanket away so that the frayed edge slipped over Jo's shoulder. Her front, close to the wall, was now exposed and cold and she wondered whether to reclaim her piece of the cover and curl her legs up into the short nylon slip and tuck the blanket under her so that it couldn't be taken again. But she remained lined to the wall, cold and rigid, beyond caring about comfort and slept again, fitfully, ill at ease with the coming dawn.

With the wind the men had entered her house again, she screamed as they attacked but the sound of her voice was drowned in the roar of the storm. The house was wide open, the bright blue painted doors swinging back and forth, the curtains flying out. They'd returned with others, she thought she saw Isaiah coming towards her with a panga in his hand, but when she tried to look he turned his face away. They were ripping the curtains from the strings above the windows and kicking over the furniture, flashing the torch around the room. She called out his name, 'Isaiah!' but when he turned it was Rick's face she saw.

CHAPTER THREE

'Africa? When?' Rick asked, 'I mean how soon? When did you decide all this?'

He looked at her in disbelief. His eyes had misted over and he seemed to be trembling slightly. 'Josie, you can't leave me – not after all these years.'

It was almost five years since they'd shared a cab back from a party, and she'd come in for a cup of coffee – faking innocence to mask her desire. She'd seen the piano and persuaded him to play and had sat on the floor with her back against the wall and her knees hugged up to her chest feeling a glow of admiration. The room was long with the piano at one end – she summed it up as he played; not many books but stacks of old records, a ceramic pot of dried flowers, a bust of Beethoven, an old wind-up phonograph in the corner and modern paintings on the walls. There was nothing careless about anything, these were possessions that spoke of a confident, discerning person. Hand-printed curtains, a deep armchair and an old red rug where a cat was sleeping. On the wall above the stereo was a black and white photograph of the trunk of a tree, it had been taken at an angle looking up to the branches against the sky, and beside it was another photo, of a cathedral taken at the same angle. She'd felt a sudden urge to rebel against the order of the room and as if to test him had dragged a cushion from the chair and sprawled out on the floor, playing her body back into the music, seducing him as he was her.

'I've got to go – I've signed the contract. But it's only for a couple of years.'

'Two years! You didn't even tell me you were applying.'

'I did, you've forgotten.'

He closed his eyes and leant his head against the pillow.

'Where are you going then?'

'Kenya – to a rural area to work on a water project with a Women's Group. It's a good job.'

'And you're going to be in charge?'

'And doing other things, maybe a bit of teaching, starting a tree nursery, that sort of thing.'

'I suppose it's just what you want.'

He was now staring out of the window.

'Do you remember when you first came here?'

'Not really – it was so long ago.' She lied, remembering vividly, everything, the tremble, the desire – and saw the sting, the quiver of his lips. 'But I remember you playing the piano to me, I wanted to turn the pages over but I knew I couldn't read the music.'

'I kept making mistakes, I was so nervous, I just longed to make love to you, I didn't know what to do.'

These were the stories they'd told time and again to each other, always slightly different, re-inventing, re-interpreting each detail, each feeling, and in so doing affirming their love, saying that this would always be there, this beginning. She had a flash of how he'd seemed to her then; self-assured and brilliant.

'Josie, you can't leave me just like this, I love you so much.' There were tears in his eyes. 'You're not really going are you?'

She wanted to hug him and say no, it was only a wild idea, she'd just got restless, there was nothing more important than being with him. But she'd been with him for five precious years of her life – his life, their life – and it was no good, the binding passion had died. Her love for him was something different now.

'We've got to move on,' she said, 'It's no use putting up with things that aren't quite right.'

'But life's never perfect, it doesn't mean you should destroy what we've got. You can't do that.'

'It's just I've got too much energy – I want to do something – I've had enough of being comfortable, I need a challenge.'

He'd closed his eyes again. They were still lying in bed, ten o'clock on a Sunday morning, a tray of breakfast things on the floor beside them.

'It's not easy for me either,' she said, 'I just know it's the right thing to do now, before I get stuck in some dull academic job that makes me grey and serious.'

She hadn't meant to sound defensive, she'd worked it out so many times; she would be confident, she'd got to be honest about this, life had become boring, there were too many things she wanted to do that he wasn't interested in so she was going to go off and try them by herself. It didn't mean that everything had to end, they'd just take a break, do different things, then who knows, maybe or maybe not they'd get back together again, at least they'd be certain about it. How logical she'd been with only herself to reason with.

'So what am I supposed to say? "Great, that's what I've always wanted, you to go off and leave me here alone."'

He gazed at the ceiling for a long time so she couldn't tell if his mind was empty or grappling with something he couldn't express.

'I'm sorry,' she said, 'I don't want to leave you but I've got to do it.' A plea for absolution, a shallow hope that he might understand and think it right.

'Why didn't you tell me before? I thought you were happy here.'

'I am. I can't explain. I just wanted it to be all sorted out so there'd be no going back.'

'But surely it's got to do with me as well.'

'No, it's my life. I've got to make my own decisions.'

Hard cold words, hoping that he would hate her for them. But he just looked hopeless.

'What am I going to do?' He gestured feebly round the room. 'What's the point of anything any more?'

'You should take that teaching job in the States,' she said, 'Then we wouldn't be leaving each other, just doing something different for a while.'

'But you know I don't want to. I'm happy here. Anyway I wouldn't go without you.'

'Why not? You should go – take the chance while it's there. Take a risk.'

He held her forearm.

'There'd be no point without you.'

'That's not true,' she tried to shake him off, 'We've been through this before. It's just comfortable together, it's crazy to pretend.'

'I'm not pretending.'

If only it had been some other breach of trust, a love affair perhaps, then she could have expressed regret and sought forgiveness. There could have been a reconciliation. But now all that seemed to loom ahead was months of sad and angry talk, her explanations not understood, her feelings not believed. She should have told him later, at any time but now, first thing on a Sunday morning with all the day ahead. She'd been waiting for the right moment; a pause, a lull, a slight annoyance, anything that could convincingly precede the declaration. But the time was never right and she'd blurted it out when she didn't mean to, in the middle of making love.

'*I'm going to work in Africa.*'

Only a minute before she'd been stroking his stomach and he'd been kissing her ear – she'd never forget it, the thud of that ordinary moment rendered ridiculous.

'You're just running away aren't you?' he said, 'You're the one who's the coward.'

She looked up at him, furious.

'I'm not running away. It's what I want to do. Why don't you ever understand anything?'

It was sunny outside with Spring birds singing and the park was full of slow afternoon walkers. Rick paced along with their friends' child slung high on his shoulders, chattering to him as if he were his own. He was a tall man, loose-limbed, always dressed in easy well-worn clothes which made him seem relaxed and confident. Watching him striding through the park with the child on his shoulders, kicking its heels against the familiar black jacket, Jo was stirred with an old admiration. He looked such an open person, the sort of man you'd expect to have lots of friends. How wrong had been her first impressions. He didn't like people much, they didn't interest him in the way they did her. He was happy with just a few others in his life; just Josie, the friends he knew well and the kids at school. He chased the child round and round a tree, this way and that, until the small boy was bursting with laughter.

When they were exhausted they sat on a bank next to a clump of purple crocuses and ate ice creams with chocolate flakes.

I've come to the end, Jo thought. Soon all this will be for the last time. Sunday. London. Spring. England. Suddenly these intangible things had immeasurable value. She watched a duck preening itself on the bank of the river, the patches of sun on the water, a fragile shudder of the breeze through the willows.

'OK. Home for tea.' Rick said, 'Let's buy some biscuits.'

They got up from the damp muddy bank, and went on, running and swinging the child between them. And when the little boy stopped to pick up sticks she clasped Rick's hand possessively.

It was a moment of emptiness, at home alone again. Rick turned on the television and settled down in front of it with the packet of biscuits. She followed him into the front room and lay on the floor reading the paper without taking in the meaning of the words.

It didn't seem long since she'd sat, back against the wall, feeling the floor hard on her bones, loving him with that first passion. Nothing had changed, the tall ceramic vase still with its dried flowers, the bust of the composer that he'd had as a child, the blue-horned phonograph, the photos that had intrigued her. But now she had no expectations, no curiosity about the man to whom these things were precious. She wondered why comfort disturbed her so much and cosiness made her panic, why she resented being part of a home. It wasn't that she didn't appreciate the beautiful things with which he chose to surround himself, but they never changed, year after year the same things in the same places, their very beauty and constancy surrounding them both like a screen, cutting out the unpredictability of life. And with time she'd felt the screen grow stronger, keeping back the world about which she cared so much.

She stared at his face, the face she still found attractive, to capture it and know it for ever, so that if memory cheated her and let it fade she'd be able to think of this moment and call it back. The long blue curtains were slightly ajar letting in the reddish glow of the warming street light, there were people passing along the pavement. The Sunday papers ringed with marks of coffee cups were strewn about the floor, the half-eaten packet of chocolate biscuits on the table. He'd fallen asleep stretched out in the chair. His belt hung loose across his hips, there was mud on his trousers from the park, a hole in the ironed checked shirt – he always ironed his shirts, even the very oldest.

'I'm a failure.'

'No you're not.' She laughed.

'I am. You know I am. If I were any good I wouldn't still be teaching lousy secondary school students.'

'Rick, you are good. You know you are, everyone says so. And you're a great teacher.'

'I don't want to be a teacher. I want to play.'

'Well, play then, no one's stopping you. You're always being asked to perform.'

'I know what it takes and I haven't got it.'

'Don't be stupid – you're talented. Why don't you just decide to believe it?'

'How can I? It's obvious I'm not cut out to be successful.'

'Of course you are, it just takes time.'

'But it never changes does it? I always think, well, next year I'll be better, next year I'll really do something. Then next year comes and I haven't and it's all just the same.'

She stared, willing him to wake up and catch her eye, but he was far away, twitching like a cat. So relaxed. Home, his world, her, utterly perfect. It was enough for him.

'You've been staring at me! Come here and let me give you a cuddle.'

She went over to him and sat on the arm of the chair. He pulled her down onto his lap.

'Don't go, Josie. Think of everything we've got here, everything we've built up together. You mustn't just chuck it all away.'

She let him hold her hand. He was stroking her fingers as he spoke.

'I understand about being bored. I know you're clever and energetic. But there are other things you can do. You don't have to go all the way to Africa. Maybe it seems important now – but it won't be what you think. No one there's going to thank you for giving up things in England. Of course you'll do a good job and have new experiences, but what about your life here, all your friends and family?' He was squeezing her fingers hard. 'Human relationships are far more important than experiences. You know that in the end it's people that really count.'

'It's only for two years, I'll be back.'

'And then what will you do? Start all over again? You're just leaving because you're frightened of letting things work.'

'I'm not frightened.'

'You are, you're frightened of struggling to make our friendship work. You're only safe when things are difficult, because then there's nothing to lose. Just be honest with yourself. And you may come back and find there isn't room for you any more. People aren't going to hang around waiting forever.'

'I don't want you to wait for me.'

'But don't you see, you're not just chucking me away – it's everything, Josie, when you come back things will be different here, two years will have gone by that you won't have been part of. People will have changed, got married, gone away. You'll be left behind. You won't belong any more.'

'Maybe you're right, but I've had enough of your lecture.' She got off his lap. 'I'm going outside to finish the garden.'

'It's almost dark.'

'That's my look-out.'

He followed her to the door and shouted. 'Damn you. You're a selfish bitch. All you ever think about is yourself the whole time. What about us, the rest of us, left here while you're away? Oh no, we don't matter. We're good for a nice safe easy life while you need it and then when you've had enough we're finished with. Dumped.

To hell with you! You go off to bloody Africa! And I hope you rot there.'

He slammed the door.

She tore the brambles out of the hedge, crying through the mud and thorns. On and on, the back and forth of truth and lies, over and over again, until piece by jagged piece the hopes and fears were revealed, the bitterness and kindness exposed. And in so doing they'd come to love each other more.

She worked until she was exhausted, clearing the length of the border, pulling up the weeds and dandelions and hurting her hands as she tugged on the roots of thistle and creeping buttercup. When it was dark she came in and washed her face and scrubbed her hands at the kitchen sink. Rick was playing the piano in the room next door. He'd made some salad and put out a plate for her with a slice of bread and cheese and a handful of nuts. She sat down and ate, surrounded by him, his sad music coming through the wall, his things around about; the china with bright orange flowers and green and yellow rims that he'd picked up in the market, the kitchen gadgets, the jars of herbs and spices arranged on the rack he'd made last winter, the string of garlic brought back from France, and the black and white photos of jazz musicians. Conspiratorially the cat came and twirled its soft black body around her ankles. She opened the fridge and got out its food, glad to have something to do. How many more times will I put out the food for the cat? she wondered. Twenty? Thirty? And then it will be the last time and I'll give it a final hug goodbye and that will be that. Perhaps it was all quite unimportant, the coming and going, the loving, the living and dying of people in the world. And if it were, did that mean she should stay? Settle down here, be content with everything that was good?

She heard the music stop. Rick came in and put the kettle on.

'I'm sorry about what I said.'

'I'm sorry too.'

'You haven't told me when you're going.'

'I'm not sure yet.'

'When do you think it'll be?'

'In a couple of months, June, I think.'

'Maybe I'll come and visit you for the next summer holiday.'

'That would be good.'

He made two cups of tea.

'Shall we go next door, or to bed or something?'

'It doesn't really matter where we are does it? I suppose we might as well go to bed, nothing's going to make it any easier.'

Hours later to the sound of birds and the first London buses, as the darkness of night thinned into morning lightness, they made love – violently, pulling and hurting each other – hating themselves for the terrible sadness of this moment, loving each other across a distance never known before.

CHAPTER FOUR

In the last few days before she left, Rick drew her closer to him, speaking more with gestures than with words, burdening her with his need. He kept buying her presents, small things; a pair of earrings, expensive chocolate, and then a book.

'You've already given me a present.'

'No, this is different.'

It was about Africa, a book she might have chosen for herself and as she flicked through the pages, not knowing what to say, she thought: he does know me after all.

'Thanks. Thanks very much.'

'I know you've read her other stuff, but you once mentioned that you hadn't got this one. And I'll be able to think of you reading it by the light of your hurricane lamp.'

'Don't say that,' she wished above all else that he couldn't still stir her heart like this, and felt tears coming to her eyes.

The first night in Africa she had no paraffin for the hurricane lamp. She stumbled around the house lighting matches and jumping back as rats stirred and hurried over the piles of rubble. Then she found a stub of candle attached to the lid of a tin and lit that. It gave out a good light and she could then see quite clearly a large rat crouching in the corner of the room. It frightened her slightly.

'You're only a rat,' she said out loud.

She opened the back door and picking up a broken broomstick from the floor moved towards the motionless creature.

'Get out. Shoo! Out!'

It suddenly shot away, startling her – she hadn't realised that rats could move that fast – and when she'd bolted the door again she felt quite shaken. It must have been the sudden release of tension after the long journey from Nairobi with the sleazy Assistant Chief. Seven hours in and out of that battered old car. Now she felt better, more herself again, in control of things.

The house was quiet and lonely. It was bigger than she'd

expected, yet had a feeling of emptiness rather than space; the grey concrete walls were bare, there were piles of dirt and rubble on the floor and the only piece of furniture was a broken chair without a seat. The air was stale and dusty, she tried to open a window, but the catch had been secured with a piece of wire. She ran a finger through the layer of dust on the window ledge, it was the heavy dust that settles down from building work. *Rick*, she wrote and then blew it off. Odd that it hadn't been cleaned before she arrived.

She dragged her rucksack and the big polythene bag of blankets and cooking equipment into the bedroom. This room was smaller and had a large mattress on the floor with a stool beside it. It was at once apparent that someone else had been living here until quite recently, on the stool was a dirty plastic plate with some food still stuck to it, and a tin with a half-smoked cigarette balanced across the top. Whoever it was must have left in a hurry, forgetting the cigarette which had been carefully stubbed out so that its length was hardly bent. Jo moved the dirty plate and the tin of ash to the floor and put the candle on the stool. The mattress was made of thick foam and still covered with a sheet of protective polythene, she sat down on the edge and watched the candle flame flicker and bend. It hit her then; the emptiness of having arrived. What if she wasn't welcome, what if no one really wanted her here? She picked up the cigarette and held it in the flame till it blackened and began to smoulder, then she took a few puffs and shifted up the mattress so that her back was to the wall.

Dear Rick, dearest Rick, you're right; I've been consigned to the middle of nowhere and am living alone in a filthy house with rats.

One a.m. in Britain, he'd be asleep beneath the duvet, she could see herself there beside him, leaning over to give him a kiss. But there's no going back now, she thought, this is home for the next two years, I'll just have to make the best of it.

The flame was beginning to dip and fade in the last of the melted wax. No point unpacking in darkness into all this dirt, the only thing to do was to go to bed and sleep. She rummaged around in the top of her rucksack, found her toothbrush and a towel and made her way to the bathroom. There was a brand new loo and a shower and basin with hot and cold taps. Dark red cockroaches shot down the plug hole as she approached with the light but they remained within sight, their antennae wavering up at her. She turned on the tap to wash them down – it spun round on its screw. The other one did the same and when she pulled, it came off in her hand. Bending down she found that the outflow pipe ended about a foot above the floor.

She picked up the loo seat, a dry bowl teeming with more cockroaches. She peered down with uneasy fascination. They seemed to be mocking her. It was as if a cruel joke had been played and someone somewhere was watching.

Outside in the cool night air she squatted by the back door and peed into the dry sand. There were a few small stunted flowers at her ankles, and some old tin cans in the rough grass. She stood on the doorstep before going back in, confident now that the Assistant Chief had left her in peace. Her house was half way down a hill and not in the village as she'd imagined, but it was hard to get rid of the detailed picture that she'd built up in her mind, of a home amongst the others, in a circular village with mud and thatch houses. There were no immediate neighbours here but further up towards the top of the slope there were trees and she could just make out the dark outline of some other houses.

It was so quiet, she'd hoped to hear people, perhaps singing or children playing, and to smell the smoke of evening fires, but the night was still and the smell on the air was of grass and the dung of animals. At least there didn't seem to be any mosquitoes. She was about to turn indoors when out of the silence she registered the sound of the cicadas, humming continuously like electric wires. A sudden buzz went through her: *this is Africa, I'm in Africa!*

In Nairobi, Geoff, the Field Director, had briefed them on their projects. There were twelve new workers, all crowded into his small office. Jo had made friends with a woman called Sally whom she'd sat next to on the flight from London. She was a nurse going to work with a small team of doctors in southern Sudan. She'd passed a huge box of chocolates around the plane and then settled down to chat to Jo; she was the sort of person who found out everything within the first few minutes; 'Was that your boyfriend waving?' 'Have you left him then?' They stuck together now, sitting at the back of the group, sizing up the others.

Geoff was dressed in pale khaki trousers and a faded blue shirt with the sleeves rolled up, his arms were dark and he wore a bracelet made of twisted metal. When he left the room Sally nudged Jo's leg,

'What do you reckon to him then?'

'Seems alright.'

'I think he's gorgeous, very sexy!'

He came back in with a tray of coffee.

'Help yourselves.' He sat on the edge of his desk swinging a leg and lit his pipe while they got their coffee. She saw what Sally meant, the casual confidence that made him attractive.

'OK, I'll just run through all the projects to give you some idea of the country and what we're doing out here.'

He stood by the wall pointing to little coloured pins on a map as he described each project. She was going to Ukambani, the area where the Akamba live, in eastern Kenya. She'd looked it up before she left; the Akamba used to live around Mount Kilimanjaro – the Mountain of Whiteness – but at the end of the sixteenth century had migrated across the plains after fighting with the Masai. Ukambani was dry, there were frequent droughts and famines, and towards the end of the eighteenth century the Akamba had emerged as traders, exchanging ivory and brass, arrows, chains, poison, snuff containers, beaded clothes and tools for grain and cattle from the Kikuyu. 'Kuuthua', the name of this trade, meant 'searching for food'.

Geoff stuck a pin near Kizui town.

'It's a dry area,' he said. 'And drought's a frequent problem.'

There weren't many pins in the North and East of the country, most of them seemed to be clumped in the Central Province around Nairobi and in the Western Province near Kisumu on the shores of Lake Victoria and straggling up to the border with Uganda. The people who were going out there had already got to know each other, they were mainly teachers. The rest of them were on their own. There was a big Scottish builder who was going up to Meru, an older woman of about sixty who was a librarian going to work in Turkana, Jack, a metal-worker going to a 'deaf school' in Mombasa, a Dutch vet who was a specialist in tick-borne diseases going to work with the Masai on the border with Tanzania, and Jo. Hundreds of miles from each other, they were unlikely to meet again.

'Well that's where you're all going, now who you are. It's probably a good idea just to introduce ourselves properly – and I guess we'd better kick off with me,' Geoff paused to gather their attention, 'I've been Field Director here for coming up to a year. I'm actually a Kenyan myself, I was born here, but was educated in the UK and I did my doctorate at an American University. I spent about five years in the Far East and then the next six years as an economic adviser in Botswana. Then I returned here. My job is to assess new projects and to keep a check on those that are running. But my main responsibility as far as you're concerned is your welfare. If there's something you're not happy about or if anything goes wrong, whether it's personal, medical or to do with the project, then you should come straight to me.' He twisted the bracelet on his wrist round and round as he spoke, then pulled it off and squeezed it in the palm of his hand. 'You're actually responsible to the heads of project – that's local headteachers in the case of the teachers, the Ministries of Health and Agriculture for doctors, nurses and extension workers and in some cases Chiefs and Assistant Chiefs – but if you're worried about the work and can't sort it out with them then I'll be happy to help. Anyway there'll be plenty of time later on before you go to have a chat and clear up any worries about the details of your projects.'

There was a tension of newness and nervousness amongst the group. He smiled encouragingly, put the bracelet back on and lit his pipe again.

'Can I ask a question?' It was the big Scottish bloke. 'What's all this "mzungu"?'

'It just means white or foreigner. That's what everyone will call you, to start with at any rate.' He smiled again, this time looking at Jo and catching her eye. 'Right. Now perhaps each of you could just say a bit about yourselves, what you were doing before and what project you're going to be working on out here.' His eye roved round the group and came back to her. 'We'll start at the back of the room – Jo?'

She hated this sort of thing, he must have picked on her because he'd sensed her scrutiny of him.

'I'm twenty-four. I've got a degree in Engineering, up till now I've been with a research team at London University. I'm going to be working mainly with women's groups setting up small scale water supplies for the villages.'

She ran out of breath and felt a hot flush of embarrassment come over her as soon as she stopped talking; almost as if she'd lied.

'Thanks. Sally, you were nursing in Newcastle?'

Jo stared at the map dotted with pins and began to decode the colour system; blue for water engineer, red for doctor and nurse, pink for teacher, green for forester and agriculturalist, a few miscellaneous black ones. The country was many times the size of Britain, what possible impact could fifty or sixty coloured pins have?

Jo was the first to leave, the Assistant Chief arrived before the briefing session was over. He was the regional administrator for Kingangi village and had applied to the organisation for a water engineer for small-scale projects. Jo didn't have a chance to ask Geoff more about her work.

'You'd better go,' he said, 'You won't have missed anything. Don't forget your household equipment.'

There were twelve large polythene bags packed with identical equipment for each of the workers, she picked the nearest one with the bright green bucket and said goodbye to the rest of the group. Most of them were travelling together on the night train to Kisumu. Sally and the doctors were flying to the Sudan.

'Cheerio love,' Sally called out, 'Take care.'

Geoff shook her hand.

'See you in a couple of months time for the language course. Good luck. Enjoy yourself.'

She was out on her own now, excited and glad to be going again. She got into the front of the battered car, the Assistant Chief heaved himself into the back and they waited while the driver loaded the luggage onto the roof and roped it down. The Assistant Chief was a small fat man, dressed in a tight blue suit with a fat orange tie, he'd shaken her hand and gone on holding it as he talked although she'd tried to ease away. His face was beaded with drops of sweat and his breath smelt of beer. As the car juddered onto the main road and began to pick up speed he leant forward, squeezing between the two front seats in order to direct the driver, and she wished she'd insisted on sitting in the back.

'How far is it to Kizui?'

'Not far. Not far.'

'Three or four hours?'

'Yes. Yes.'

'I'll be quite glad to arrive, the plane got in at six this morning,' she paused, 'In fact I've been travelling since yesterday afternoon.'

The Assistant Chief didn't reply. She struggled to find something else to say. Perhaps he didn't understand her. She spoke more slowly.

'I'm looking forward to living in the country, London's very crowded.'

'Yes. Very good. Fine.'

Rick flashed into her mind, yesterday afternoon at the airport, standing back so her mother and father could give her the last hug goodbye before she went through the passport check. '*Was that your boyfriend waving?*' It was more of a gesture than a wave; a hand held outwards, have strength it seemed to say.

'Hapo. Hapo!' the Assistant Chief shouted at the driver, waving his arm as if to take the wheel and the car took a sudden swing into a crowded side street. The change from high-rise buildings and smart banks and shops was immediate; here the shops were small, many with Asian names above the windows, there were cheap coloured clothes, cooking pots and suitcases hanging outside. Cars and people blocked the road. She was excited by the commotion; it seemed familiar, the noise, the smells, the people, the rush of life in the down-town city. At the corner of the street was a barrow piled with green pineapples, a man was peeling them with a large knife, letting the spirals drop to the pavement and spearing the slices of fruit onto wooden sticks. There were stalls with 'shoeshine', newspapers, loose sweets and cigarettes, bundles of red-stalked leaves that people were chewing. Young men walked along hand in hand. Many had shirts open across their chests, some wore tight leopard-spot printed nylon tops or faded t-shirts with slogans: 'Marlboro' Safari Rally', 'Jumbo! – Kenya', 'Globetrotters – U.S.A.' Bare feet, flip-flops, platform shoes and boots. Music was blasting out from a couple of speakers on a makeshift record stall.

The driver stopped on the corner next to the pineapple barrow in the middle of a stream of traffic and at once hooting started up behind. He wound down the window to shout back. The Assistant Chief had got out and was bargaining for a couple of pineapples and a slice of yellow fruit which he passed in through the window. This was for her; she blew away the fat black flies that hovered after it knowing she'd have to eat it.

A few young men had already stopped by the car and were loitering there looking at the rucksack and polythene bag of household equipment roped to the roof.

'You, mzungu! Where are you from?'

'England.'

'Mzungu. Mzungu!'

People were pushing to look at her.

'What's your name?'

'Can we drive on?'

'One minute.'

The Assistant Chief called to a boy across the street. He hurried over and passed in a couple of cigarettes. Within seconds others had joined him, thrusting their goods in at the window, waving them in front of the windscreen: handkerchiefs, clothes pegs, packets of biscuits, bright yellow pills, green and blue perfumes and fistfuls of digital watches.

'Is this the quick way out of Nairobi?' she asked.

They'd left the busy down-town streets and were plunging deeper and deeper into shanty town. There were corrugated iron houses patched with sheets of cardboard and polythene, and low-hanging cables looped across the makeshift homes. The road was no longer tarred but had turned into a rough track and the driver drove haphazardly over the ridges spinning the wheel this way and that to avoid the pot-holes. He seemed to be enjoying himself.

'This is the way out of town is it?' she asked the Assistant Chief.

'Yes. Yes. Just one minute.'

She knew he was lying and felt annoyed.

'Where are we going?'

'Just some small business.'

They stopped in the middle of a run-down estate. He struggled out of the car and hurried away across the track.

'Where's he going?' she asked the driver, but either he didn't understand or else he didn't know as the question went unanswered. He sat chewing a matchstick, with his hands splayed out on the steering wheel. He was a thin man, but with thick fingers, he had a metal bracelet and a piece of leather around his wrist, a yellow woollen hat on the back of his head. It was hard to know how old he was, probably less than he looked.

Her fingers were sticky from the pineapple and she had bits trapped between her teeth which she began to pick out with the end of the wooden stick.

Already the light was fading and a few fires of burning rubbish had been lit by the side of the road. It wasn't just a housing area, there seemed to be tea houses and small kiosks selling loaves of bread and bottles of Coke, there was a car repair shed and a furniture workshop in the clearing ahead. Some children were playing in the dirt with a car made out of old tin cans and driven by a steering rod; they negotiated a track round rocks and rubbish. A girl swung a small child up from the dust onto her back and disappeared down an alleyway, another woman came hurrying past with a battered cardboard box on her head. There was something about this poverty – the shanty dwellings and people whose homes they were – that was almost beautiful. She was ashamed of the thought.

A shout across the track; the Assistant Chief was waving. Reluctantly the driver, with whom she hadn't yet exchanged a word, pulled down his hat and got out of the car. He returned with the Assistant Chief and two other men, struggling beneath the weight of a large blue sofa. A crowd of children followed. They clapped and cheered as the sofa was hoisted onto the roof of the car. The driver roped it down. Her rucksack and the bag of equipment were jammed in next to the Assistant Chief with a roll of chicken wire and a couple of tins of paint, and they set off again.

'Miss Jo, what's the time, please?'

'Almost six o'clock.'

She wound back her watch, changing it to Kenyan time, severing the last sentimental link with home. Rick would be watching telly in bed by now, if only she could be there, out of this beaten-up car, away from this fat sweaty man. She would have given anything to have a hot bath and curl up in bed.

'Miss Jo, Miss Jo.' He was tapping her shoulder.

'Please just call me Jo – Jo's fine.'

'OK. Fine. Can you take one beer before we go?'

'No thank you. I'd rather be getting on to Kizui if that's alright.'

'I think we can take one beer. It's too hot.'

He disappeared again in Diego Road and she and the driver sat once more in silence looking out through the windscreen. They were parked half on, half off the pavement outside a butcher's shop, and people passing on the pavement had to squeeze between the car and the shop front. A man spotted her white face and slowed down to stare in. Darkness had come very suddenly and little was visible to her but the meat in the shop; hanging carcasses, whole tongues hard and curled, skinned sheeps' heads, a pile of legs with hooves.

Inside the New Tip Top Board and Lodging Jo followed the Assistant Chief up the dimly lit back stairs, pausing behind him every time he stopped to get his breath back. At the top was a room with a few plastic chairs and tables and a broken pinball machine. Some young women were lounging indolently against the railings. The Assistant Chief pushed past and crossed the room to an older woman who was scrubbing the floor with a thick grey rag.

'Habari Mama?' he greeted her.

'Nzuri, nzuri. Is this the mzungu?' She got up from the soapy wet lino and offered Jo her forearm.

'Shake, shake,' the Assistant Chief said to Jo.

She tried to take the woman's hand.

'No, her hand is too wet to take, you must shake her arm.'

They followed the woman down a corridor that was lit by a low-hanging bulb and had narrow bedrooms off to the side. In one a couple of women were dressing, another was full of crates of beer. At the end was a door marked in large white-painted letters: MANAGER'S OFFICE. The woman knocked.

'Samson, the mzungu is here!'

Samson was a stout man with a flabby face. He had a silky cravat around his neck and his hair was parted at the side in Western style. He got up from behind the table where he'd been sitting reading a paper and greeted Jo.

'Habari?' He asked, shaking her hand, and then roared with laughter as she hesitated over the reply.

'I'm asking you "How are you?"' he said and chuckled again.

'Nzuri,' she said 'Nzuri sana.'

'Ah, so you know some Kiswahili – very well, yes, very well, fine, fine. So you have come to work at Kingangi.'

'That's right.'

'You will be our first "mzungu".'

'I thought there were some Irish missionaries there.'

'They are very far, maybe fifteen miles. You are the very first.'

'I'm looking forward to it.'

He'd been holding her hand all this time but now let go and turned to the Assistant Chief, 'This one is going to be very good. Very good.'

The woman came in with a tray of bottles, she dusted and opened three beers, flipping the tops off onto the floor.

'What will you take? Beer? Soda?' he handed her a beer. 'How do you like our country?'

'I only arrived this morning, but it seems very nice, I've heard it's very beautiful.'

'Very beautiful. So many tourists come here. We have lion, giraffe, elephant, the Indian Ocean.'

She sat on the large leather sofa next to the Assistant Chief and tried to follow the gestures and expressions as they spoke in Kikamba. The beer was warm but not bad, she refused a second one, but it was opened and put in front of her and then a third and fourth lined up beside that. The two fat men were soon drunk, she saw them looking at her, imagined that they were talking about her. Perhaps they wouldn't be driving to Kizui that night . . . but the driver was waiting.

'What does your father do?' Samson suddenly asked.

'He's a lecturer, at a university.'

'A big man.'

'Not very.'

'But he is important?'

'Yes, important,' the Assistant Chief interrupted, 'That's why she's very well-educated.'

Jo hoped the woman would return but when she did it was only to bring another tray of beers and a packet of cigarettes.

'Can you take some cigarettes?' Samson asked.

'No thank you.'

'Bad for the lungs.' He coughed heartily as if to prove the truth of his statement.

'Do people smoke in London?' the Assistant Chief asked.

'Some, but not as many as used to.'

'Women – do they smoke?' Samson asked.

'Yes, some women do, but quite a lot of people have given up because they're worried about their health.'

'But they like to drink.'

'Most people do.'

'And women take beer.'

'Yes.' She was enjoying herself.

It was two more hours before they left. As they passed the young women, now sitting at a table by the pinball machine drinking beer with a couple of men, one of them touched her arm.

'You, mzungu!'

Jo smiled. Another one asked her something.

'Sorry, sorry,' the Assistant Chief said, pushing her in front of him down the stairs. 'They are very rude.'

He turned and shouted at them. They laughed and called back.

'They are very rude.'

'It's OK, I just didn't understand what they were saying.'

'Don't listen, they're not good women. Watembezi, you understand? Streetwalkers.'

The driver was asleep in the car, his head resting awkwardly on his woollen hat on the wheel, he woke with a jump as they got in, started the engine immediately and got out to kick the headlights into action.

The Assistant Chief had bought meat before they left and she had to sit with it on the shelf in front of her pushing the damp newspaper packages back on every time they slipped forward. On the straight but pot-holed Mombasa road overnight coaches swayed past them, blaring their horns, she read their names, 'Disco Dancer', 'Sleeping Coach'. Gradually she began to relax and her frustration subsided, it was too dark to see the countryside around so she kept her eyes on the road. The Assistant Chief was asleep behind her, the driver was chewing leafy red twigs which he pulled from a bundle on the dashboard. He offered her one and she took it for something to do, she guessed it was some sort of stimulant, it tasted dry and grassy.

It was more of a sensation than a thought; that this was a day she would always remember, a small point, a moment out of time, with everything lying ahead.

When they turned off the main coast road the Assistant Chief woke up and tapped her on the shoulder.

'Machakos.'

'Sorry?'

'This is Machakos.'

They were about half-way; she remembered Machakos from the map above Geoff's desk, it was the only other main town between Nairobi and Kizui. They stopped for petrol and went on again. The road became more hilly and they travelled slowly with the old car straining up the slopes and the driver pumping the brakes as they went down round the bends. Every so often he pulled off the side of the road to secure the ropes on the sofa and to kick the headlamps on again, and the Assistant Chief got out to relieve himself against the wheel.

They'd turned off the main road through the back of what must have been Kizui town, past the Police Station where a light was burning, and had gone several miles up a rough track when she felt the Assistant Chief touching her shoulder again.

'We have arrived.' It was pitch black all around, but she tried to see into it. 'I think you can stay at my house tonight.'

'If you don't mind – I'd rather go to mine.'

'Maybe it is better with me.'

'No thank you.'

She'd bolted the door with relief and waited a long time until she was certain that he'd gone. Then she'd lit the matches and seen the rats on the heaps of rubble.

CHAPTER FIVE

She slept the night in her clothes under a blanket on the polythene covered mattress and in the morning woke covered with flea bites. Someone was knocking on the door, she got up and drew the curtains, the sun was already bright. There was a child at the door, a young girl in a green sleeveless dress which was torn and falling apart at the waist. She handed Jo a dirty bottle full of milk.

'Who's it from?'

The girl kept her eyes to the ground, her head was closely shaved and covered with small smooth patches, circles of baldness. She looked about ten or eleven and had long thin arms and legs, her feet were dusty. She answered softly in Kikamba.

'I'm sorry,' Jo said, 'I don't understand. How much?'

'No,' the girl said in English, 'From mother,' and turned and raced away, scrambling out of the garden through a hole in the hedge. There were other children there, waiting, watching, Jo could see the brightly coloured jerseys through the thorns and greenery.

'Mzungu! Mzungu!' she heard.

'Hello.'

'How are you?'

'Very well. How are you?'

'Quite fine thank you.'

She came out of the house and went towards the hedge but as she approached a cry went up and they raced away giggling. She saw a tiny child in shorts that were falling to its knees stumble as it struggled to keep up with the others. It let out a terrified yell as it fell to the ground. The older girl in the green dress stopped, picked it up on her back and leaning forward tied a cloth around it, knotted the ends across her shoulder and walked on up the slope.

Jo watched till they'd disappeared behind the trees, then she turned back to her garden. Her vague impressions of the night before were confirmed, her house was whitewashed with a corrugated iron roof and stood alone on the sandy slope surrounded by a few tussocks of grass and sharp thorny plants. At one side was a corrugated iron tank with a pipe running down from the gutter. She banged the side to see how much water there was; it rang hollow to the bottom, at most a couple of inches left. The tap was dripping and a small pool of water had collected underneath. She tightened the bolt. Until the rains came she'd have to fetch her water from the river. Today I'll go walking, she thought, and find out where the river is and how many homes there are in the village.

From here she could see for miles – down to a forest and beyond to great boulders and distant hills – not simply into the distance but seemingly further than that, to smooth blue mountains blurring with the sky. Nearer to her house she could make out part of the road along which they'd come and the pattern of other dirt tracks along the lower ridges, the clusters of thatch houses with splashes of pink bougainvillea around the compounds and the green line of trees along the river.

It was already hot, the sun warmed her skin, there were lizards basking on the bricks by the house and bright coloured birds in the trees. A couple of donkeys were tethered at the bottom of her garden. Some women had stopped on the path that ran alongside the hedge and were staring in at her, they had large drums of water roped on their backs, one of them called out,

'Mzungu! Wimuseo? Habari?'

'Nzuri!'

They laughed and called out something else that she didn't understand and then walked on barefoot up the dry slope bent under the weight of the drums.

Rick, it's beautiful, beautiful beyond all expectation, miles and miles of unfamiliar land, strange trees and unknown birds, far from anything I know; bushland and rough vegetation and burning sun. And women calling out; a sound that doesn't break into words.

Hard to believe that there were towns and cities out there, that boys were hawking sweets and watches on the streets of Nairobi, that somewhere in London in a stuffy music room Rick would be giving a piano lesson. If only he could see this; the sun shimmering on distant roofs of corrugated iron, the clear blue sky, the turquoise bird on the thorns, its feathers glimmering like silk, the shiny fig-like leaves on the tree beside the house and high up, the green and yellow pawpaws clustered round the trunk.

The house was still cool, but dry and dusty. It was being repaired, the inner walls were crumbling and there was a bag of cement and some workmen's tools beside one of the heaps of rubble. The ceiling had fallen in and a broken beam jutting out from the wall was hanging with a piece of rotten hardboard, the rest was in pieces on the floor, damp and mouldy. From a crack in the roof where the sheets of corrugated iron didn't meet a shaft of light was coming down illumining the dust.

She picked up a bit of broken chair from the rubble and let it fall again. She felt suddenly cast down, aware that she'd been observed but left alone. All those faces at the hedge, staring in, laughing, knowing her before she could know them, taunting her in a language she couldn't understand. She'd just waved back, called out and smiled, uncertain, hoping for friends.

I wish you were here. I feel so lonely. It's ridiculous, I don't even know where I am.

But someone wanted to make her welcome and had sent the milk, carried by the thin girl with the ringwormed head. The glass bottle was sticky and dirty and warm, it smelt of animals and woodsmoke, but the milk inside was clean and sweet, she tasted a drop on her finger and realised how hungry she was.

In the corner of the room was a small stove. She looked around for wood or charcoal so that she could light it and boil the milk, but opening the door to the kitchen found the floor strewn with blood-stained shreds of paper and splinters of broken bone. It looked as if there'd been an animal fight, that something had been killed. Then she remembered that the Assistant Chief had given her one of the parcels of meat and she'd left it on the side. The rats must have returned while she slept and torn into the soft package of flesh. She was sweeping it up with the broken head of the broom when she heard a voice behind her.

'Good morning. How are you?'

It was the Assistant Chief at the door, dressed in the same tight blue suit but with a different coloured tie, yellow and purple. He was already sweating and mopping at his brow with a handkerchief.

'Please, please, you mustn't clean. I will send a woman to sweep for you.'

'It's OK, I was just clearing up a bit. I'm afraid the rats must have got at the meat.'

'Sorry, sorry. You forgot to put it in the foodsafe.' He bent down and picked up a bit of bone. 'They have eaten well! But I can buy some more for you, even in Kizui we have good meat.'

There were a couple of young men behind him, their arms straining beneath the weight of the blue nylon sofa that had been carried on the roof of the car from Nairobi, they struggled up the step and pushed it through the door. It was a large and ugly piece of furniture, obviously expensive.

'So here is your sofa.'

The Assistant Chief smiled as the men shoved it close against the wall in the place that he'd directed. They were panting, their faces shiny from the heat, looking away from Jo, waiting to be told what to do next.

It's the ugliest thing I've ever seen, and it takes up the whole room. But I haven't the heart to tell him I don't want it.

'Thank you.'

'Are you ready to go?' the Assistant Chief asked her.

'Where to?'

'Town. Town.'

'What for?'

'To buy a cylinder for the gas cooker and a good bed. We can go now.'

'I was going to use this for cooking.'

'No, no, a jiko is no good for you, how can you know how to use that, it's just for local people.'

He was embarrassed about the state of the house and anxious to get out.

'I'm sorry, this is too dirty, these men are very lazy, it would have been better if you'd slept at my house.'

'It was fine here.'

'They will finish today, there was just some small problem, today they will clean all this rubbish and mend the ceiling and I will get a woman to wash the floors for you.'

As long as he doesn't expect me to have a servant as well as a sofa.

The car was waiting on the track above her house. The driver had slept the night in it, there was a blanket bundled on the back seat and it was stuffy with the strong smell of an unwashed body. She sat in the front as before with the Assistant Chief behind her. They'd only gone a short distance when a man came running towards them in the middle of the road, waving his arms. He wore trousers torn off at the knee and layers of ragged shirts and jerseys. The driver drove on and tried to nudge him out of the way but the man put his hands flat on the bonnet and forced them to a halt. Then he pressed his lips to the metal and kissed the car. He hurried round to Jo's side, stuck his head through the open window and before she realised what was happening had kissed her shoulder. It made a yellow stain on her white t-shirt and he backed away laughing.

'Sorry. Sorry.' The Assistant Chief was leaning forward trying to mop at her shoulder with his handkerchief, 'Here, take this.'

'It's alright, don't worry.'

'He's not in his right mind. It is very bad.'

A mad man. She could feel the damp spittle soaking through to her skin, but she ignored the mark and passed the handkerchief back. They drove on, leaving him standing at the side of the road, grinning and clattering the tins which were hung from a string about his waist. The driver said something to her which she didn't understand but she nodded.

'He smokes too much bhangi – dagga,' the Assistant Chief explained, 'It's destroyed his mind.'

'Who is he?'

'Moses Ndeti. But we just call him "Bhangi".'

'Where does he live?'

'Not far.'

'Where?'

'Up from your house. Maybe you have seen, there is a hut just made of leaves, that is his home.'

They drove down along the sandy tracks that she'd seen from her house, past the whitewashed school and a small wooden church. There were women working in the plots beside the road, digging the soil with long forks which they swung from their shoulders. Clumps of leafy banana trees, coloured washing draped over the hedges, compounds with mud and thatch houses. Children came running to the roadside when they heard the car, waving and shouting. But somehow the madman had dulled her interest, his slobber had dried on her shoulder and the yellow mark kept catching her eye. She wanted everything to be perfect, to have peace and tranquillity, the gentleness of rural life, without the ugliness of madness, its unpredictability, the sudden swings of laughter and aggression.

'Is he violent?'

'No. No. You needn't be fearing. He won't disturb you. He's too much afraid of the watchman.'

'I didn't know there was a watchman.'

'I've appointed a man to guard your house at night.'

She wondered if the watchman had seen her the night before, peeing by the side of the house or standing on the doorstep staring into the darkness.

The car skidded on the downhill slope, the rear wheels sliding away on the smooth sand as the driver pumped the brakes, it skewed sideways and approached the edge of the track. Jo gripped the side of her seat and closed her eyes, ready in that fraction of a second for life to end, to spin over and over down the deep eroded gulley, but they stopped a few inches from the edge. The Assistant Chief leant forward.

'He's not a good driver, he's too young.'

'That's alright. It's difficult on the sand.'

The car edged forwards, the wheels slipping nearer and nearer to the side until it suddenly pulled away and they shot on down to the riverbed. The river looked completely dry, just a wide sandy bed, crossed by a concrete slab. There were a few children with plastic jerry cans scooping up water from depressions in the sand.

'Isn't there any water at all now?'

'There is further up, at the waterfall, but not here, not until the rains. Then you will see. In the rainy season we can't pass here, we have to go the other way, right round on the hilltop, maybe ten miles. Sometimes there is so much water that old men are swept away!'

The Assistant Chief laughed and repeated it for the driver who also laughed.

I just don't like him. He's different here, more confident on his own territory, very much the boss.

There were a lot of people out on the road, mostly women with heavy baskets on their backs, piled with bananas and vegetables. The driver hooted to get them to move from the middle of the track. Some waved but most just stepped up on the bank and lifted their heads to watch the vehicle pass. They stared at the white face. She would have preferred to walk, to have taken the path across the hills and met the people along the way. But they weren't to know that.

We just went by in a cloud of dust. The Assistant Chief has captured me. I am his new status symbol – 'To add to a car and smart suits what more could the perfect African gentleman want than a female "mzungu" fresh from England.'

They emerged through the eucalyptus forest onto the pot-holed tarmac and drove into town the way they'd come the night before, past the Police Station where crimson bougainvillea hung over the wall. A couple of women were sitting there weaving baskets. A landrover was parked outside and some men in khaki uniform were leaning against the bonnet smoking, one of them waved to the Assistant Chief as the car went by.

The town was hot and dusty, it was a run-down place with thin dogs crouching at the roadside and dirt and rubbish everywhere. The market was small, just a few women sitting beneath the trees on a triangle of earth in the middle of the road. They had a couple of sacks spread out in front of them with a few bundles of leafy green vegetables and piles of sweet potatoes. As soon as the car stopped some girls came running up holding out fistfuls of bananas.

'How much?' Jo asked, 'Shillingi ngapi?'

They pushed each other to get closer to her. From behind someone touched her hair. One girl peeled a banana and gave it to her.

'Itano, shilling imwe. Five is one shilling,' she said.

The older women looked on from their seats on the ground. She only had a twenty shilling note, about a pound, it caused confusion, they backed away. Then the girl who'd given her the banana took the money and ran across the road into a shop.

'What's happening?' the Assistant Chief asked.

'I'm just buying some bananas, but I didn't have any change.'

'You don't need to buy here, I will give you bananas from my shamba, and maize and beans.'

'Thank you, but I'm happy to buy my food and I'm very hungry, I haven't eaten for two days.'

The girl returned, gave her a handful of coins and some grubby notes that were soft and worn and then another couple of bananas.

'Would you like one?'

'I don't take fruit in the morning.' the Assistant Chief replied.

She followed him through the town, eating as she went along. They were tiny yellow finger-bananas, soft and sweet, she held onto the skins for a while then dropped them in the road on a heap of rubbish. The Assistant Chief was in a hurry. They passed a couple of small stores with tinned food and biscuits stacked in the windows, then a butcher's shop smelling of blood and sawdust, and on past a row of cloth shops where curtains of low-hanging clothes and khangas waved from wires across the pavement. The bedmaker was at the bottom of the row; he was a crippled man without legs. He sat up on a table, just a bundle of body in dirty brown rags, balanced there, the unoccupied flaps of his trouser legs folded beneath him. He was working on a length of wood, planing it with the tool gripped awkwardly in his deformed hand, a pile of shavings was heaping up around him.

'She wants a good bed,' the Assistant Chief explained, 'It must be very good, not weak. Metal, good metal, and springs.'

There were a few wooden beds on the pavement outside, simple frames with rubber and sisal thongs, which she liked the look of.

'One of these would be fine, these look very nice.'

'Those ones are not good, they're too cheap, this is better.' The Assistant Chief tested a huge metal-framed bed with a fat foam mattress. Its price was double that of wooden ones.

'I'd prefer one of these.'

'They are very bad, those ones, they're just made by this man here, you know they're made from bad wood and old car tyres.'

'I'd prefer one like that, if that's alright, I'm not used to a metal bed.'

'If it is what you want, but this one is not big enough, he must make a big one for you.'

The Assistant Chief engaged in a prolonged negotiation with the crippled man, and handed over a thousand shillings from a bundle in his pocket. The bedmaker took the notes and put them beneath his hat.

'He will make it in one week.'

'Thank you.'

'OK. Fine. Now I think we can take one beer.'

The bars ran in a tumbledown row along the back of the square that was both a larger marketplace and a bus park, their walls were painted in bright colours, a few feet of one colour at the bottom and then another above it; yellow and blue, pink and brown, red and green. They went into the Hotel Relax, she had no choice but to follow, and sat opposite each other at a small table. An old man dressed in a polo-neck jersey and ragged trousers, brought them beers, dusting the bottles with a cloth. He greeted Jo warmly, shaking her hand first one way, then the other, gripping her thumbs.

'I would have been happy with a cheaper bed, I don't need a big one.'

'No, no. It is better.'

'I can't really afford so much.'

'It's not for you to pay.'

'Who is paying?'

'It's no problem. We have money for your comforts.'

'I think I should explain; I don't need comforts, I'm very happy with the same as everyone else.'

The Assistant Chief looked up from his beer, which was already half drunk.

'It's good to make the money flow. Chippo there is my good

friend, we were in school together, when we were boys we were too close.'

'I see.'

'He fell off the back of a matatu van.' There were tears in his eyes. 'They had to amputate his legs.'

'I'm very sorry.'

Some young men had come into the bar. They were crowding round a small table drinking sodas and playing draughts with bottle tops. One was wearing a denim jacket, another had a dark blue beret pulled at an angle on the back of his head. She knew that they were talking about her but looked away to the wall at the end of the room. There was a large painted picture of a lion eating a man and above it a photograph of the President and a message, 'God is the Head of this House.'

The Assistant Chief had finished his beer and called for another.

'How are you? Katambo!'

An old man with white hair came up to the Assistant Chief and extended his hand in greeting. He held his arm with the other hand, showing respect.

'Wimuseo?'

'Ii, nimuseo. Ii.'

There was a singsong to the Kikamba greeting.

'This is Ben Kyalo, from Kingangi. He is your neighbour.'

They shook hands. She noted the purple shirt with the zip at the neck, his khaki hat and honey-brown skin. He had a warm, smiling face.

'I'm afraid I don't know your name,' she said to the Assistant Chief when Ben Kyalo had gone.

'I am Gabriel Kivuto Katambo – the Angel Gabriel!' he said and laughed.

'So what do I call you? Mr Katambo?'

'Fine, fine.'

The young men had finished their game and left the bar, looking back at her as they went out. The one in the beret had a handsome face.

'When will you start work?' Mr Katambo asked.

'As soon as possible.'

'Good. Good. And they have given you money for equipments?'

'No, I was told that the village and the women's groups had already raised enough.'

'Yes, yes, we have some money, but we're expecting a

contribution. I think they have quite some money in Nairobi for you to use in this work.'

She looked across at his eager face.

'I'm not being given any money from Nairobi; they've just sent me here to plan the project, to co-ordinate the installation of the water pumps.'

'But when the Field Director comes perhaps he will award some small grant for you.'

She looked at his eyes, the whites stained brown with broken blood vessels, the nervous hands turning the ring in the groove on his fat finger.

'There's only a small amount available for individual projects, at most I can ask for fifty pounds. It's not our job to provide money. The funds have got to come from somewhere else.'

'But you must make some contribution before you leave.'

There was no room for misinterpretation, to suppose that she hadn't quite understood him.

'I thought you'd requested a water engineer, not a grant, I thought that was clear from the contract.'

'But it is possible that you can raise money.'

'I'll have to inform the Field Director if you don't want me here.'

'You've misunderstood. Sorry if there is some disagreement.'

'I think there is.'

She felt intense disappointment; the thought of the project collapsing before she'd even begun, of there being no job for her here, of returning to Nairobi to wait for a flight back to Britain. Never living in the white house with the view across the bush to the mountains. Mr Katambo was mopping the sweat from his face again. She felt something tapping on her arm.

'Give me one penny.'

It was a runny-nosed child at the table, with a smaller child, just a baby wearing only a t-shirt, held on his hip. She looked in her purse and finding nothing but shillings gave him one, it made her feel calmer, and less angry with the Assistant Chief, after all it was inevitable that she'd be asked for money.

CHAPTER SIX

On Sunday Jo made her way up the scrubby slope at the back of her house to the home of Ben Kyalo. He was there waiting for her, standing in the shade beneath the mango tree, dressed as before in the purple shirt with the zip at the neck, but looking younger and less stooped than she remembered from their meeting at the Hotel Relax.

She'd hoped to be introduced to his wife and children but although she saw faces peering out from houses in the compound no one else came to meet her and she was shown instead into a dark narrow room.

'Welcome,' he said, 'Please sit.'

He moved the radio covered with a crocheted cloth onto the table in front of her, turned it on to the 'Voice of Kenya' and disappeared. There was an education programme on in English, a monotonous lecture on the geology of the Rift Valley. She tried to listen but soon lost interest.

The room was small and had the shabby feel of one which is lived in by too many people, it seemed dirty, the furniture was broken and there was a musty smell of bodies. At one time someone had tried to make it nice and had nailed to the wall a few sheets of an old newspaper, pictures from a calendar and a United Nations map of the world. The sofa had been covered with ugly coloured crochet squares. She hadn't expected to find familiar things, the refuse of her own culture; the vinyl-covered sofa and bright acrylic knitting, the copper vase and plastic flower. A large gourd was all that she admired; it had been scorch-marked with a pattern of stars and figures of men and cows, and was a perfect shape, rounded as a goat's belly. It hung by the door from a long leather strap. Above it was a wedding photograph of Ben Kyalo and his wife. Jo was intrigued. From the date at the bottom she saw that it had only been taken a few years before. Ben Kyalo was wearing platform shoes and a suit which was too large, the sleeves of the jacket hung over his wrists, the woman looked plump in the tight white dress. They both seemed awkward, standing straight, arms at their sides, their faces dull and serious.

A few small children were peering in at the door but they ran away as soon as Jo came out. A sack of charcoal had been propped against the trunk of the mango tree in the middle of the compound and there was a half-woven sisal basket abandoned beside it, but no people around. Smoke was coming from one of the mud houses and a sweet smell of maizemeal hung on the air. The women were probably in the kitchen. Yet Jo had been hidden away as a special guest. She expected Ben Kyalo to return but it was a child who appeared from one of the houses carrying a large tin cup of water. It was the girl in the torn green dress who'd brought the milk to her house.

'To wash,' she said, holding out the mug of water.

Uncertain of quite what she was meant to do, Jo hesitated and the girl took her hands and poured the water over them letting it splash down onto the hot sandy earth.

Boiled chicken and potatoes and a white mound of stiff maizemeal – ugali. Jo and Ben Kyalo sat at the low table with the food in big tin dishes piled in front of them. The liver was served on a separate plate. No one else joined them.

'What do you eat in England?' he asked.

'The same sort of thing, meat, potatoes, vegetables.'

'And ugali?'

He was squeezing the sticky white meal in the palm of a hand and mopping it in the juice. She'd been given a spoon.

'No, we mainly eat potatoes or rice and bread.'

'How big is your father's shamba?'

'About a quarter of an acre.'

'How many children?'

'Three.'

'He is still young.'

She ate another potato, there were still five to go.

'What does he grow?'

'Tomatoes. Beans. Onions. Potatoes.' He nodded to each. Asparagus. Artichokes. Courgettes. 'But people buy most of their food.'

Ben Kyalo had finished his plateful and was dividing the remaining meat between them.

'Eat. Eat. This is for you.' He put the gizzard on her plate.

'No thank you. It was very good.' She patted her stomach.

'You must taste it. This bit is too sweet.'

When they'd finished an older woman came in to take away the tray of bones and to pour them cups of sweet milky tea from a large enamel teapot. Then Ben Kyalo called the children in and asked them to sing for her. They crowded into the corner of the room, a ragged bunch in an array of clothes which were either too big or too small. The older girl in the green dress began, clapping her hands as she sang, and the smaller ones joined in the chorus. At first Jo thought it was a traditional African song but then some of the words became clear, it was in English, a church song, 'Praise God, Praise Him.'

She began work the following day. It started badly. She'd asked Mr Katambo and the local headmaster to announce that there'd be a meeting for women to give their views on the water scheme. It was to be held in the school at one o'clock. Only five turned up.

They sat in an empty classroom that smelt of chalk and sweat. Outside, the schoolchildren were eating their lunch in the shade of the trees. A few boys wandered over to have a look in and before long a small crowd had gathered, faces pressed to the windows. She sent them away and addressed the women.

'As you probably know I've come here to set up a water supply for the village. But before I do anything I want to know what the problems are at the moment and what sort of supply you need. The idea is that it's going to be a women's project; women will raise a lot of the money, do a lot of the work – which will be worked out as a financial contribution, and they, you, will learn how to maintain the pumps and have complete control of the whole scheme.'

It was all wrong. But her ideas had piled up, how else could she begin.

A couple of the women were knitting, another was weaving a basket, yet their eyes remained fixed on her. She picked up a stub of chalk, wiped the board with a screwed up piece of paper and drew two columns: problems / solutions.

'How far do you have to go each day for water?' No answer. 'More than two hours?' They nodded.

'We have to leave now,' one of the younger women said. They all got up to leave at once, shook hands with Jo and hurried off, chattering as soon as they were out of the classroom. She cleaned the board, packed up her papers and hurried away, hoping not to be seen by any of the teachers or children.

'Excuse me please.' One of the women had lingered behind, waiting for Jo at the school gate. She was taller than Jo by a couple of inches, well-built, with a strong-boned face. Her skin was lighter than that of others, a golden brown. 'I don't think they understood you,' she said.

'I know. I'm sorry, I don't speak Kikamba.'

'You can speak English, but maybe more slowly, then we can understand.'

'Did you understand anything?'

'Of course. But you ask us questions and we don't know what you want to hear. We're not used to planning these things. There isn't a proper Women's Group here.'

'Who were the women who came today?'

'My mother and her sister, the wife of Mr Katambo and the wife of the headmaster.'

She was called Jerusa and was Ben Kyalo's daugher. Now Jo knew she saw the similarity; the same honey-coloured skin, the ready smile and deep warm eyes. Her hair was plaited in lines running from her forehead down to the nape of her neck where the ends were twisted together. She wore a chain with a cross, her toenails were painted. She brought Jo tea and they sat on the sofa in Jerusa's house.

'Me, I'm just working here at home,' Jerusa said, 'Waiting and praying.'

'What do you want to do?'

'I applied to teachers' college in Mombasa. I've got good grades but they can't let me in.'

'Why not?'

'I don't know anyone to help find the way. Maybe you know someone there.'

'I've only just arrived. I don't know anyone in Mombasa.'

'Perhaps in Nairobi?'

'The only person I know there is the Field Director of my organisation. I suppose he might be able to help, I just don't know.'

Jerusa was pulling on the cross around her neck.

'Why have you come here?' she asked.

'To work on this water project. Mr Katambo asked for a water engineer and they've sent me.'

'The women are saying that you've come to teach them marketing and accounts so that they can earn money.'

'Who's saying that?'

'Many people. We don't know about the water.'

'I thought you'd raised money for a water project, that's what Mr Katambo told us.'

Jerusa shook her head. 'Maybe he was fearing that they wouldn't send anybody.'

Some of the children came into the room. Jerusa called them over to shake Jo's hand.

'What are they saying?'

'Witawa ata? It means, what is your name?'

'How do I ask them their names?'

The children giggled and hid their heads behind their hands.

'Witawa ata?' she asked the girl in the green dress.

'Museo.'

'She's my daughter,' Jerusa said.

The girl had dark skin, but her eyes were like Jerusa's; deep and warm, made pretty by short curled lashes.

The impressions of those first days were to colour the feelings of all following days, there were many things which began in the time spent at Jerusa's home.

In the daytime she was Jo, the white woman, the engineer, but in the evenings there was little to do but visit people's homes and join in the life that was going on. She enjoyed eating with her fingers, squeezing a ball of ugali in the palm of her hand and dipping it into the dish of sukuma wiki, dark green kale, chopped fine and fried and boiled till it was soft. It was good to feel the hunger of a day without food which ended with a meal of githeri, the maize and beans that distended her stomach. She joined the women carrying wood from the hills and cooking in the kitchen hut until the smoke stinging her eyes drove her out. It wouldn't have been possible without Jerusa.

Until she met one of the priests from the mission at the start of the rainy season, she saw no other whites. She was aware of the stares, the shouts of 'mzungu', her weakness compared to the strength of the other women; not knowing how to milk a cow, expecting the teats to be soft and easy to pull, not rubbing her fingers sore, blistering her hands shelling maize and slashing grass with a panga, refusing to stop, pounding maize in a hollowed out tree trunk until her shoulders ached and burnt with the effort of lifting and dropping the heavy pole, unable to stop because she pounded in tandem, one, two, one, two, with Museo chanting and working with ease. She did these things to try and belong. They seemed to like her for it. Jerusa showed her how to catch a chicken and hold its neck and cut with the sharp blade of the panga, how to plunge it in hot water and pluck out the feathers. Her hands were bloody and trembling but she was too proud to give up and plucked the skinny bird, trying not to think how the pink folds of skin and deep-bedded feathers belonged to the nervous creature that she'd slaughtered.

She was often asked if she had a husband, sometimes she lied and said he was in England. She was pitied because she hadn't borne children, no infants suckling at her breasts or bundled on her back. 'Maybe you'll be lucky one day,' Jerusa said, 'You can marry when you go home again,' and Jo realised that she couldn't begin to explain. What did the women think when they watched her playing with the children and holding the babies close to her? And what when the babies woke and saw her white face and screamed and screamed until she handed them back?

'It's never seen a white face,' Jerusa said the first time she rescued a wailing child from her arms. But the baby was sick, it had healing weals on its cheeks, raised red scars where the grandmother had cut its skin with a razor to bleed out the evil spirits that were sucking the air from its lungs. For weeks it continued to rasp and vomit and flies settled on the cuts and on the scummy stickiness of its eyes and mouth. Then it died and was buried in a small grave by the plot of bananas. Jo cried, it was the first time she'd seen a dead child, its tiny body tight and thin, she didn't even know whose child it had been.

That night, there were screams in the compound, the wailing of a woman, the shouts of a man, a scuffle, screams, screams, breathless shouts. Jo was sitting on the sofa in the narrow room with the children clambering around her when she heard the first cries. She hurried into the compound, saw a light on in Ruth's house behind the mango tree and silhouettes of people at the window, an arm raised and beating down, again and again, like the thwacking of a man herding cattle. She banged on the door but it was bolted, the noise from within continued. Then Jerusa appeared from the garden with green bananas to cook for supper.

'Come away,' she said, 'That's their business.'

'Can't you do something?'

'That woman neglected her child – and she's been with another man.'

It stopped as violently and as suddenly as it had started, Jo turned away from the door, ashamed that she'd listened.

'I'm going home.'

'But you haven't eaten.'

'I'm sorry, I'm not hungry.'

'Let me escort you.'

'It's OK, I'll go with the children.'

Jo lay awake on her bed with the wick of the lamp wound down low, unable to banish the sounds from her mind. It wasn't easy to be friends with Jerusa; they clashed more often now, always over things Jo felt the women shouldn't accept.

The following morning Ruth's husband left the compound. When Jerusa came down to bring Jo milk she told her that the man was walking to Machakos with the cow, that he was going to sell it and use the money to buy another wife.

Did the women pray in church for kindness from the men, for release from beating, for protection from pregnancy, for the life of their children? Jerusa wanted Jo to go to church, for many Sundays she refused, but in the end she gave way. It was a small wooden hut half way up the hillside. Inside were low benches made from logs roped together with sisal. There was a paraffin burner on the altar. The women and children brought drums and tambourines, her spirit was uplifted. Everyone looked smart and beautiful, in bright coloured dresses and scarves, radiant with the rhythm and power of the hymns. Up above the corrugated iron roof warmed and creaked in the hot sun.

On the way home they approached some old men drunk with beer who were straggling across the track. As they drew near one of them veered towards her, put out his hand and pulled her breast. He pinched hard, hurting. She pulled away.

Jerusa had picked up a stick from the roadside, she hit him with it, then hurled a stone at his feet. He raised his hands for mercy and cried out.

'You ignorant old man!' Jerusa shouted, 'God will punish you.'

Then she wiped her hand on the khanga tied around her waist, and turned away.

'Why did he do it?'

'He says he's never seen a white person, he wanted to make sure you were a woman. But he's just drunk. That's all they do these old men, they sit watching their crops grow, drinking honey beer. Even my father and he's a Christian.'

Sometimes friends of Jerusa's would ask to touch Jo's skin or hair and then she was reminded how much she was envied, how they would save their money to buy creams from town to make their faces lighter and prettier. Jerusa plaited Jo's hair one afternoon, sitting outside in the compound with the children gathered around to watch. It hurt as she tugged at the roots, pulling them tight into tiny plaits. Museo brought out a mirror when it was finished and Jo had to laugh at the white skull that was revealed and the puny look it gave her, like an albino, odd creature, outcast.

Work still wasn't going well. Jo and Jerusa visited women in the village and surrounding areas, finding out how far they had to go for water, how much they carried and how long it took them. Jerusa translated, Jo paid her fifty shillings a week. A few women had been persuaded to start a Women's Group; Kasyoka, the headmaster's wife, was elected Chairwoman and Jerusa, Secretary. They would meet each Sunday at Jerusa's home but at most ten women came. Others saw little to be gained and even those who were interested stayed away for fear that they'd be asked to pay.

There wasn't any money for the project, Mr Katambo finally admitted it. Jo wrote to *Maendeleo ya Wanawake* (Progress for Women) and the American Women's Association – both keen to support self-help projects – they each sent two thousand shillings, about a hundred pounds, welcome but scarcely enough for a few lengths of pipe.

'I've come up with a new proposal,' she said to Mr Katambo, 'We're going to start some income-generating schemes – basket-weaving and vegetable gardening to begin with. The profit is going to be pooled to buy tools or clothes or corrugated iron mabati roofs or whatever else people need. It'll be a bit like the Mabati Groups.'

'What about the pump?'

'I've applied for a grant, but at the moment there just isn't enough money.'

He heaved himself up from the sofa in her room.

'We were expecting a proper engineer,' he said. 'A man.'

In September Jo travelled to Nairobi to speak to the British High Commission about the grant for her project. She'd submitted a detailed proposal with drawings, requirements, costings, and a careful assessment of the impact. A pompous young man was in charge.

'You realise you'll only be able to buy British and Commonwealth equipment if we award you a grant.'

'That's ridiculous, it's far more expensive.'

'That is the rule.'

'When will I hear?'

'Your application was too late to go into this year's assessment so you'll just have to wait and see if there's anything left over from the small projects scheme at the end of the financial year. Otherwise you can apply again next year.'

'What are the chances?'

'I'm afraid I can't tell you that. Good afternoon.'

Things were hard in Ukambani, after months of dryness the land was parched and cattle were dying. The smell of the meat factory seeped into the bus when they stopped at Athi River on the way from Nairobi. There were whole animals dead at the roadside, cattle that had collapsed before they could be sold, driven mile after mile through the arid land only to drop dead before they could be exchanged for a meagre fifty shillings.

Jo had found a co-operative business in Machakos which agreed to buy traditional baskets, kiondos, from the Women's Group for sale overseas. A local forester gave them seeds to start a tree nursery. But the rainy season was approaching, and interest flagged. The women stopped coming to the meetings, sometimes it was only Jerusa and Jo.

People were busy planting the shambas. The women were going further afield for water. Some had donkeys and would come to the village to sell water for as much as five shillings a drum. The animals returned home foamy white with sweat, and with sores on their backs which attracted the flies. Jo put out water and cabbage leaves for them and sometimes when no one was around took them handfuls of sugar.

Then on October 18th the rains came. Jo and Jerusa were returning from Matundu market. The sky darkened, a few heavy drops fell and then the clouds burst. People came running from their homes and danced in the rain. Children tore down banana leaves for umbrellas. Suddenly the air smelt musty sweet. Jo and Jerusa sheltered beneath a tree.

'Will I be giving you a ride?'

A landrover had stopped beside them. A middle-aged Irishman in a sporty green t-shirt shouted out of the window. The back of his vehicle was already full.

'We're only going to Kingangi.'

'Well take my umbrella.'

He thrust a large black umbrella out of the window and the 'Lamb of God' landrover sped on.

'He has an African wife,' Jerusa said.

'But he's a Catholic priest.'

'It's a secret.'

The land turned green with the rain, the first shoots of maize and beans appeared, there was a green haze on the distant acacia trees. A few bright flowers opened. She loved to wake in the early mornings to the sound of rain thundering on the corrugated iron above, hearing it let up and then start again with increased ferocity. When it stopped she would get up and stand at the open door, drawing in the strange earthy smell. The air was suddenly alive with voices; shouts and calls as people emerged from their houses to see how much water had been collected in the drums and buckets and cooking pots put out the night before. Water dripped from the trees in her garden and down below on the hillside steam was already rising from the dark thatch roofs.

It was many months before the madman, Bhangi, came to her house. He arrived one evening and gave her two brown eggs from his tins. His face was ugly, his teeth had rotted to small brown stumps, his fingernails were cracked and horny like toenails. He knocked at the door and then stood at a distance rattling his tins until she came out. She gave him a couple of shillings, he dropped the coins in a tin and then hurried away through the hole in the hedge. When Jo cracked the eggs she found half-formed chickens inside, feathers slimy with yolk, the ugly head of a young chick surfacing in the pan. Later she heard that Bhangi stole the eggs, that he crept into people's compounds and scoured the long grass looking for those that had been laid apart from the others.

'If he doesn't find eggs he catches grasshoppers and eats them without cooking. He can eat even snakes,' Museo told her.

Bhangi was often about, hanging around the shops in Kingangi, hoping for cigarettes and beer, begging scraps for himself and the dog, a hopeless wasted creature which tagged after him, its head low and its ribs heaving beneath tick-ridden fur. The dog cowered away from people and was beaten when Bhangi was mad.

'You shouldn't trust that man, he's a thief,' Jerusa had told her, but he only took things from the rubbish pit. Jo got used to seeing him there with the dog, turning over the rubbish and picking out things to put in his tins, an old toothpaste tube; a bit of string, a broken biro.

CHAPTER SEVEN

She recognised him at once when he stopped her on her way to the shops at Kingangi and had a feeling that he'd been waiting for her, he seemed to be doing nothing in particular, going nowhere, just passing time. It was the young man in the dark beret who she'd seen that first day in the Hotel Relax.

'Hello. How are you?'

'Fine.'

'Can I escort you?'

'I'm only going to Kingangi, just to buy bananas and bread if there is any.'

They walked a while in silence, she had no particular wish to talk, to answer the inevitable questions, to play the role of the stranger to which she'd become so accustomed, and hoped that they would reach the market without need for this.

'What are you doing here?' he asked.

'What do you mean?'

'Why have you come to work here, why aren't you working in your own country?'

He spoke aggressively. This wasn't just idle curiosity.

'I'm an engineer, I'm working on the water project for Kingangi.'

'What good do you think you can do here? It's like the missionaries isn't it, you coming out here to live like us and spread your word around, to develop these backward people?'

'No, not at all.' There was something menacing about his serious face, the dark beret, the confidence with which he spoke. 'I haven't got any message to spread, I'm just doing a job. And I don't live like most of the people here.'

'But I've seen you, I've watched you trying to be an African, walking with your basket strapped over your head and eating with your fingers instead of using the spoon that you're given.'

Blood rushed to her face, she quickened her pace, hoping there might be someone on the track around the corner who she could stop and greet, but it was early afternoon, still the hottest part of the day and people were sleeping or working in the shade of their shambas.

'Who are you anyway?' she asked.

'Isaiah Mutisya. And you?'

'I'm sure you know my name.'

'No. Tell me.'

'Jo.'

'But your full name?'

'Josephine.'

'Josephine,' he rolled the word, 'A beautiful name.'

She ignored his sudden smile.

'I don't think you understand, I'm not trying to be an African. I just want to fit in a bit, to belong while I'm here.'

When they reached Kingangi, half a mile further on, he left her, went over to greet some friends and took a cigarette from one of them. There were always a few people hanging around the shops, sometimes the butcher's was open and people came to buy meat, at other times women had carried boxes of bread up from town and were selling it under the trees. There wasn't any bread that day, but Jo bought some bananas from the fat woman who was always there, a pile of limes and oranges from a friend of Jerusa's and a thin bunch of onions from the old lady. Isaiah and his friends were watching from the shade of the bar. She walked past them and into Kilonzo's shop to ask for bread, he didn't have any so she bought maizemeal instead.

Inside the small chai shop with the splatter-painted walls she asked for water and a cup of tea.

'May I sit with you?'

Isaiah had come in. He pulled out a chair from another table and moved it to sit opposite her. Then he took the half-smoked cigarette from behind his ear and lit it. He was wearing jeans and a thin black shirt and had a digital watch which hung loosely on his wrist. He tipped back his chair.

'What do you think that picture is of?' he asked gesturing to the wall-painting at the end of the room.

'It's a man and woman dancing. With a crocodile watching.'

'And have you seen what colour the woman is?'

Her face was brown, the dress was blue, the bulging breasts and arms and legs were pink.

'It's a white woman,' he said, 'A mzungu like you, that's the ideal, to be white. Is it? What's so special about white people?'

Mwanza came over to the table with the kettle of sweet milky tea and refilled their cups, then he brought over a plastic plate of mandazi, triangular oily doughnuts.

'Eat, you're too thin. Do you know what the women of my home say. That mzungu, she's not strong, she doesn't eat! It's better to be plump here.'

Jo tore off bits of mandazi and dipped them in her tea.

'Do you know why there's a crocodile?' he asked.

'Kingangi means crocodile.'

'So you know some Kikamba.' He smiled, his face opening up to her, 'And you know the story?'

> In the old days, before the people knew about God, a crocodile came out of the river. He walked up the hill and wherever he saw a person out in the shamba, he called to them and said 'Please help me, I am very thirsty, I have left the river, bring me some water.' And when they arrived with the water he ate them too. By the time the crocodile reached the top of the hill he was very sleepy because he had eaten so many people. There was a very beautiful woman in the village who all the men wanted to marry. When she saw the crocodile approaching she called out, 'Whoever wants to marry me, come now!' But the men had seen the crocodile and all were afraid. Except for one. He ran up the hill and when he neared the crocodile he began to dance. And the beautiful woman danced with him, and they danced and danced, until the crocodile became more and more sleepy. Then they sprinkled magic powder on the crocodile and took a rope and tied him up and rolled him down the hill back to the river. So the crocodiles can never visit this village again.

'So you've met Isaiah?' Jerusa said the following day as they were walking down to Matundu market.

'Do you know him?'

'Of course, we were in school together.'

'What does he do?'

'He's at the university.'

'But his home's around here?'

'He comes from Matundu. When the university is closed he stays here to teach at the school.'

'He seemed intelligent.'

Jerusa laughed. 'That man is too clever. When he was in school he was even teaching the teachers. They were so much frightened of him.'

'He thinks I shouldn't be here, that white people should leave Africa alone.'

'He was only joking with you.'

'Maybe. I'm not sure.'

Everywhere Jo went she hoped to see Isaiah. She took to walking past the school and following the long route to Kingangi round through Matundu village. It was late December, Christmas had passed with celebrations at the church and a huge meal of roasted goat and traditional Kamba food at Jerusa's home. Jo bought clothes for the children and cloth for Jerusa and her mother, Mutanu. She gave Ben Kyalo a new hat.

January was the hottest month, she slept naked, flapping the sheet, turning over and over, sometimes lighting a candle and reading till she fell asleep. Letters from home spoke of snow and blizzards, ice on the inside of the window panes, the school heating had broken down and Rick had to wear gloves to play the piano, her mother had taken in a stray cat.

At the end of the month the co-operative in Machakos rejected the first load of kiondos, saying that only natural-coloured baskets would sell overseas. Mr Katambo had leased an acre of land down at the river and the Women's Group cleared it ready for a tree nursery and vegetable plot. It was covered with thick scrub and thorn bushes, they left the trees but tore down everything else, slashing their way through the undergrowth with pangas. Then one afternoon when they were resting in the shade Jerusa told her that Isaiah had returned to university.

'He asked me to tell you.'

It was as if Isaiah had forced a gap in her life which hadn't been there before. It was six months before she saw him again. Work went well but no longer meant so much to her. She even grew tired of Jerusa and spent more time alone in her own house, reading and listening to the radio. She questioned her belonging in Kingangi. In February it was the mango season, heaps of musty sweet fruit were for sale in the marketplace and all along the roadside, discarded hairy white pips. Children brought presents of mangoes to her house and in return she would let them come in and draw with coloured felt-tips. A girl and her mother came to ask for help with money for school fees, she gave them three hundred shillings, about fifteen pounds, but had to refuse the others who followed. In March the long rains began and the first vegetables germinated in the shamba by the river. It was an experimental garden with new crops; tomatoes and peppers, courgettes and different kinds of beans, as well as cassava, cabbages and sweet potatoes. She went there every day to pull out the weeds and water the seedlings. The tree seeds had been planted in polythene pots and stacked beneath a dry grass shelter to shield them from the sun. The local forester came up to Kingangi to give them advice on how best to grow the different species. A Danish volunteer came out from Machakos to show the women how to make traditional dyes from local leaves and flowers and bark to produce the colours wanted for export baskets. Afterwards the women complained that they didn't have time to dye sisal, that it was easier to weave in wool or coloured plastic bought from town. And Mr Katambo was still unhappy with her work; he came every few weeks to ask about the grant.

'What about your Field Director? He is an important man. He can visit that office and request some help.'

'He's already written a letter for me. We just have to wait till April.'

'I think you can go to Nairobi and make another request.'

'There's no point, they'll only get annoyed if I keep bullying them.'

'What about the United States?'

'They said they couldn't give us anything, apart from schoolbooks.'

'And Canada, you asked them?'

'I'm waiting to hear.'

Then in April she received a letter from the British High Commission awarding the project three thousand pounds. Saying nothing to Mr Katambo she went straight to Nairobi.

'How much water will this scheme provide?' It was the same young Englishman in city-striped shirt, looking more bronzed and overweight than before.

'It's based on an estimate of eleven gallons per person per day,' she said, 'Ten gallons per cow and four for goats and sheep.'

He jotted it down. 'What about population growth?'

'That's already taken into account – for twenty years at four per cent. It's all tabulated in the proposal.'

'We just have to check that you know what you're talking about. Too much money's already been wasted on these sort of schemes.'

She signed the papers then went to the Field Office to discuss the work with Geoff. He was away on safari assessing new projects in the north of the country. There was a letter for Jo on the board; a short note from Sally saying that her project had collapsed due to fighting in the area and she and the two doctors had packed up to go home. *It makes me wonder if we should ever have been sent in the first place.*

It was a Saturday in June, Museo was sitting inside doing a page of sums that Jo had written for her and Jo was hanging the washing out on the line when she saw a man standing on the track looking down to the house. He waved when she looked up and then walked on. It was Isaiah.

She went out that afternoon, knowing that she would meet him. He was sitting on the bank by the school and got up to greet her.

'I thought you were away at university.'

He was almost as she remembered him, wearing the same clothes and dark beret, worn-out shoes. But he'd grown a bit of a moustache.

'I'm just here teaching, until the 11th of July.'

Isaiah was living in a room behind the school. There was a row of these cell-like rooms, each measuring scarcely more than eight feet by four, with a bed and chair and desk. The male teachers lived here. A couple of them were sitting in the shade in the yard outside drinking cloudy local beer from tin mugs. Another bottle was standing in a bowl of water beneath the trees. They greeted Jo warmly, swaying as they got to their feet to shake her hand.

'You must taste some uki, come and join us. This is local beer, the best, very strong.'

One of the young men staggered across to the tree and poured out a mugful of honey beer from the bottle in the water. Isaiah unlocked the padlock on the door of his room.

'That beer's not clean, you shouldn't drink it,' he said to Jo.

But she was keen to try it. It was sour and faintly fizzy, a honeyed yeasty taste, cool, a few bits of sediment and dirt floating in the bottom.

'Thanks, that's enough.'

'It's good?'

'Very good.'

'Take some more.'

'No, that's enough.'

'What's your name?'

'I thought you knew – Jo.'

'Where from?'

'I live half way down the hill, the other side from here.'

'Where Mutisya was before you came.'

'Who's Mutisya?'

'You don't know?' the two men laughed, 'Mutisya, oka, come here!'

Isaiah came out into the yard, he'd changed and was buttoning up a clean white shirt. The men began to banter in Kikamba.

'Come inside,' Isaiah said. It was obvious he was angry.

Jo sat on the edge of the bed. The room was dark and cramped, Isaiah had shut the door and the shutter to the small window was only slightly ajar. There was a pile of tatty exercise books on the desk and a few university text books. On the floor by the door was a charcoal jiko, a pan and a couple of potatoes.

'Can you take some lunch?'

'OK. Thanks.'

He went outside to light the jiko and Jo got up from the bed and flicked through the exercise books, page after page of identical work in each, copied no doubt from the blackboard. Then she came across the most recent work: 'What is education?'

'Is this what you set?'

'What?'

'About education?'

'Yes, but those boys can't think. Look at what they write. They just think education is about coming to school each day. But they only come here because it's better than working in the shambas – here they can sit around, copy down what the teacher writes on the board, eat a good lunch and spend the evenings playing football. They pretend they're learning.'

'Where did you go to school?'

'Here, to this school and then to sixth form in the town.'

'And you've done OK.'

'I was the only one. There were only five of us who passed – out of sixty – and I was the only one who went to the sixth form. The others couldn't find money for fees.'

'How did you manage?'

'Mr Katambo gave me help.'

Isaiah was chopping a potato in the palm of his hand with a large sharp knife. A few bits of onion were already frying in some fat on the jiko, he dropped in the potato and a handful of maize and beans from a sack beneath the bed, then poured in water and covered the sufuria with a tin plate.

'And you've seen those teachers,' he said, 'They're just boys, they don't care, they go to class drunk, they smoke bhangi, how can they teach when their brains are sky-high?'

'Surely the headmaster keeps a check on things?'

'He's a drunkard himself.' Isaiah had taken off his beret and was standing close to her with one foot up on the chair, his arms resting on his knee, the knife still in his hand. 'He's respected because he's an educated and wealthy man, but everyone knows he steals from the school fees to buy beer for his friends and furniture for his home.'

'Maybe it's just a rumour, people are probably jealous.'

'No, I'm telling you that's the truth.'

'Can't the governors sack him and appoint someone else?'

'They wanted him to be headmaster because he's a Kamba. They got rid of the last headmaster even though he was good because he wasn't one of us, because he was a Kikuyu and they didn't trust him.'

There was a newspaper on the floor, Isaiah tore off a page and screwed it up to wipe the dust from the seat of the chair.

'Can I have a look?'

It was months since she'd seen a paper.

'The news is bad,' he said, 'They've detained another of our lecturers from the university – Mukaru Nganga – that's seven held without trial. They detained George Anyona because he was against the one-party state, and John Khaminwa, his lawyer. How can these people have fair trials if even the lawyers are arrested?' He was thumping one hand on the palm of the other as he spoke. 'And you know Al Amin Mazrui?'

She didn't.

'He wrote *Cry for Justice*. He was detained on the seventh of June. The government is suffocating the voice of the people, arresting anyone it fears. It destroyed the people's theatre at Kamiriithu, now it's interfering with what we can learn, controlling what books are taught in the schools and university, what plays we can see, what journalists and writers are allowed to say. I tell you this country is rotten at the top.'

'What about Oginga Odinga?'

'He was expelled from the party in May.'

'I know, but do you think he'll try to overthrow the President?'

'I can't talk, even walls have ears.'

She was surprised at his sudden reticence.

'What do you mean, surely you can say what you think.'

'People are arrested for saying what they think.'

'But no one's going to arrest you up here, anyway who's going to hear. There are only two drunken teachers outside.'

'You don't understand.'

She picked the hard black weevils out of the githeri and put them on the side of the plate, they sat side by side on the bed, eating slowly without talking. He was very thin, but muscular. His hands were slim with neat cut nails. He smoked another cigarette when he'd finished eating, but only had a few puffs before he stubbed it out and balanced it across a mug on the desk. She felt him move closer to her, he seemed to be looking at her in a different way.

'Thanks for the food, it was very good. I've got to get back now.'

She stood up and opening the shutter saw that it was already dusky outside. Darkness came quickly in Africa, sweeping down like a blanket over a fire.

'It's Saturday, why are you so busy?'

'I enjoy it, I'm working on the first water pump.' As she spoke she knew that a moment was there, but something held her back, a flash of what it would be like, flattened on her back, his pent-up energy spurting out, and the drunken men outside listening through the door.

'I've got some drawings to finish tonight.'

'They can wait one day, we can just talk some more.' He stood up and was close behind her, almost touching, she could smell the faint tobacco smell on his breath. 'You can stay here.'

'No.'

He moved away immediately, took his beret from the hook on the door and put it on.

'I'll walk you home.'

'It's alright I can make my own way.'

'It's not safe to walk alone at night.'

He picked up the panga and torch from beside the bed and they went out into the grey night. The moment had slipped away like a snake through the grass. As they walked along the track and down the hillside he shone the beam of light far ahead of them, flashing it from time to time into the bushes. When they reached the hedge by her house Museo was there waiting for her on the doorstep.

'Thanks, I'm OK now.'

He turned off the torch and held her hand, 'Have you ever been to the waterfall?'

'No,' she was interested, 'I didn't know there was one.'

'Beyond Matundu, about three hours walk from there. I'll take you.'

'OK.'

She climbed through the hole in the hedge and found herself half-running over the rough dry grass up to the house. Museo had brought milk as she always did and a soft yellow pawpaw from Jerusa, they slit it open with a panga, scooped out the black seeds and sat eating it together, the sweet yellow juice running over their mouths and fingers.

Later, when Museo had left, Jo undressed and washed in a bowl of cold water. She dried herself and lay down naked on the bed. Outside, the familiar sounds; a far-off cry of a child, a dog barking, the cicadas. It was a long time since she'd felt this thrill of anticipation.

CHAPTER EIGHT

As soon as it was light Jo and Jerusa and Museo got up from the small uncomfortable bed.

Jo went down to the corrugated iron shed at the bottom of the compound and washed quickly in a bucket of river water, shivering with each splash and feeling the soap stinging the sores on her wrists. Her body was bruised and aching, there were dark patches on her shins and thighs where she'd been kicked. She felt numb to what had happened; it seemed very distant, true and yet not true, the violent rape. Museo had given her a small rough towel, she began to dry herself but then decided to wash again, lathering the soap all over her body and then tipping the whole bucket of water over her head. She felt warm afterwards as she walked back across the compound, dressed in one of Jerusa's nylon dresses. The dress was made of thick material and smelt of soap powder and sweat. She belted it tightly but it had been stretched to cover a child-bearing figure so it bulged across her stomach and hung loose over her bosom. In it she felt disguised and safe.

Jerusa was cooking thin uji porridge for breakfast. She'd put on her best clothes, a tight red skirt and see-through blouse that was straining at the buttons, she'd got fatter in the past few months, her tummy bulging as if she were pregnant.

'When we've taken breakfast we must go to the police to report everything that was stolen,' Jerusa said.

'I don't really care about my things. I just want to make a statement about what happened.'

Jerusa poured the uji into tin mugs and handed Jo the largest.

'It's different here from England,' she said, 'It's best if you just say that your money and possessions were stolen. Don't mention anything else.'

'But they're bound to ask.'

'You can say you were beaten. Say they tied your hands. But don't tell them that the man had intercourse with you.'

'Why not?'

'The police are not good.'

They drank the uji sitting on low stools beside the fire in the kitchen hut. Jo felt dull to the world. A boy came in and herded out one of the goats that were sleeping in the corner. Then the grandmother arrived with a bucket of milk from the cow. She had one of the babies tied on her back, a newborn child with tiny clasping fingers and a yellow knitted bonnet. She told Jerusa that Ben Kyalo had gone to town to report the 'magic' to the Chief and Assistant Chief. He'd sent some men to change the locks on her house and put bars on all the windows. Mutanu, Jerusa's mother, had gone to clean and wash the floors.

Jo wanted to go to her house but Jerusa set off in the opposite direction taking the short cut along the track towards the village and then branching off down to the valley. They brushed through a thick banana plot and then skirted along the edges of the shambas and tobacco fields, following the fierce hedges of sisal plants with their thick spike-leaved bases, until they reached the sandy goat track which cut down the hillside to the river site they'd been working at. It was hard to believe that she and Jerusa and some of the other women had been there only the day before. There were still the prints of bare feet in the sand and the irregular tracks where the heavy sandbags had been dragged from the bank to the water. She thought how suddenly an unexpected event can change the course of life, how it killed the meaning of everything. They stopped under a tree at the edge of the bank to take the thorns and spiky burrs out of the soles of their rubber 'slippers'.

'Jerusa?' Jo hesitated; it wasn't easy to talk now the intimacy of the night had gone, 'If you were raped would you report it to the police?'

Jerusa continued to pluck the thorns from her slippers without looking up. She looked strong, standing with her feet planted wide apart, her back straight, breasts and tummy curved outwards.

'It wouldn't be possible for me to report it,' she said, 'Even the same for you. The police are just men like the man who raped you. If you tell them you've been raped maybe they will just want to have you themselves, they'll be jealous of that man, especially because you're white. Or they'll say that he was your boyfriend and you refused him.'

'But I'm not going to pretend it didn't happen.'

Jerusa turned away and unwound her khanga, shaking it in the air. Then she pulled it tight around her waist and rolled it over to secure the top. She stood waiting to go.

'Maybe you don't know about these things,' she said quietly, 'It happens to many women here, even girls, even quite young girls who don't know about intercourse.' She picked up the kiondo that Jo had been carrying. It was a woven purple basket given to her by one of the women from the Women's Group, and contained her notebook with the address of her friends in Nairobi and the hundred shilling note which Ben Kyalo had brought back from her house.

'Let's go,' Jerusa said, 'It's still far.'

They crossed the river at its lowest point and scrambled up the long slope, reaching the top out of breath and with sweat trickling down their faces. Jerusa wiped her forehead with the corner of her khanga and went on, but Jo paused for a moment longer, looking back in the direction in which they'd come, across to the hill on which she lived. She tried to make out where her house was but it was hidden behind the trees, she could only see the school with its sloping football pitch and the ramshackle row of teachers' houses that ran along the back. She could get to Nairobi in a day, find Isaiah and tell him what had happened.

There was a steep fall dropping down to the eucalyptus forest which marked the far edge of town. The earth beneath their feet was already hot, warmed by the morning sun. Parts of the path had been destroyed by the rain; it led along the side of a gulley and whole sections of the bank had dropped away so that it was difficult for people to pass. Half way down the slope they stood aside and pressed into the hedge to let a chain of women go by with heavy plastic drums of water on their backs. They were on their way from another part of the river; labouring up the hill with the containers tied with ropes that ran in the grooves on their foreheads.

The policeman behind the desk was asleep on his arms. He woke when Jerusa called out in Kikamba and ordered them to wait. They sat on the wooden bench facing the photograph of the President and a tatty poster advising people to beware of pickpockets. Jo hadn't been into the Police Station before but had often passed it on her way to town and noticed groups of people hanging around outside. It was a dingy place, grey and tatty. Even the outer room smelt of the cells behind; a faint odour of sawdust and urine. After a few minutes the policeman got to his feet and called them over.

'You say you work at Kingangi?'

'That's right.'

'And someone stole from your house. At what time?'

'About ten o'clock.'

'And where were you?'

'I was there, in the house.'

'I didn't know there were whites at Kingangi.'

'I'm the only one.'

He looked at her with idle fascination, as if he'd heard it all before but was faintly curious. Then he took a biro out of his pocket and began to write in the log book.

'So if this man was caught you'd recognise him?'

'Yes, I think so, I can't be absolutely sure.'

'Perhaps you know him?'

'No, I've never seen him before – it wasn't just one man, there were two of them.'

'What did they take, a camera, radio?'

'A short-wave radio, . . . '

He interrupted, 'What do you mean, "short-wave" – for cassettes?'

'No, it doesn't matter, just a radio. And money, a camera and clothes,' she paused, he was writing slowly, 'A chair, a gas cooker and cooking pots.'

'And what was the value?'

One by one she went through the value of each of the things she'd listed, and watched in silence as the policeman added it up incorrectly and then tried again.

'But he didn't hurt you?'

'No.'

He was a heavy-jawed man with a scarred face, and when he turned to call another man from the office behind, Jo saw that one of his ears was missing.

'This mzungu is complaining her things have been stolen.'

The second policeman was a sharper looking man, tall and thin. He glanced over Jo critically and then turned abruptly to Jerusa.

'You, wait outside!' he said. 'Come this way,' he commanded Jo with a flick of his head.

She followed him through the back of the police station to a small room with a large desk heaped with papers. He sat down and pushed them to one side, pulling out from under the pile a hardbound book. He repeated the questions she'd already been asked, writing carefully and neatly, spelling words wrongly, mouthing to himself as he wrote the dates and times. Then, leaning back in the chair, he laid down the pen and lit a cigarette.

'Where is your husband?'

'I'm not married.'

'So you live alone?'

'Yes.'

'But you know this man – maybe he was your boyfriend?'

'No, I've never seen him before.'

'But you have a boyfriend?'

'He's away in Nairobi. Look, I want to make a statement.'

He pulled a form out of a drawer behind him and pushed it across the table to her.

'You can write in this space.'

While she was writing two old men, handcuffed together, came into the room followed by the policeman with the missing ear. He picked a pad of ink off the table, spat on it and put it in front of the men. They were frightened and didn't understand what to do, he started to kick them and then in fury seized their fingers, rolled them on the ink and pressed them to the paper.

'Cattle thieves,' he said, 'But we always catch them in the end. Don't we?' He cuffed the head of one of the men, knocking his hat to the floor. Jo didn't look up. 'They were up at Matundu last night but we caught them red-handed.' They were cowering against the wall, heads hung. 'They're just stupid old men, they can't even read or write.'

The younger policeman had finished his cigarette and took the paper from her. He had long fingers and his face was fine, different from those she was used to, with softer hair and holes pierced through his earlobes. He was probably not on Akamba but from one of the northern tribes, Samburu perhaps or maybe even a Somali.

'What was this man wearing – the one who entered your bedroom?' he asked.

'Trousers, not jeans, and a shirt which was a light colour and had a darker V-shape on the front, like this.' She described in the air the pattern on the shirt, two dark strips running from the shoulders to meet at the buttons in the middle, it was the thing that was clearest in her mind.

'And how did he look?'

'He had quite long hair, it wasn't combed, his face was . . .' She'd stared at him, but now she wasn't certain that she was getting it right, it was there in her mind, the face, looming over her, forcing her down, 'I'd recognise him, but the face is hard to describe, he was ordinary-looking, quite young, maybe 25.'

'How tall?'

'It's hard to say – it was dark, I was knocked onto the floor.' Standing over her, kicking, thrown back on the bed, his body forced onto hers. 'About five foot nine or ten.'

'And you say you would know him again.'

'I think so, I can't be certain.'

'You must say you are certain if you want us to catch this criminal.'

'I'm certain.'

He read back to her what she'd written, slowly, hesitating over her words, 'Is that correct, is that everything?'

'No. I was also raped.' She said it bluntly, factually, looking the policeman in the eye. 'When they'd beaten me and taken my things, this man, the one with the V on his shirt, returned. He forced me onto the bed and raped me.'

'He had sexual intercourse with you, is that what you're saying?'

'*Were you a virgin?*'

'*Did you promise him sex?*'

'*How many times?*'

He called the other policeman and told him the story. He stood over her, asking the same questions again. She was on the brink of tears as she repeated what had happened and the older man, brutal and mean-looking with his flat-sided head, asked,

'How can we believe you? Who is your witness?'

'I was alone, there weren't any witnesses.'

'If you live alone you must expect these things.'

When she came out of the police station hours later Jerusa was waiting for her. She'd found a patch of shade against the wall under the hanging bougainvillea.

'What are they going to do?'

'Nothing, they can't be bothered.'

'What about your things? Are they going to look for them?'

'They said it would be hard to find them, that the men had probably gone straight to Nairobi to sell them there.'

'They just want money, we'll have to bribe them before they do anything.'

How? Jo wondered. She hadn't got any money, no one round here had any money. How do you go about bribing the police?

There were a few women sitting on the step of the police station, they'd noticed Jo come out and now were staring at her. She didn't bother to smile but took Jerusa's hand and hurried into the road. They headed towards the main part of town without speaking. A man passed by on a bicycle with a long saw strapped to the back, the metal flexing up and down as he went over the bumps. Further on there was a broken-down truck at the roadside with a couple of men working underneath it and a crowd gathered around to watch. Life went on the same for everyone but her.

'We can go and take tea now,' Jerusa said.

'I'm going to try and get a bus to Nairobi. And go and see the Field Director.'

'That's good. You'll be alright when you tell him. He can give you help.'

Jerusa seemed so strong and certain, her physical strength matched by character. They crossed the large market square, ignoring the shouts to buy oranges and bananas, and went into one of the small chai shops to sit and wait for a bus.

'I'm going to find Isaiah,' Jo said.

'He won't like to hear this,' Jerusa said.

'But he'll understand.'

Jerusa had picked up the spoon and was playing with the sugar. 'Perhaps an African man won't respond in the way you expect. Maybe he'll blame you.'

'I told the police I was raped. It's a fact, I can't pretend it didn't happen just because people don't like to hear it.'

'You know that if a man is convicted of rape he can be given the death sentence.'

A white Nissan van had started circling the square. It was blaring its horn and a couple of men were running behind banging the sides.

'Hurry, you can take that one.'

Jo rushed out and climbed in, she was pushed over the people in the front to a place jammed between four others on the back seat. Someone thrust her basket in to her and the van had already moved off, racing another one out of town before she had time to turn and wave to Jerusa.

CHAPTER NINE

She thought they would never arrive in Nairobi, the Nissan van broke down just after Machakos and they had to wait at the roadside for a bus and then stand the rest of the way, ducking down through the police checks. As so often happened, the bus was waved off the road on the outskirts of the city, the police came aboard and ordered everyone without seats to stand. One of them singled out Jo and asked for her passport and for a moment she thought she was going to be taken off the vehicle, but the turn boy who took the fares gave the policeman money and the bus was waved on. A plump woman made room for Jo on the end of the seat and she balanced there for the rest of the journey with her knees pressing hard into the metal ridge of the seat in front to stop her from falling.

She looked around her as she hurried up River Road, searching the faces for the man who'd assaulted her, watching for the shirt with the black V, suspicious of everyone, noticing the shades of skin, the eyes, the mouths, the facial hair – did he have a beard? She wasn't sure. She felt conspicuous, convinced that someone was following her, that they knew where she was going, and would stop her from reaching Geoff's office. She jumped as a man came hurrying past brushing her bag. The suddenness, the moment of attack, repeated. She walked on as fast as she could without running, past the chai shops and photo studios, the bargain stores with windows of watches and secondhand radios, dodging on and off the pavement to get round the parked cars and people who got in her way. It was a hot afternoon, the sky was a backdrop of blue, the modern city buildings up ahead rising clear against it, postcard-like. The air was heavy with exhaust fumes.

She crossed Moi Avenue, darting in front of a city bus, and now that she was over the boundary between the down-town territory and the smart city she stopped to buy a newspaper. The stall was stacked with international magazines: *The Economist*, *Newsweek*, *Mayfair*, *Penthouse*, some new, some dog-eared, acquired from tourists, airports, hotel rooms and lounges, traded and re-traded. The smiling faces of politicians and naked women.

It was only a short distance to Geoff's office but she went in the opposite direction and walked without thinking till she came to the Thorn Tree cafe at the New Stanley Hotel. It was packed with tourists and travellers; foreign faces, suntanned and unfamiliar, crowded round the outside tables drinking beers. She walked in purposefully, looking around as if she'd come to meet someone, half-believing that a friend might wave and call her over to their table. But only a few people glanced up in her direction and then turned away. There were always messages on the board around the trunk of the thorn tree, notes that people had left for travelling friends. Nothing for her. She hesitated a moment looking for an empty place, but there were only a few spare seats at already crowded tables.

The terrace swam before her, the noise rising and falling. A crowd of faces staring.

'Stop being so frightened,' she said to herself in the mirror in the Ladies, 'No one's going to hurt you here.'

She washed her hands and face in the warm running water and stared at herself again, noticing the freckles on her nose and the muddy colour of her skin under the bright electric light. As when drunk, she was observing herself as if it were someone else.

'It's alright, you're alright. It doesn't look as if anything has happened to you.'

The face in the mirror tried to smile, she saw its lips quivering and tears collecting in the eyes. Then another woman came in and asked her for change for the toilet and she guiltily turned away.

Outside she sat at a table with a couple of African women who were drinking beer. She felt more comfortable with them than with the tourists but when she smiled they ignored her. It was as if part of her person had been taken, her confidence diminished. She wished Jerusa had come with her.

The two women soon got up to go. They were both wearing high-heeled shoes and short skirts, they strolled onto the pavement laughing and swinging their hips, enjoying the stir they caused.

A young man immediately came and sat down next to Jo. He was wearing a blue roll-neck jersey with holes in the shoulders and had a bundle of looseleaf papers which he laid in front of her. He perched on the edge of the chair with his hands on the table and leaning forward intently asked for money.

'I'm a student from Uganda.'

'I've heard that before.'

'No. It is true. Some people try to cheat you but this is the truth. I've got nothing. Only my papers. You come from a rich country, you can give me just some small help.'

'What's your name?' she asked him in Kiswahili.

'Michael Mwangi.'

'A Kikuyu name.'

'No.' He laughed. 'OK. I'll tell you the truth. My wife is sick. She is pregnant. I have come to find work, to get money for the hospital. But there are no jobs in Nairobi.' He raised his hands and then pressed them to his stomach. 'My family is hungry. I just need ten shillings for the bus back to Thika.'

She gave him her coins.

'God will bless you. Asante, mama. Thank you.'

He backed away. When she left the Thorn Tree he was still hovering on the pavement, round the corner, not quite out of sight.

Geoff wasn't in the office when she arrived so she waited. He returned from the swimming pool with wet hair, looking bright and energetic.

'Hi! How are you?'

'Fine.' He was smiling, holding out his hand to shake. She suddenly wanted to blurt out what had happened, to be hugged and held, to cry, but he didn't notice that anything was wrong.

'Just a sec.'

He went next door, put the kettle on to boil, hung up his towel and swimming trunks and combed his hair in front of the mirror. He returned with a couple of mugs of coffee and a packet of biscuits and showed her to a chair on the opposite side of his desk.

'Something pretty bad has happened . . . '

'Go on – '

'I've been raped.'

'Oh my God.'

He came and stood behind her holding her shoulders. He didn't know what to say or do. It would have been easier for them both if she'd broken down in tears but now the need to do so had drained away. She spoke flatly, it was no longer difficult to say the words without feeling them. *I woke with a knife at my throat, they dragged me onto the floor and tied me up. Then, then, I was raped.*

He let go of her shoulders – his hands had lingered too long – and walked over to the window.

'Have you any idea who it was?'

'I didn't know them but I'd recognise them again, one of the men at any rate, the one who raped me.' She said it again to make it true – to get used to it – to make sure he'd heard her.

'You must go and see a doctor,' he said.

She wanted to stay in the safety of his office, but he seemed anxious to get rid of her. He dialled the doctor and she listened as he explained to the receptionist over the phone.

'This is an urgent case, she's got to see someone today.'

The woman he was talking about didn't sound like her.

'I've got you an appointment for five o'clock. Dr Macleod, in the British High Commission building. Come back here afterwards.'

'I've got to go and see a friend.'

'What about tonight, have you got somewhere to stay?'

'Yes, that's fine.'

'You're sure.'

She nodded.

'You'd be welcome at my place. Seriously – I'll take you out for a meal or something.'

'No, it's OK thanks, I've fixed up to stay with someone.'

'Well, listen, come back here tomorrow then. I think the best thing I can do is drive you down to Kizui. I'll sort out the Police and have a word with the Assistant Chief. Then you can pack up some stuff and stay here until it's been cleared up.'

'I was planning to go back to work.'

'We can talk about that tomorrow. But I don't think it'll be safe for you to go on living there until the men have been arrested.'

The phone went and Jo slipped out.

'Ask the accountant to give you some money now,' he called after her.

Out in the warm afternoon sun she felt happier again, momentarily special. She went to Woolworths to buy Hair Glo for Jerusa and cigarettes for Isaiah. Then she headed for the university, turning off Kenyatta Avenue, past the back of the market where the Kikuyu and Akamba women were selling woven baskets. There were bunches of flowers in buckets on the pavement; firm orange Birds of Paradise, purple orchids, and speckled Tiger lilies.

Voices were rumbling in her head, jumbling unintelligible words that she couldn't stop. Madness.

She spoke out loud, 'I'm going to find Isaiah,' but the voices went on, laughing back at her.

Outside the main university building a man was mowing the grass. It was a sweet English smell. She went straight into the central building and asked at the desk for Isaiah.

'He comes from Kizui District, he's an Akamba.' She couldn't remember his family name. The man had his arms folded across his chest, he stared back blankly, too lazy to help.

'It's very important,' she said, 'Could you just look at the list? He's studying Literature and Politics, a third year.'

'I can't find someone without a proper name.'

'I've got to see him, it's urgent.'

'What is it – has someone died? If it's so important why don't you know the name?'

A young man in spectacles had come up behind them and was listening.

'Who do you want?' he asked.

'I'm looking for a third year student,' she described Isaiah, 'He often wears a dark beret.'

The student directed her to the accommodation block across the highway up towards Uhuru Park.

'Students aren't allowed visitors staying in the rooms,' the man behind the desk called after her.

She passed the Norfolk Hotel; an impression of tables heaped with food and bottles, well-dressed foreigners. A row of taxis was parked outside, shining black in the sun, the drivers called out to her as she went by. She smiled and shook her head. A smell of roasting maize, sweet and burnt, drifted towards her as she cut down the path at the back of the Boulevard Hotel. There was a man on the corner roasting maize in an upturned oil drum. She stopped to buy a piece.

'For one shilling, please.'

Using a bit of broken metal he cut a couple of inches from a cob and sprinkled on some salt and red chilli powder.

'Asante sana, thank you.'

It brought relief to talk to people, pretending nothing had changed. Letting them see her; bright, white, smiling, fortunate. Or did they glimpse the fear beneath the surface, the shattered confidence and lack of trust?

Pop music was blasting out of the rooms into the corridors of the student accommodation block: '*This is the Voice of Kenya, Nairobi, the time, five o'clock.*' A young man came past swinging a huge radio cassette player and singing to the music, 'By the Rivers of Babylon'. For a split second she thought it was Isaiah, he was wearing similar black shirt and trousers.

'Excuse me!'

When he turned, his face was quite different. He stood jiggling to the music while she tried to explain who she was looking for.

'Yeah, I know him, just follow me.'

The door to Isaiah's room was locked. The student waited while she knocked, no answer, she knocked again – harder, louder, longer.

'I don't think he's there,' the young man said, 'Maybe he's staying someplace else.'

'I'll leave a note then. Can I borrow a piece of paper and a pen?'

She followed the student into his room. On the walls were posters of Mandela, Guevara and Marilyn Monroe. There was a heap of folders on the floor by the bed. He put a pen and sheet of paper on the desk for her.

'Are you his girl?'

'Just a friend.'

She smiled at the put-on American accent.

'Cig?'

He offered her a 'Sportsman' from a packet by the bed.

'Thanks.'

She hadn't imagined it like this – typical student accommodation – loud music, unemptied ashtrays, unmade beds, pictures and cuttings on the wall, piles of library books. Isaiah's description had been of somewhere grey and austere. A place of seriousness.

After she'd seen the doctor she wandered aimlessly. It would be best to remain alone and take a room in a cheap hotel. All formalities were over, there was no one but herself to blame for what had happened. She passed a cafe with bowls of salad, slices of cheese and brown bread rolls in the window, the sort of food she hadn't seen for months. She joined the queue but as she drew nearer to the counter her stomach caved in and she turned and pushed her way out.

Jeevanjee Gardens were beautiful when the purple jacarandas were out but at this time of year the trees were bare. A few old men were asleep on the benches in the patchy shade of the scraggy branches. She sat on an empty seat in the sunshine, hugging her kiondo on her lap, and stared into space. She could go to Westlands, to the smart suburbia of the city where friends of her parents lived, to Diana's motherly welcome, to hot bath and clean sheets. But it was all too serious to tell a mother, these things don't happen to girls who could be daughters. So back to Geoff, a virtual stranger? Or find a safe hotel, with bolts on the door? She postponed the decision and got out the postcard that she'd bought in the kiosk at the bottom of the High Commission building, it was of elephants with the flat snowy peak of Kilimanjaro behind, another for Rick to pin on the kitchen wall. She only told him that her house had been broken into, and said she'd got a week's holiday coming up, how about coming to visit? She knew he would read the plea between the lines.

She was lucky and got straight on a number 16 heading up to Westlands. It was crowded with people leaving the city centre at the end of the day; schoolkids in smart uniforms, shoes and socks, who were chatting in English. The woman next to her had polished nails and a gold bracelet, she was reading a copy of 'Drum'. Jerusa should be here, working in the city, dressed up and looking beautiful, not stuck in the country doing endless washing and cooking and carrying.

'Make sure you go to a doctor,' Jerusa had said before Jo left, 'Go to a good doctor, not an African.'

He was an old white man, stout, bald, with a little moustache and tweed jacket.

'Come in. Now what can I do for you young lady?'

'Hmm. Raped. Raped were you? Is there actually anything wrong? Any pains, bleeding?'

'No. Probably nothing to worry about, not a lot I can do, anyway can you get undressed and hop up here.'

'Now, this man you say raped you, was it once or twice?'

'I hope you don't mind me asking this sort of thing, but did you fight or were you relaxed?'

'So you just lay back – very sensible, a lot of women find if they relax they suffer no pain and it's almost enjoyable.'

'Just one more thing for the record – did you reach orgasm?'

'But he did?'

'I'm not upsetting you am I? They're difficult for me too, these personal questions. I can sense it's been disturbing, a bit of an emotional upheaval.'

'But you know, some women consider rape a compliment. That's what the African girls think, it shows they're sexually attractive to men.'

The bus stopped at the Westlands shopping centre and Jo got out. Some boys were polishing the parked cars and others were hawking punnets of strawberries. She bought a couple of boxes to take to Diana, and then tried to phone her again but there was still no reply.

It was almost dusk and not safe to walk the next three miles up the road to their house but she didn't care. It was only when she was half way there and it had become dark that she felt frightened again. She started to jog. It was a windy road darkened by close trees on either side, there were padlocked gates which led up to the smart houses secluded in this affluent suburbia. Guard dogs, hearing her footfall, came leaping to the gates, snarling. She stumbled on her flipflops and dared not look behind her.

The guard came to unlock the gate and Diana's dog, a friendly old labrador, snuffled around her dirty blistered feet as she walked up the drive. The flipflops had rubbed away the skin between her toes.

Diana opened the door. She was dressed in a low-cut evening dress, with a turquoise necklace, huge silver earrings and her hair piled up.

'How wonderful to see you. You've come at just the right time. We're having a surprise party for Jeremy, it's his 50th birthday!'

Jo was swept in and up the stairs.

'You will stay the night?'

'If that's alright.'

'And you must join the party – everyone will be delighted to see you.'

It was a strange relief to be caught up in Diana's enthusiastic welcome. She treated Jo as both child and woman, in the way a mother would.

'Borrow one of Lucy's dresses, and help yourself to my makeup.'

Jo washed and pulled on the first dress that she took from the cupboard. She didn't look in the mirror. A gentle hubbub of chatter drifted up the stairs as the first people arrived. She went to the landing, looked down and saw Fidelis standing in the hall with drinks on a silver tray. She couldn't face a room full of whites – the small-talk and jokes – she should have stayed in town and gone back to the university. In the bedroom she looked at the sculptures, carefully lit in alcoves in the walls; a soapstone woman, thick-featured, legs curled beneath her, breasts hanging uneven, a 'shetani' carving of polished ebony, the face distorted, open mouth, square teeth, one breast small and round, the nipple pointing high, the other hanging low and heavy, nipple held between finger and thumb. A chameleon balanced above the body, tail curled round. Above the bed, carefully positioned, was a small fertility goddess and beside her a tree of life; climbing, distorted figures, large heads and thin limbs intertwined with one another. She couldn't sleep with such things around her.

She sat at the dressing table. She brushed and pinned up her hair, put on mascara, eye shadow, lipstick, deliberately overdoing it.

Outside, the swimming pool was floodlit. A sweet smell of moonflowers drifted in through the open window. She sprayed perfume on her neck and wrists, got up and twirled about the room, then flung herself flat on the bed and stared at the ceiling.

She wandered down to the crowded smoke-filled room. Diana was at the door, smoking a cigarette in a long holder.

'You do look lovely, but far too thin,' she stuck the cigarette in her mouth and adjusted the shoulders of the dress in a motherly way, 'I don't know who you're going to find to interest you, there aren't many young things here I'm afraid. Though there's a rather sweet woman from the university who should be coming.'

'I don't think she'll make it,' the woman in pink interrupted, 'Martin saw her this afternoon and she was in a terrible tiz.' She turned to Jo, 'I expect you've heard, things aren't very healthy up there these days. After those left-wing lecturers were arrested the students have been determined to stir up more trouble.'

'I heard a group of them chained themselves naked to some railings,' Diana said, 'But it may have been a rumour.'

The pink lady chuckled and ate a sausage roll.

'Well, a beautiful new face I haven't encountered before.'

A dark-haired man had appeared at Jo's side. He was wearing an expensive suit with spotted yellow tie.

'James, you must meet Jo, daughter of my greatest friend. She's terribly brave and works out in the bush, all on her own, on one of these water schemes for the villages.'

His eyes roved over Jo as Diana spoke, noting the lipstick and the dark eyes, straying to the hands with chewed nails clutching the glass.

'Is that with one of those volunteer schemes, that plonk you out in the bush and see how long you can survive before you come down with malaria or hepatitis?'

'Not exactly.'

She knocked back her wine.

'What do you do?'

'I'm with the Bank.'

'Barclays Bank?'

He smiled tolerantly, 'The World Bank. We deal with the big schemes. The fact of the matter is . . . ' Diana and the pink lady had left her, Jo looked around in search of someone else to talk to but knew no one. 'I was saying, the fact is that Africa's in a bloody mess and really it's only the chaps like us who can begin to sort it out. The trouble is, of course, that Africans are basically lazy and greedy, they all just want something for nothing. So no sooner have you propped a nation back on its feet than it topples over again.'

'I don't think you can put all the blame on the Africans. The World Bank is always devising these unrealistic superschemes and then blaming the people when they don't work.'

'For example?'

'The Tana River irrigation project. Which didn't work, so more money was poured in and then, when that didn't help, they turned round and blamed the people who'd been forced to move there.'

He seemed not to be listening. His eyes had strayed again to her neck and breasts, the safety pin in the front of the dress.

'I agree that the necessary finance and infrastructure has got to be developed,' she went on, 'But people here are as hard-working as anywhere . . . '

'Cigarette?'

She refused.

'I didn't think you'd smoke. Well, to be honest I don't know what a pretty girl like you is doing out in the bush. You can't exactly be having a whale of a time.' He lit his cigarette, 'Unless you've got a thing about black men, which I somehow doubt.'

She left the room without a word, pushing through the people, passing through alcohol, perfume, smoke, as if in slow motion. Diana was at the door, her words followed Jo out.

'Poor girl, she's terribly tired, she's come all the way down from the bush.' Jo stopped to listen. 'It must be quite a strain living out there all on her own – and working so hard.' She fled up the stairs and threw herself onto the smooth-covered bed.

Isaiah, where are you, what the hell am I doing here?

As she cried the mascara ran and blackened the pillow.

CHAPTER TEN

The day Isaiah took Jo to the waterfall she woke to see a lizard in a patch of sun on the stool beside her bed, it was poised motionless only a foot away, its tail curled round behind, and as she stirred its red head began to click up and down. She could see the pattern of its skin in the folds around its neck; the deep ancestral lines.

She washed standing in a plastic bowl in the bathroom, pouring a mug of water over herself, then another and scooping it up and using it again. It was only seven o'clock but already hot, her body felt sticky after the restless night on the soft foam mattress. It had been airless in the room, she'd woken and fanned the sheet but then still tossing and turning and unable to sleep had got up and gone outside. The sky was jet black and crowded with stars, she'd hung her head back and looked up, and had a mad desire to get dressed and run up the hill to knock on the door of Isaiah's room behind the school. But she'd returned to bed and slept at last. Now she tipped the bowl of water over her head and combed back her hair.

She took longer than usual deciding what to wear and having discarded one shirt after another and then discarded that she pulled everything from the cupboard and dumped it on the bed. She found a thin white Indian shirt that she'd forgotten about, put it on and hung the string of coloured beads that Museo had threaded for her around her neck. There was Zairean music on the radio. She tidied away the clothes dancing and singing along, her own invented sounds to the African song. The sun was streaming into the room, casting a pattern through one of the torn curtains onto the dusty concrete floor. She looked around for the lizard but it had disappeared. A couple of geckoes were now clinging to the underside of the stool catching flies.

There seemed to be nothing to do when she was ready. She put away the milk and the remainder of the pawpaw in the food safe and washed her cup and knife in the last drop of water from the bucket in the bathroom. Then she rearranged the papers on her desk. There was a letter from Rick she'd been meaning to answer and a reminder to renew her subscription to the *Guardian Weekly* but she postponed both again. An hour later Isaiah still had not arrived.

She was sitting on the doorstep, dreaming into the distance, when she spotted him on the hillside. He was some way off, coming down from the direction of the school, strolling slowly. He had a package in one hand and a stick in the other with which he was flicking at the bushes along the path. She went indoors and pretended to be busy at her desk. He must have stopped to light a cigarette just before he reached the house, he was drawing on it as he knocked, and bent to stub it out on the step before he came in.

'Wimuseo?' he greeted her in Kikamba and she smiled at the gentle teasing in his voice.

'Ii nimuseo. Fine,' she said.

He shook her hand, clasping it one way and then the other, confirming his own excitement. She was struck by how good he looked; he was wearing trousers that she hadn't seen before, they looked as if they came from a suit, a white t-shirt and the dark beret.

'I've brought you some books.'

Inside the piece of tatty paper torn from a maizemeal bag were four of the African Writers series, all of them soft and battered.

'You should read Ngugi first, then Marechera and Alex la Guma.'

'Which of the Ngugi books?'

'*The River Between* is easy – I've been teaching it in school. *Petals of Blood* is a bit difficult but that book is so good.'

'What's it about?'

'It's a political novel. If you read it carefully then you can really know about Kenya. He can see what's rotten. It's satire. You know that Kenyatta locked him up in 1977, then Moi let him out in 1978 but he couldn't get another job at the university. So he went back to the country and talked to the people, wrote in Kikuyu, and produced plays at Kamiriithu. He thinks writers should rediscover their mother tongues and speak out for the people.'

'Do you agree?' She smiled but he needed no encouragement, he'd picked up the book and was flicking through it as he spoke.

'Of course. He's a revolutionary. He wants to smash the neo-colonial state and build socialism and a true democracy.'

'It sounds like political dogma to me.'

'You must read the book.'

He turned to a page that was marked with a scrap of paper and read,

And you, traitors to your people,
Where will you run to
When the brave of the lands gather?
For Kenya is black people's country.

Or read Marechera – he was thrown out of the university in Harare and went to Oxford. I want to know what you think of him.'

She admired the seriousness with which he spoke, his sudden wide smile which first she'd thought was mocking her but now she knew was a mark of modesty, denying his own intelligence. She envied him his unassuming manner, as if it were nothing special to have gone from here – a rural home, parents who couldn't read or write and had no money – to the university in the capital.

It was a long walk to the waterfall, first down along the dirt tracks through the villages and then out across the scrub land where there weren't any homes. They met Jerusa and her mother on the road to the village and walked with them as far as the turning to Matundu market; they were going there to sell chickens and baskets to buy more maize for the family. Jerusa had one of the babies tied on her back and was in high spirits, laughing and joking with Isaiah, exchanging a quickfire of banter which Jo couldn't follow.

When they'd parted Jo and Isaiah went on, taking short cuts through people's compounds and across the shambas, until they reached a market clearing where they stopped to buy mangoes.

'When I was just in primary school,' Isaiah said as they sat in the room behind the tailor's shop drinking tea, 'We had this old teacher. We thought he was so stupid because he could only count to a hundred. And when he was meant to be teaching us English he'd tell the old Akamba folktales. We used to mock him so much, shouting rude things in English that he couldn't understand.' He tipped his tea from one glass to another cooling it. 'Two years ago I went to visit him. He's very old now. I had to write a paper on oral literature. We sat together in his small house and he told me all those stories again. It was the first time that they really became important to me.'

'Didn't you remember them?'

'Some I did, but we didn't realise they were important then. We just wanted to break away.'

'Most people still do don't they? Even you.'

'I may wear jeans and speak English but I'm an Akamba here.' He thumped his heart. 'To be an Akamba is to be something inside – it's like magic or God, it is belief, it's not like Western culture.'

'We have beliefs too.'

He finished his tea and called for more.

'Do you believe in God?' she asked.

'No.'

'In magic?'

'Yes, I believe it can happen.'

'Tell me about it.'

Isaiah looked about him then leant towards her. 'It's not something that can be explained. Witchcraft exists because every Akamba talks about it. But no one has ever seen it, no one can define it.' He twisted the metal bracelet on his wrist. 'It's the art of secrecy and imagination.'

The heat seemed to swell around them as they dropped down towards the plains. The landscape changed and passing through a thicket of trees she heard a troop of baboons barking and crashing away over the treetops.

The stony track led down to the open scrub; there was dry wood all around, bleached bones of animals, curled cracked seed pods, and brilliant birds perched high on the trees. A startled dik-dik that had been browsing near the path leapt away, zig-zagging frantically into the bush.

Isaiah motioned her to stop and be silent, he pointed through the bushes and she saw the crouched figure of a man stalking silently through the undergrowth, a bow and arrow in his hand.

'He's looking for meat.'

'What sort of meat?'

'Anything – birds, maybe a gazelle, snakes even. They come out here when there's not enough food in the villages.'

Further on Isaiah stopped to pick a handful of yellow marula fruit, she'd seen them in the market place, piles of bruised round yellow fruit, sold for only a few cents a heap.

'Try one – this is what people eat when there's drought, the old people and the children come down here to pick these fruits.'

It tasted sweet and watery, he tipped the rest into her hands and she chewed them slowly, spitting the slippery brown seeds onto the ground.

They heard the roar of the water before they saw the fall and had to push their way through dense spiky undergrowth to reach the river's edge. A fine spray blew across to them, Jo set out across the rocks to get closer, the crashing sound deafening her ears. The waterfall was about seventy feet high coming over a rocky escarpment. She bent and splashed the river water up into her face and sipped a little from her cupped hands to slake her thirst. When she looked around Isaiah had disappeared, then she heard the faint echo of his voice and saw him half way up the dry rocks at the side of the fall. She crossed back to the bank away from the spray and followed, it was an easy climb up the edge of the escarpment, hauling herself over solid boulders almost step-like in their arrangement and then finding footholds in the cracked rockface above. If it was dangerous she didn't care, she found a faster route and was soon higher than Isaiah, showing off, heading for a ledge just a few feet from the top. When she got there and looked back she was frightened, it was a long way down, there was no way on, above was an overhang of rock and to the right the falling water, as she looked the movement seemed to be pulling her down. Giant creepers hung over the fall, they were thick and twisted and covered with moss, dripping with moisture. Isaiah arrived beside her on the ledge, his face was wet, there were bits of undergrowth caught in his hair.

'That's how a thief got away, he ran from the village and when he reached the waterfall he leapt over.'

'I can't hear,' she shouted.

He leant towards her, putting his mouth close to her ear, 'The men who were chasing knew the fall was there, they thought he'd die but the man grabbed the roots, he slid down to the river and the next week he turned up back in the village again.'

She looked again at the hanging roots, it wasn't clear where they were coming from, they didn't look secure enough to hold the weight of a man. Yet she almost believed the story.

The ledge narrowed towards the falling water, Isaiah started to crawl along it, she waited and then followed, looking only forward at the slippery wet rock and the pale soles of Isaiah's feet ahead. As she neared the water the spray blew back wetting her hands and shoulders and trickling over her face. But then they were behind the curtain of roaring falling water, the ledge had widened to a small cave, the noise was different; captured, quieter. He was kneeling in the back of the hollow watching her, she went towards him.

He was trembling, his eyes were wet. She looked at him, hoping he wouldn't speak, but his lips began to move and she heard words she couldn't understand, singing Kikamba words. She smiled and slowly leant towards him, forwards on her hands and knees, closing her eyes but holding his face there before her. He touched her, his hand slipping inside the shirt, brushing the necklace of beads, he took her breast in his hand and bent, licking it, kissing it. She looked down, it seemed the most beautiful thing, his black hair pressed against her skin, his thin brown eyelids closed.

He ripped his clothes off. He was naked but for the metal bracelet around his wrist, and she still dressed with her shirt unbuttoned and his body kneeling up in front of her. No uncertainty. No restraint. He was lean and muscled, smooth black skin, short curled hairs on his thighs, he took her hand and pressed it against him. He was for her utterly different. He pulled off her clothes and pushed them to the back of the cave and they forced each other down onto the hard roughness of the rocks, feeling the pain, not caring, their skins brushing and pressing together, soft and yearning. Out of one body into another; for a long moment her body surged upward with his.

They looked out through the curtain of falling water, down to the shallow river.

'We could have fallen.'

'I wouldn't have minded.'

They laughed, foolish meaningless conversation. She went on stroking his body, running her hand along the long limbs. For the first time they talked without fear of each other – gently, stupidly. He asked if her mother was alive. Would she like me? Yes, of course. Did you know this was going to happen? I hoped so. Why? I liked you. You can stay longer here, you don't have to go back to England. I've got a whole year more – it's a long time. Not long enough. Don't talk about it. You're so beautiful. So are you. He was beautiful; strong, still naked. Nipples cold and hard. She looked again at his body, wanting it to remain unclothed. He said, suddenly, pulling away from her gaze,

'You only like me because I'm black.'

'Everyone's black here.'

'I wanted a white woman.'

'I know.'

She saw some women far below down at the water's edge.

'Can they see us?'

'No, not here.'

'Have you been here many times before?'

'Only when I was a child.'

Hidden behind the veil of falling water she wanted to stop the flow, to pull aside the curtain, arrest the ceaseless falling and turn off the noise. She could see that the women were laughing – one was washing her legs in the water – a picture without sound, their motions slow and distant.

Isaiah had dressed and was touching her again, exploring with a single finger, his eyes following, she bent her head and watched. She wanted him again. Later. Now. They laughed.

She dressed carelessly, enjoying the touch of her crumpled clothes, and they edged on out of the cave through a gap between two boulders which was scarcely wide enough for them to pass. She squeezed from side to side pulling herself through with her hands, all she wanted to do was lift her head and stretch. Isaiah reached the sunshine and stood upright, tucking in his shirt, putting his hat on again, straightening it. They were now high up on the other side of the waterfall. A small boy was standing, not far away, on the rocks level with them and as Jo appeared he moved, an almost imperceptible shift of his foot but enough to distinguish him from the boulders behind. He was wearing khaki shorts and a grey jersey with sleeves that hung from holes in the elbows, he had a stick held across the back of his neck, and one arm up, loosely draped over it, the wrist hanging limp. His face was serious, older than the small frame suggested. She passed close by, uncertain whether or not to acknowledge him, but he didn't move so she walked on down the path following Isaiah. The women on the opposite bank saw them and waved.

'Did you see the boy?' Jo asked.

'Yes.'

'When?'

'When you were climbing up ahead.'

'So you knew he was there, watching?'

'It doesn't matter, it's good to learn – I saw my mother and father when I was younger than that. I slept in the same room with them.'

She turned and looked back and saw the boy crawling through the gap in the rocks behind the water.

They waded across the river and stopped to talk to the women; they hadn't seen Jo before and were excited, what was a white woman doing there, why didn't she come to visit, what was her name? They were younger than she'd first assumed, playful and overexcited, one of them tried to touch her hair and Isaiah shouted at her.

'I don't mind,' Jo said.

'They shouldn't do that; you're not an animal.'

'I'm used to it.'

The girl was embarrassed and hid behind the others, her bright spontaneity crushed.

'They can't just treat you as if you're some strange creature, they should know better. They should respect you.'

She resented his interference.

They walked home fast, knowing that they'd stayed too long and would be caught in darkness before they reached the village. Men were driving their cows home from the grazing grounds, thwacking their sticks on the hard protruding bones of the rumps. A boy in a bright orange jumper ran by, racing after a herd of goats, darting in and out of the bushes to chase out the ones which strayed from the track. The dust rose about the herd of animals, blurring their hurrying legs.

Darkness came before the village was even in sight, a brief burst of amber light warmed the sky and for a short while everything was caught in unnatural light. Then it was dark. They were now on familiar ground and followed the river path by instinct, jumping across the irrigation channels, feeling the spear-headed leaves of arrowroot brushing their ankles. The bullfrogs had begun to croak, sounding like water glugging from bottles.

'Can we go more slowly now? It's not much further.'

'We can rest when we reach the village, it's not good to walk at night.'

Isaiah pulled a stick out of the bushes, broke it in two and gave her half.

'There are too many youths around, they can beat up people here down by the river. Sounds are muffled in the valley.'

She was glad to reach Kingangi. The shops were shuttered and locked except for Kilonzo's where a hurricane lamp was burning; inside a woman was sitting on a sack of maize nursing her baby and a few old men were drinking bottled beers perched on a narrow wooden bench with their backs to the wall. The goods were kept on shelves behind a wire mesh cage and Kilonzo was standing on a ladder dusting the tins of margarine and cooking fat and rearranging the bottles of orange squash. Isaiah called him down to ask for a cigarette and Jo stood at the doorway waiting. She'd seldom been to the village at this time of day, it had a different feel. From somewhere there was the sound of a radio and people shouting. A couple of children came running to the shop for paraffin which they pumped into old squash bottles and stoppered with dry maize cobs. There was something unpleasant about the atmosphere; the lack of light, the fatty smell of boiled meat that hung in the air, the absence of women. They left the shop and passed a group of men leaning against the tree where the women sold vegetables by day. There was the sweet grassy smell of marijuana thick in the air. One of the men called out to Isaiah. He turned back but she waited where she was, running the stick through the sand, listening to the low tremors of their voices and the laughter. A man shot past on a bicycle, startling her, silent in the sand; it was J.K., a friend of Isaiah's and she saw him wobble and wave as he turned the corner. It was a man's world in the village at night, another sphere of life she knew little about.

'What did those men say, the ones under the trees?'

'They were just joking with me.'

'About me?'

'It's alright, they were my friends.'

'But what about people who aren't your friends?'

'Everyone has sex.'

'But not with a mzungu. I know what people say; that they want to know what it's like with a white woman.'

They were nearing Jerusa's home and Jo hoped they'd be able to pass unnoticed, but a child came running down across the dry earth shouting her name. She stopped and waited for the child to reach them, then picked it up not certain who it was. It was one of the smaller ones, a boy, dressed only in a t-shirt with his little bottom bare and dusty.

They went in to visit, most of the family were crowded in the small 'table-room' eating ugali and a stew. Jerusa had bought meat from Matundu market, the veterinary inspector had been the day before and all the butchers had slaughtered cattle. Jerusa fetched two more plates from the food safe and took the meat and bone from her own dish and gave it to Jo.

'Go on, eat,' Jerusa said.

'No, this is yours.'

'You're hungry.'

Later when they'd finished the meal and were drinking tea, J.K. appeared. He leant his bicycle against the mango tree and came in with a couple of beers which he opened with his teeth and put on the table. He was a tall, dark-skinned man with a wide expressive face. He could make the children laugh with just a twitch of mouth or eye and never spoke without wink or smile or frown, conveying the slightest change of thought or mood. He had a beard and wore a floppy black hat, purple shirt and green flared trousers with dark patches where the pockets had fallen off.

Ben Kyalo, Mutanu, Ruth and the children went away to bed.

Isaiah rolled a cigarette and passed around the beers. Then he leapt up.

'Where's the "gram"?'

He took the record player from under the sofa, brushed off the dirt, put in the batteries and loaded on a stack of records. They were scratched and dusty.

'Dancing, sisters!'

He moved the table out of the way and started dancing in the middle of the room, with his back curved and his bottom stuck out, his head nodding to the beat, smiling, his feet in the beaten old leather shoes shifting back and forth. J.K. got up to join him. They held hands and danced together.

'This is music, man!' J.K. said.

Isaiah clapped his hands.

'Dance, dance,' he said.

Jo and Jerusa got up to join them. There was scarcely room for four to dance in the tiny room, their bodies knocked and swung together. Jerusa was singing. Isaiah's eyes were fixed on Jo. The music went on and on, sweat running, her body rising through exhaustion.

CHAPTER ELEVEN

Isaiah came down to her house the following afternoon as soon as school had ended, she was digging the garden and realised that he must have been standing there watching her for some time before she became aware of his presence. She put down the forked jembe and went to shake his hand.

'What are you doing?' he asked.

'Digging.'

She was pleased that he'd found her here, working as hard as any other woman.

'You can't plant at this time of year.'

'It's for next year.'

'But you can buy food.'

'I want to grow it.'

She enjoyed swinging the jembe, feeling the sweat trickling down her face, bending to pull out the roots and grasses, looking back to the newly turned soil, not allowing herself to stop until it was finished. She liked the smell of the earth, its dry sweetness, her mind floating as she worked.

Dreams had surfaced; of living here forever, of the cycles of cultivation and harvest, of the brown coloured children with wide eyes and soft curly hair; images she would never speak of to anyone, that came from deep within.

'I've brought your mail,' Isaiah said.

Her letters came to a post office box in Kizui town which she shared with the school, a teacher would usually bring them to her house, but they were often mislaid – forgotten in the headmaster's pocket or under a heap of books – and wouldn't turn up for months. She took the bundle from Isaiah and flicked through them quickly looking for the airmail letters from England. There was, as there nearly always was, a letter from Rick and one from her mother. She ripped them open, dirtying the thin paper with her muddy hands, and scanned through them eagerly. There were the usual reassuring messages from home, amusing, loving, she read her mother's letter hastily, keen to know everything, and then put it away to save for later.

Isaiah had picked up the jembe and was digging from where she'd left off, swinging the fork with an ease she hadn't mastered. A steady rhythm of swing and fall and heave.

The letter from Rick was only a single page, much shorter than usual. He was spending a weekend with friends in the country, and had written it over a pint of beer at the pub. The scene flashed into mind: the tables in the garden of the village pub, a crowd of friends, brown-legged in summer clothes, eating bread and cheese, laughing at the smallest things. She felt a tinge of jealousy, wanting to be there, wondering who he was with, who he wasn't telling her about.

'What's the news from England?' Isaiah asked.

'Nothing really. It's sunny for the first time this year.'

She folded Rick's letter away and put it with the others in her pocket.

'How is your mother?'

'Fine.'

Isaiah had paused to throw out an old tin can that he'd dug from the soil. He was wiping the sweat from his face. 'She will be missing you so much,' he said.

For days now she'd hardly thought of home, it had slipped from her mind, suddenly no longer needed. She'd written to her family but it was ages since she'd sent a letter to Rick. Those she'd begun had been wrong; flat, untruthful, and now she'd lost the desire to write.

She picked up the tin, it was an old paintpot which might be useful for something. She scraped off the clods of earth with a stick – a channel of white ants was exposed, they hurried frantically into the grass.

'Come here!' Isaiah shouted, 'I've found the queen.'

Several feet underground where the earth was still moist the soft pale body of the queen termite was lying, swollen and regal, attended by scurrying workers. He poked the pulpy body out of its secluded tunnel and then squashed it with the fork.

'Why did you do that?'

'You can't let them breed, they destroy everything, the crops, the trees, even furniture and books. Last year they ate the school library.'

'I don't believe you.'

'No, it's true; it happened in the holiday when no one was there, they ate all the wooden shelves and then all the books. Even thirty copies of *The Government Inspector* – it was the set book.'

She laughed.

'It's not so much of a joke. Now the students have no texts again.'

He destroyed the rest of the nest and continued digging, terracing as he went, heaping earth from one level to the next in a neat step. She followed behind him with a panga, digging up the tough roots of weeds.

It was almost dark when they came inside. What had begun as a simple vegetable patch now looked like a proper shamba. She cleaned the prongs of the jembe with grass and put it with the paint tin in the corner of the room.

'Can I wash?' he asked.

'Of course, there's water in the bucket in the bathroom.'

She listened to him splashing in the water, then sweeping it out through the hole in the wall, and felt again a deep charge go through her. He appeared dressed in his trousers but without his shirt, the light of the lamp made his body look warm and strong.

'Are you hungry?' she asked.

'Later I'll cook for you. I've brought sweet potatoes from my mother's shamba. She sent them for you.'

They stood at the open door, looking out to the glow in the valley, not speaking, only feeling the gentle pulse of their bodies close together.

Then she went to wash. He came to the door and pushed it open.

'Can I watch?'

It was dark but for the faint glow of the lamp coming from the room next door. He watched as she tipped the water over herself, then he put out a hand and pulled her to him. He closed the door and pressed her hard against the wall. It was rough sex, shivering, thrusting, hungry. Passionate in its violence. She drove her nails into his buttocks. He lifted her off the ground and she clung around his neck. Afterwards they laughed.

It was only later when Isaiah was cooking the green bananas and sweet potatoes on the jiko outside and she was dressing again that she remembered the letters in her pocket. They'd fallen onto the floor and lay there as if watching, spying on something secret. She put them face down on the table but for the one from Nairobi which she opened. It was a brown envelope, addressed in large slightly childish writing.

It read, '*The Assistant Chief, Mr Gabriel Kivuto Katambo and Mr Samson Nwambete Nwanza wish to announce that they will be coming on a visit of inspection to the Kingangi water scheme on 5th July. Please be in attendance.'*

'What does this mean?'

Isaiah stopped stirring the food, moved the sufuria to the edge of the heat, and took the letter. He read it once and then again, out loud, sticking out his chest and puffing up his cheeks in imitation of Mr Katambo.

She laughed, 'You're a bit too thin.'

'One day I'll be fat.'

'I hope not.'

'It means they expect a proper reception – they'll want the pump to be working by then, and you should provide beer and get the women to cook.'

A couple of weeks later, only a few days before the visit was due, the pump still hadn't arrived. She'd hired men from town to finish digging the trenches. The pipes were laid, the standpipes were fixed in concrete in the village and the first storage tank had been erected, but there was still no pump. Jo paid J.K. to cycle to Kizui to send another telegram to the manufacturers.

Isaiah came down to visit after school and sat on the doorstep marking books. Jo was watering the flowers and passion fruit tree in her garden, scooping the paint tin into the bucket of bath water and letting the water spray out through the holes she'd punched in the bottom.

'What am I going to do? I can't impress him with just a few underground pipes, an empty tank and taps that don't work.'

'If he's decided to come now he's decided. And everyone is prepared.'

A small celebration had been planned; other important people had been invited, there was going to be singing and dancing, the slaughter of a he-goat, and the women were going to cook traditional food.

'But you know what he's like, he'll expect everything to be working. He's probably even told Samson that there's running water in the village.'

'It's the least of our problems.' Isaiah was chewing a matchstick, when he had no money for cigarettes he chewed matchsticks. 'I am fearing that he will know that I am sleeping the nights in your house.'

'It's none of his business.'

'But it is his house and you are his mzungu. Some people are already talking.'

'Saying what?'

'That the mzungu is going to marry an Akamba.'

For those first secret nights he'd come after dusk and left before dawn. She would watch him disappear up the hill in the early morning, strolling from the hips like a long-limbed animal. He never turned to wave. Later, the schoolkids came past and called out in greeting. She thought of them in the crowded classroom, three to a chair, in front of Isaiah. She wondered what he taught, how much they understood.

But before long Isaiah grew lazy and careless; he lingered longer and they laughed when they heard first the students passing and later the bell for morning assembly. Isaiah never hurried; even when he was late and the bell had already rung he would stroll slowly up the hill.

On Mondays and Fridays they raised the flag in the school compound. Jo would sometimes make a detour to pass there on her way to work. The teachers stood beneath the tree, the children in lines in the sun – bare feet, pink and grey uniforms, straight-backed and serious as the headmaster patrolled the rows looking for those improperly dressed or the ones who'd sneaked into school without paying fees. He would drag them out and beat them later. They stood to attention, hands at their sides, the senior boy saluted and hoisted the flag. The national anthem was sung and then the Evangelical Christian group would sing hymns to the accompaniment of a guitar and tambourine. She sat on the bank out of sight, listening.

She now used one of the school classrooms in the evening for a literacy class. Most of the women from the Women's Group came to it, some wanted to learn how to read recipes, others wanted accounts and business management. She devised simulation games to relieve the struggle of straight reading and writing. The students looked in, eager to see their mothers in school.

Before long she got to know some of the students. A few of the older ones would come down to her house after school, pretending to want help with their work but only really keen to sit on the blue sofa and look around, at the radio, the typewriter, the books and cut-out pictures on the walls. One day she put cassettes into the tape recorder and let them record their voices, they sang and beat a rhythm with a ruler on the side of the table. They were men and women really, disguised by the grey school shorts and skirts and short-sleeved pink shirts, often she wouldn't recognise them when she met them at the weekend in the village dressed in long trousers and t-shirts, with hats and platform shoes. Or in dresses and headscarves with babies on their backs. Some had children of their own and many earned their schoolfees through work on their tobacco plots. They sold the tobacco to the company in town.

Time stood still for the spontaneous moments she had with Isaiah and the students from the school. But as Mr Katambo's visit approached she became reluctant to waste her time with them.

'Can't you tell them not to come today?'

'You're too busy,' Isaiah said, 'No one works all the time.'

On the day before the visit, Isaiah accompanied her to the village shop to buy sugar and bread and margarine.

'Do you remember the first time I met you?'

'Were you waiting for me?'

'Of course.'

'Why were you so unfriendly?'

'Because I wanted to see you get angry. You seemed so good, you were always smiling, greeting everyone.'

She bought the sugar and bread and Blue Band and a packet of flour that she'd promised Jerusa. She gave Isaiah money for cigarettes. Kilonzo, the bull-faced man who wore a dirty yellow waistcoat with biros in the pocket, was unsmiling as always. He seemed to dislike her for no apparent reason. He would often make her wait behind the children for paraffin from the drum and sometimes would pretend he couldn't understand her or that he didn't have the thing she wanted. 'Toilet paper', she could see it there on the shelf behind, 'No, it is finished,' he said. She remained patient, there was nowhere else nearby where she could buy paraffin and toilet paper.

That day he short-changed her and Isaiah noticed.

'You've been given the wrong money.'

'I know, it doesn't matter.' She wanted to get out of the shop without making a fuss.

'You've been cheated.'

'It was probably a mistake, come on let's go.'

But Isaiah had begun to argue with Kilonzo.

'He says you owe him money, is that true?'

'No, but it doesn't matter.'

'He owes you money.'

'It's only a few cents.'

They left the shop and took the back route down to Jerusa's home.

'Not all Africans are wonderful,' Isaiah said.

She didn't reply.

‘Why do you think you have to like everybody, you’re not a stranger here any more? You can be yourself.’

It was disconcerting; the way he saw straight through her act, for that is what it was, she saw it now, she’d been playing a role that she’d invented, that of the perfect foreigner. She’d pushed respect for a different way of life too far, making it sacred, never criticising, suppressing her feelings about the things that annoyed her: children pulling her hair, the man in the shop cheating her of money, the madman hanging around her house, the young women who just came to her house to sit and stare.

‘I’ve never liked Kilonzo,’ she said.

It made Isaiah laugh. ‘No one likes him. They say he sold his wife to a rich Kikuyu so that he could have enough money to build the shop.’

Mr Katambo was coming the following day. They went to bed soon after dark. She woke Isaiah in the night, unintentionally reaching out for him and feeling him hard in her hand, starting to kiss him, hearing him sigh, drawing him onto her and still half asleep tumbling with him for pleasure and sinking back into his arms.

It was a day of celebration and the sky cloudless above. Mr Katambo and Samson Mwanza arrived in the car and took up their seats in the shady banda that had been constructed near the bank of the river. It didn’t matter that the pump hadn’t arrived. Mr Katambo was in his element, dressed in a cream safari suit with a silk handkerchief tucked in the breast pocket, he rose to his feet and delivered a long and resounding speech, praising the Kingangi project, praising the women, praising God and the mzungu, calling on the crowd to cheer and clap and chant her name. There was honey beer and bottled beer and they ate the traditional food with their fingers from banana leaves. In the afternoon Mr Katambo and Samson Mwanza made a tour of the village. They turned the taps on and off, expressing approval, and then slapped the side of the storage tank as if it were the flank of a fine cow. Samson Mwanza had brought her two chickens from Nairobi, packed in polythene bags with the giblets neatly stuffed inside. They drank tea and ate bread and margarine in her house and then drove off back to the city. Mr Katambo spent as much time there as he did in Kingangi.

That night Isaiah was sullen, as if he were jealous of the attention she’d been given.

‘I want to get back to Nairobi,’ he said, ‘It’s too cut-off out here, I never see a newspaper.’

It was only a week till the university term was due to start.

'I think you should come too,' he said.

'I can't do that.'

'You could easily get a job in Nairobi.'

He hovered in the kitchen getting in the way while she was preparing the chicken, she didn't feel like eating it and wished she'd given them both to Jerusa.

'You're in my way.'

He went next door and turned the radio on loud. Then he scoured the bookshelf and pulled out the Brandt Report.

'Have you read it?'

'Bits.'

'Can I borrow it?'

'Sure.'

He stretched out on the blue sofa and started to read. When it got dark she lit the hurricane lamp and put the small paraffin burner beside him on the stool. She watched him for a moment, the light on his face, jealous of the book, its sudden hold on him.

She went outside to fetch water from the tank. There was a small child waiting for her on the doorstep, she almost tripped over it.

'What do you want?'

'Water.' The girl had a kettle and cooking pot. Jo unlocked the tank and let her fill them up. People often sent their children to ask for a little water. The following day the same children would return with presents of bananas.

Isaiah seemed not to notice Jo moving about the house, washing in the plastic tub and lighting the jiko. When she came back dressed in a khanga she found he'd fallen asleep.

'What do you make of the Brandt Report then?'

He woke and looked surprised to see her, then seemingly out of nowhere he said,

'I would like you to be my wife.'

'You're dreaming!'

'No. What is your answer?'

'I can't answer.'

'I want a white wife.'

'There are plenty of whites in Nairobi.'

'I want you.'

It wasn't in the village but in the town that Jo felt friendliness drawing away from her. In Kizui people stared when she went there with Isaiah, the women at the market no longer gave her extra fruit and now they cheated her on the piles of tomatoes, giving her bad ones. Before, she'd always been given the best meat, now it was often fatty with chunks of bone. The man who'd sold her honey now said he had none left. Isaiah appeared not to notice; he greeted his friends and joked with the older people in the market square where he liked to hang around the bars. Then the day before he was due to leave for Nairobi something happened which changed his feelings.

They'd gone to town to buy bread and meat so they could have a small party with Jerusa and J.K. that evening. They'd left the butcher's shop and were crossing the market square when a man shouted out in Kikamba.

Isaiah tensed, his eyes darted round, he clenched his fists. The shout came again and Isaiah turned and leapt upon the man. They scuffled in the dirt like fighting dogs, raising a cloud of dust. Within seconds people had gathered to watch, a woman hastily gathered up her bananas from a sack on the ground. Jo moved back against the tree. There was blood on Isaiah's face and the spittle from his mouth was trailing with dirt. His hat was knocked off and kicked away, a small boy picked it up and put it on. Then an older man rushed foward and dragged them apart.

Isaiah was panting, he got up and brushed the dust from his clothes. He picked his hat off the head of the child and walked over to Jo. The crowd dispersed as quickly as it had gathered and the other man vanished with it.

'What happened? What was it all about?'

'He insulted me.'

The blood on his face had dried, there was dirt in his hair. She hadn't seen him like this before, dirty, ruffled, hurrying away, walking fast.

'But why did you fight?'

'That bastard insulted me.' He took his hat off and ran his hand over the back of his head. 'I don't believe in turning the other cheek.'

'What did he say?'

'It doesn't translate.'

They went into the Hotel Relax. The old man there had seen the fight, he gave Isaiah a cigarette and brought them sodas without saying a word.

'Was it about me?' she asked.

Isaiah wouldn't look at her, she tried to take his hand across the table but he drew away.

'I know it was about me, go on tell me, there's no point protecting me, I want to know.'

'I can't translate it,' he said again. He rocked the bottle on the table, and drew his other hand across his face dragging down on his mouth.

'Go on,' she urged him, 'Just roughly. Tell me.'

'He said: "When you've finished can I fuck the white bitch?"'

She felt a lump in her throat. She'd smiled at the man only a minute before.

'You should have ignored it. He probably only said it because it sounded good.'

Isaiah got up and washed his face at the basin in the corner of the room. He took a bit of broken wooden comb out of his pocket and combed the dirt out of his hair.

'I don't want to leave you here alone,' he said.

'I'll be OK, I'm not alone, I've got Jerusa.'

'I'll come back to visit one weekend.'

Jerusa and J.K. came to eat with them that evening.

'Hey, this man is a hero!' J.K. said, clasping Isaiah's hand and making him turn his face to the light so that J.K. could examine the bruises. They joked, the fight became unimportant. They drank the warm beers carried from the town and ate the roasted meat with salt and chillies.

When Isaiah had gone back to Nairobi Jo threw herself into her work with more vigour than before, she was buoyed up by the Assistant Chief's visit and the prospect of installing the first pump.

'I'm pregnant,' Jerusa said, smoothing both hands over her tummy.

'Who's the father?'

'I think you can guess.'

'J.K.?'

'We are going to get married.'

It made little difference to Jo's friendship with Jerusa; J.K. was seldom around in the early evening, preferring to spend his time with his friends in the village and coming to Jerusa's only when he was hungry. Jo slept less than she used to. It was getting colder at night and she would curl under a sheet and blanket and read the books that Isaiah had left behind. She missed his company, his argument, his liveliness. She longed to make love with him. She wrote a long letter to Rick talking of everything but Isaiah.

One evening, several weeks after Isaiah had left, Jo was pouring the bath water onto the garden, when she noticed three men hanging around on the track above her house. They moved on quickly but were there again when she drew the curtains across the open windows – it wasn't the place where people usually stood to smoke and talk.

CHAPTER TWELVE

In the morning Diana was reading a magazine in the garden, she had her silvery-blonde hair tied up in a pony tail and was dressed in cream cotton trousers and a t-shirt, from a distance she looked much younger than she was. She leapt up and waved.

'Breakfast!' Diana's voice carried down the garden.

Jo pulled herself out of the swimming pool, and still panting from the exertion of the last few lengths hurried barefoot up the lawn to join her at the table on the terrace.

'How was it?'

'Lovely.'

Jo wound a khanga around her waist and sat down on one of the comfy wicker chairs. Her hair was dripping onto her shoulders.

'You're terribly energetic, I just go in to cool down.' Diana poured the coffee into the white china cups. 'I'm afraid the pool really needs a clean,' she said, 'But Fidelis won't do it because he's frightened of falling in – he can't swim.'

Fidelis was hovering in the background waiting to be asked to cook eggs. The conversation didn't include him.

'I think it has been cleaned,' Jo said. 'There were hardly any leaves.'

'Perhaps Jeremy did it.'

The water had been cool and clear. Jo had dived deep and swum the length underwater. She surfaced and clung to the edge, getting her breath back. She scooped out the struggling insects that had fallen into the pool, then raced against herself, up and down, somersaulting at the ends. It was a way of putting off the day, pretending that she didn't have to plunge back into the fume-filled city and face the world. In a couple of hours she'd be driving to Kizui with Geoff – back to the urine-smelling police station and her plundered, devastated home. If only she could return and find it hadn't happened.

'Tuck in, you must be ravenous. What about eggs, one or two?'

It was the same whenever she visited; she would swim, Diana

would read, Fidelis would lay the table. She always asked for one egg and was given two. It was a pleasant taste of another life, a brief escape to the land of the rich, to peace and luxury that she could sip of without responsibility, knowing it wasn't a retreat to her own kind.

In the early hours of the morning Diana had crept into Jo's room. She came close to the bed and bent to give her a kiss.

'Are you alright?'

'Yes.'

'I'm sorry about that awful man. You were quite right to stick up for yourself, he's a pompous little prat.'

Fidelis went to boil the eggs; now, now was the time to tell Diana, before they began to eat. *Diana? Something awful happened – I don't know how to tell you – but . . .*

'Your mother would be horrified to see you so thin.'

Too late. Diana was once more *in loco parentis*. Mothers aren't told these things, she seemed to say. It was best not to ask, simpler by far to pretend, to disguise her suspicion that something was wrong.

There were slices of pawpaw with limes, fresh orange juice, coffee and brown toast with butter on the table.

'I'm sure you don't eat enough.'

'I eat a lot.'

'Well, not a lot of the right things, you'd better have a couple of these as well.'

Multivitamin pills from a large brown glass jar, a red sugar coating, earthy when she bit into them.

Diana began to talk about the party of the night before.

'I think it was quite a success . . . the last of them didn't leave till four . . . they got quite carried away and threw Jeremy in the pool . . . so of course we all ended up there . . . poor Fidelis, there was a terrible mess indoors . . . I've given him the day off today but he wanted to make you breakfast.'

Fidelis brought out the two boiled eggs served with fingers of buttered toast. It was something he'd learnt to do when the children were small and had never been told that it was no longer needed.

He was an old man; his hair was white, his face creased in obliging lines, several of his teeth were missing.

'Thank you, thank you – thank you,' she said as he put down the eggs, poured more coffee, took away the pawpaw skin.

Diana continued to chatter while Jo ate; it wasn't necessary to listen, the gist of it filtered through and Jo nodded occasionally prompting her on.

The sheltered corner in which they sat smelt sweet with garden flowers. There were roses, a bed of lilies and honeysuckle growing up the trellis. Against the wall of the house was a collection of African water pots, rough-fired earthenware jars, that were planted with tropical ferns and orchids. A breeze rippled through the dark-leaved trees at the bottom of the garden. Moses was down there hanging out a load of wet washing on the taut rope line. Jerusa's dress had already been washed and ironed and returned, neatly folded on the chair in her room. The stains had been rinsed from her underpants. Before the party she'd thrown her dirty clothes over the chair. She flinched at the thought of him finding them there. And washing them for her, scrubbing with soap until they came clean.

There was a sudden interchange of angry shouts from the house next door.

'There's an Asian family there now,' Diana explained. 'The Harrisons left in March, John was posted to Geneva. It's a shame for us, the new family's very nice, but it's not the same, we don't really have a lot to do with them. And now they've got a problem with the servants. There's a row virtually every morning.' She pushed her sunglasses up onto her head and squinted into the sun. 'Fidelis says that nearly all the old boys have left because they don't like working for an Indian.'

The noise stopped, a door slammed and a dog began to bark.

Diana stood on tiptoe and peered over the hedge.

'That's Mrs Patel going off in the car now.'

Diana plucked a couple of dead heads off the flowers and sat down again.

'I don't suppose you want a dog do you?' she asked.

'Not really, why?'

'They had to leave Bouncer behind and the Patels are keen to get rid of him. He's much too old to be any use so they're getting a couple of proper guard dogs.'

'I don't think I could look after it properly in Kingangi.'

'He's a very amenable old creature, he'd be no trouble.'

'It's not that.'

'I could give you plenty of food for him.'

'No, I'm sorry but I just don't think it would be fair on him – it wouldn't be quite the life he's used to. It's very hot and dry out there and I'm away from the house for most of the day. And I've got donkeys and goats in my garden.'

'The thing is, Jo, there's just no one in Nairobi who's prepared to take him – so many people are leaving.'

Diana drove her down to the Field Office with the dog in the back of the car. Bouncer was grey around the muzzle, with warts on his legs and a scarred nose where he'd been wounded by an intruder with a knife. He had a resigned look in his eye. He was too old to have much bounce left in him but he had alert expressive ears which twitched in communication. Geoff came down from his office with a briefcase and small leather travelling bag. They loaded the sacks of dogmeal, the lead, the dog bowls and old tartan blanket into the back of the landrover, then tempted Bouncer in with a biscuit. Diana put the box of food that she'd packed for Jo onto the front seat.

'Come and see us again!' she shouted loudly as Jo and Geoff drove off.

The landrover ground noisily through the traffic. They swung out onto Uhuru Highway.

'What's in the box?' Geoff asked as he put his foot down and took a hand off the wheel.

'Odds and ends.' There was cheese and chocolate, pots of chutney and homemade jam, a bottle of multivitamins, a loaf of bread and a ginger cake. Jo felt embarrassed.

'I thought it might be dog biscuits.'

He was cross that Jo had turned up late and annoyed about the dog which was now slobbering in their ears.

As soon as they were out on the open road Bouncer settled to sleep on the blanket and Geoff relaxed. It was hot, they opened the windows and front vents, but even the breeze was warm. Geoff took off his jacket and gave it to Jo to put in the bag at her feet.

The noise of the landrover was an excuse for silence.

Geoff got out his pipe and lit it, cupping both hands on the wheel as he held the match to the padded-down tobacco. It was a sweet smell, reminiscent of crowded seminar rooms. She cast a sideways glance at him; olive green shirt with the sleeves rolled up, the African bracelet, the pipe balancing in one hand on his knee. He had thick flat fingers.

'That evening, the night it happened,' – he kept his eyes on the road as he spoke – 'Did you notice anything at all odd? Were you aware of anyone watching you?'

'Not really, not at the time.' She paused, remembering the last hours when everything was normal; washing, watering the passion fruit plant. 'There were some men hanging around on the track above my house – but they went on as soon as I appeared. I didn't think anything of it.'

'Did you see what they looked like?'

'Not to remember. It could have been anybody, it was probably just students hanging around late after school.' *No, it couldn't have been students, they would have called out and greeted her.* 'But they were there again when I drew the curtains and then just before I fell asleep I heard sounds outside my house, just faint noises near the wall, I thought it was the donkeys.' She closed the window and opened the vent another notch. 'I almost got up to scare them away but I was too tired.'

'So they'd obviously been watching the house for some time.'

'I suppose so.'

'And presumably everyone knew that you lived there alone.'

She nodded.

'Everyone knows everything in Kingangi.'

They were on the straight stretch of Mombasa road. One of the coastline buses roared past them, an oncoming lorry flashed its lights and Geoff veered off the tarmac onto the rough edge of the road.

'Bloody lunatics.'

They bumped along the edge and then drove up onto the tar again. There were giraffes browsing at the roadside trees. They swung round when the landrover passed, their legs splaying out behind, and stopped a short distance off.

'Strange creatures aren't they?' Geoff said.

'I've never seen them so close before.'

'They were just young ones. They're the most graceful of ungainly animals.'

They drove on in silence until Machakos where they stopped for a soda and to fill up with diesel. Jo got out to stretch her legs. She found some water for the dog. His mouth was foamy with thirst, he gulped it down and then leapt straight back into the landrover and settled down with his head on one of the sacks of dogmeal.

Geoff had disappeared to find oil. A pick-up truck drew up alongside the landrover, a man wound down the window and shouted at Jo.

'You, mzungu! I want to buy that dog.'

'Sorry, he's not for sale.'

'How much?'

'He's not for sale.'

'I need a strong dog – I'll give you a good price.'

'I've only just bought him myself – I don't want to sell him.'

'OK, I understand. You've bought a good dog, that one is very strong. Thank you.'

The man drove off. She sat down beside Bouncer. He opened an eye and closed it again. Jo stroked his back, the fur was warm and left her hands feeling oily.

Geoff returned with several packets of cigarettes.

'A man just offered to buy the dog.'

'I can't think why.'

They passed through the police checkpoint at the district boundary without problems.

'What are you going to say to the police in Kizui?' she asked.

'It won't be a problem, don't worry.'

'They didn't believe that I was raped, they refused to take it down in my statement.'

'We'll have to see about that.'

'What do you mean?'

'Don't worry, I've been through this sort of thing before.'

And yet he didn't believe her. Was it embarrassment? Or that his competence had been challenged by her misfortune?

'In the Far East a girl of about your age committed suicide. But the parents refused to believe it, they thought that the local man she'd been having an affair with had murdered her for her money. The poor man was distraught. The father came out from Britain, there was an inquest, I was her nearest neighbour and had to deal with it all. She was an odd girl, depressed a lot of the time. I think it was the climate and being away from home, it didn't really suit her. And of course it never really works having a local boyfriend.'

'What happened?'

'The verdict was suicide in the end, the father went home and the local man disappeared, he'd lost his job of course.'

'It makes this seem pretty insignificant.'

'At least we've got you in one piece.'

It was as if he hadn't taken in what she'd told him. '*I woke with a knife at my throat. He tied my hands behind my back and forced me onto the bed and raped me.*' Flat voice, factual, this is what happened, it did, it did, it happens all the time now, over and over again, when I'm least expecting it I begin to live it again, there's a knife at my throat, I'm being punched and kicked, now as we drive along, as you sit there telling me about the suicide of someone whose life is irrelevant to mine, who doesn't concern me, who suffered more or less or differently, I'm being beaten again, I'm running up the hill, panting, tripping, this time they're behind me chasing, I'm going to fall and be kicked and raped again. It repeated scene after scene, in total detail, so that some things she'd missed before were quite clear now, his trousers, she remembered they didn't have a zip but buttons. And today his face was there for the first time, she could see it; frightened, strained, mean.

'I can't get it out of my mind, it keeps repeating.'

'That's bound to happen – just try and take it easy. I think you should come back to Nairobi tomorrow with me and have a few days off. You can stay at my place.'

'I've got too much to do.'

'There's no point going straight back to work before you're ready. You've got to be sensible. If you come to Nairobi you can forget about things. You can read, watch telly, relax. I'll take you out to a film or a meal or something. Then you can come back later when you've got over it.'

'I'd prefer to stay in Kingangi and get back to work.'

They stopped by the side of the road to let the dog out to pee. Geoff walked a short way across the scrub and stood against a small bush, she tried not to watch. He came back, put some more water in the radiator and lit his pipe again.

'Amazing view,' he said, leaning against the bonnet close to where she was standing, 'I reckon this must be the highest point.'

Ahead was the Yatta Plateau and, looking back towards Machakos, a flat sunlit tract of bushland, stretching out to the distant mountains.

'I can see why the settlers wanted this land for themselves,' he was talking more to himself than her, 'I couldn't live anywhere else.'

'Where did you stay last night?' Geoff asked when they were back on the road again.

'With friends in Westlands. They had a party, there was a lot of talk about the political unrest.'

'That's nothing new, the expats are always frightened. And of course Githii's stirred things up with his editorial.'

'They were talking about his arrest, do you know what he said?'

'I've got it somewhere in the office. I could have shown you. Basically he was calling for withdrawal of the Preventive Detention Law, but with no attempt to be subtle. He wrote something like "the nation has been gripped with fear over the past six months – fear of detention of individuals without trial".'

'I'm amazed they've detained so many.'

'It's happened before. Kenyatta was the same, clamping down on the intellectuals. But it's possible that the President's got wind of some plot to get rid of him, there was all that business about students getting arms from neighbouring countries. Now he's just following out his threat to tighten the screw of state security.'

'But do you think there'll be a coup attempt?'

'I doubt it, people get scared and exaggerate. It'll all blow over. Anyway it won't affect you out here.'

When they arrived at her house it had been cleaned and swept. The locks had been changed and bolts put on the top and bottom of the doors. There was wire mesh grid on all the windows. Sunshine was streaming in casting a distorted shadow of squares onto the floor and up the wall. Someone had washed the curtains and scrubbed the floor. Geoff looked around, opening all the doors, going into every room.

'Well it looks pretty secure to me, I'm amazed they managed to get in.'

'The bars are new – they've only just been put on.'

'You should be safe enough now – with them and the dog.'

There was a bottle of milk, a packet of sugar and stem of bananas on the chest in the kitchen.

Jo let Bouncer out of the landrover. He looked hot and puzzled and went straight under the sofa to hide. She put down a dish of water for him.

'Have you ever had a dog before?' Geoff asked, as they hauled the sacks of dogmeal out of the vehicle and carried them on their shoulders into the kitchen.

'No, but it should be OK, he's very docile.'

'Nevertheless, you'll have to exercise him and make sure you get him some bones and fresh meat.'

'Of course, there's plenty of meat available.'

'It'll cost a bit. But we might be able to give you an allowance on the grounds of increased safety.'

'I don't know if he'd pass as a guard dog!'

It wasn't as bad to be home as she'd expected. She lit the jiko and scattered some tea leaves into the pan of milk and water. Geoff watched her.

'Do you always make tea on a jiko?' he asked.

'The cooker was stolen.'

'You should've told me, I could have got you another one before we left Nairobi.'

'It's not important.'

After they'd had tea he got his jacket and tie out of the landrover, put them on and combed his hair. He was going slightly bald and took pains to cover the patch.

'OK, let's go and sort this whole thing out.'

The Chief of Police was unavailable; 'away on duty' they were told, so they ended up drinking with the two policemen she already knew, the one that was missing an ear and the younger one who'd taken her statement. The Babylon Bar was a large building overlooking the main road. It had an outside verandah with tables and chairs and coloured lights strung from the trees. It was dark when Jo and Geoff arrived there, the police had kept them waiting in the police station most of the afternoon. They parked the landrover round the back and went in through a large room where a solitary couple was dancing to some scratchy music. The police had arrived before them and were already drinking at a table on the terrace.

'So you drink beer?' the younger one said to Jo as she poured it into the glass, 'Which is better, Tusker or White Cap?'

'White Cap.' She'd made up her mind to co-operate, to humour them and play along.

'No, Tusker Export is the best, it is more strong.'

Geoff was hardly drinking. He'd placed his briefcase conspicuously on the chair beside them and now got out some printed papers which he leafed through and then tidied away.

'Gentlemen, I think it's time to discuss this case.'

The two policemen shifted in their chairs.

'I understand from my friend at Police headquarters in Nairobi that Kizui has an excellent record for dealing with crime.'

Both policemen nodded and cleared their throats.

'Now, I've got all the details of this incident from Jo, but obviously we need your assistance in finding these men.'

The man without the ear laughed, 'You know this is not easy, these criminals are probably hiding now, they are dangerous men.'

'Have you any idea who it might have been?'

'I think we can know.'

'Perhaps we can make things a little easier for you to track them down?'

'It is possible.'

Jo went inside to the loo. When she came back Geoff and the policemen were laughing together. Geoff had ordered food and more beers. A huge tray of meat arrived; chicken's legs, pieces of goat's meat, liver and ribs. She picked out a few bits of potato with green vegetable and ate slowly while the policemen concentrated on the meat, swilling it down with beer.

She was worried about the dog, locked up in an unfamiliar house.

'Eat, eat. This one is for you,' the younger policeman said, pointing out a breast of chicken. They'd become friendly, informal, wanting her to join in, seemingly unaware of her sex. She took the bit of meat, they ordered more beers, she accepted, she accepted a cigarette too and began to chat. They talked about the rains, the problems with the roads, the local football team, the smuggling of grain north across the border to Somalia.

Way after midnight Jo and Geoff staggered out of the Babylon Bar. They drove in silence up the rough track from town. A few groups of young men were still hanging around, distinguishable only by their coloured hats and lighted cigarettes. Just before the river crossing a man came running towards them in the middle of the road, waving his arms and shouting. Geoff slowed right down and drove up on the bank to avoid him.

'Can we stop and pick him up? He lives in Kingangi.'

'Not safe.'

Geoff engaged low gear and they climbed slowly up the hill. Behind them Bhangi let out a plaintive howl.

She kidded herself that Isaiah might be in the house when they returned, lighting the jiko, fiddling with the radio, typing an essay on her typewriter. She longed for him to turn to, to hold her.

She was frightened as she opened the door and fumbled in the darkness for the hurricane lamp. The dog came slinking out from under the sofa and put its head up to her knees, she bent to fondle its ears and it growled gently with pleasure.

Geoff was nervous, he double checked the bolts on the doors and took the keys out of the locks and put them in his pocket.

'There's a new watchman,' she said, 'I think it'll be quite safe.'

'We can't take any risks.'

'I may need to let the dog out in the night.'

'OK, I'll put them here,' he said, putting the keys on the table. He seemed very large in the dim light as he came over to her and bent to pat the dog.

'Think I'll go to bed now,' he said.

'Will you be OK in here?' she asked, 'The dog can sleep in my room with me if that's alright.'

'Jo?'

She pretended not to hear the questing in his voice. She turned to pick up the paraffin burner but he was in her way.

'Jo?'

'Yes?' she said.

'Let me look after you.'

Before she could move he'd taken her in his arms. He held her close, bending down his head to kiss her hair and neck. Her arms were at her side, pinned straight down, she froze, then tried to pull away moving her head this way and that to avoid his kisses, struggling to loosen his grip. He was breathing in her ear, wet and heavy, as he tried to put his tongue there. She was revolted by his slobbering.

'Come to bed,' he said.

'Fuck off! Just leave me alone. I've had enough.'

He gathered himself together very quickly, smoothing his beard. 'I'm sorry, I should never have asked, I thought it would be different.'

She picked the lamp off the table and went out of the room. In her bedroom she found the dog hiding under the bed. The bed had been repaired, there was a clean sheet and new blanket laid out on it.

'It's OK,' she said to the dog, 'Come out. We'll be OK.'

Geoff left early in the morning, he was once again the Field Director, dressed in a clean blue shirt and different pair of trousers. The incident of the night before might never have happened.

'You're sure you want to stay here?'

'Quite sure.'

'OK. It's up to you, but get in touch as soon as the police come up with anything. And if it gets too much on your own just come straight to Nairobi. There shouldn't be any problems now – the police are sorted out.'

'How much did you pay them?'

'Fifty quid.'

When he'd driven off Jo was left alone with the dog. She sat on the blue sofa with its head on her lap fondling its ears.

Did fifty quid make it worth their while?

CHAPTER THIRTEEN

Sunday, August 1st, Jo woke and turned on the radio, it was six o'clock, the news was due on the Voice of Kenya – silence, she turned up the volume and was suddenly blasted by loud pop music. Then it went off, a pause, the sound of someone shifting in front of a microphone, his clothes or the rustle of paper, nervous, breathless, inexperienced: '*The Government has been taken over by a strong military council . . .*'

She woke immediately and sat up in bed, grabbing the radio and twisting it around to improve reception, unable to believe that what she heard was going on now. The voice, it must be a young soldier, elated by the experience and impassioned with his message, went on. She listened, impatient with him, '. . . *rampant corruption and nepotism have made life almost intolerable in our society.*' But what's happening, what's going on? She shook the radio to get rid of the crackle. '*Under these circumstances our armed forces have heeded the people's call to liberate the country.*'

Stirred by the words she felt a rush of excitement.

There was gunfire in Nairobi; it woke people, they tuned their radios, gathered their children and waited, frightened. People were being shot, beaten on the head with rifle butts, bodies trampled on, there was a surge of violent fighting outside the radio station, then a core of Air Force men broke into the building. At the university, rebels had already entered the accommodation block, roused the students, urged them to take to the streets. Those who leapt up and dragged on their clothes were aware at once of the significance; the people's uprising, the overthrow of government. Some of them piled into a hijacked bus. Gunfire echoed in the city. A couple of fighter planes streaked overhead, circled and returned, enhancing fear and confusion.

Before long, troops loyal to the President were striking back, at anything with life; motorists unaware of the fighting were hauled from their cars and robbed, the bus carrying students was machine-gunned, riddled with bullets it slewed across a roundabout and crashed.

At the wheel of her vehicle, a woman was shot dead outside the Cathedral. It was Sunday.

Later Jo heard that they'd dragged one of the popular broadcasters out of bed and forced him to announce: '*The President's bandit gang is gone. People can now breathe.*'

At the time she sat in bed, her eyes fixed on the radio on her knees, still imagining the unknown nervous soldier, in sweat-dampened uniform, gripping the microphone with both hands. '*The students have pledged their unconditional support for the 1st of August revolution organised by the Kenya People's Redemption Council,*' he said.

She pictured Isaiah with others surging through the streets, fists thrusting into the air, victory cries and chants. He would be there.

But in Nairobi students died in the overturned bus. The sporadic gunfire continued, roadblocks were thrown up, cars were abandoned. Outside the Boulevard Hotel another bus full of students ran into the army, they were forced from the vehicle, made to strip and lie on the grass, then clubbed with rifle butts. Some struggled to run and hide. More soldiers swept through the capital and leapt from their jeeps, training guns on whoever moved. Others joined in the looting.

There were rich pickings in the capital, not just for the soldiers who stormed the Hilton Hotel, but for those who bent back the metal grilles and smashed the windows of the Asian shops with bricks and rifle butts and took what they could get; radios, televisions, cooking pots, clothes and food and drink. The pavements were covered with glass.

By early morning people were pouring in from the slums and shanty towns to loot and plunder, piling goods into stolen buckets and bowls, walking away with chairs on their heads. Some ventured to shout 'Power to the people', the fast ones ran, others were caught by soldiers and police and fell to their knees with hands flung up and goods strewn around them. And where there was looting there was rape, Asian women and girls were raped at the back of shops.

The radio conveyed nothing of the violence; a calm voice announced that the Constitution had been suspended and a national liberation council set up. All political prisoners were free. Freedom! Jo wished Isaiah were there to hug and spin around the room. She got dressed, looped the long sisal rope through the dog's collar and raced with it up the hill to Jerusa's home.

At eleven o'clock a burst of patriotic music came on the air, it was followed shortly by a confident voice, that of a regular announcer. Jo and Jerusa were sitting together on the sofa in the dark mud room with the radio on the table in front of them, the batteries were running down, it was now on full volume and only just audible, '*Early this morning shooting broke out in Nairobi. It originated from a small group of rebels in the Kenya Air Force. Quick action from the Army and Police put the rebellion down. The situation is now back to normal.*'

J.K. was hovering at the doorway, rocking a baby in his arms to stop it from crying.

'I'll go to Kizui to buy batteries, maybe even they will know some more details there.'

Jo gave him a twenty shilling note.

'Remember to come back,' Jerusa said as she took the child from him.

He laughed, 'Unless I can join the rebels!'

'The coup's failed – you'd be shot.'

J.K. pulled on a woollen hat, tied a bit of string around his trouser leg to stop it from flapping in the chain and got on his bike. Some of the children ran after him, chasing the bicycle until they were exhausted and unable to keep up any more. Jo and Jerusa stayed listening to the fading triumphal marches on the radio. Just before it went dead they heard General Jackson Mulinge announcing the restoration of peace and order.

Jerusa put the radio back in the cupboard under its crochet cover, then went into the bedroom to change her dress for church.

'It won't make any difference to us,' she called back to Jo.

'What?'

'The fighting. It can't affect us here.'

'But Isaiah's there – in the middle of it.'

Jerusa emerged in a tight dress that clung around her pregnant stomach. She took a pot of cream from the cupboard and rubbed it on her cheeks, smiling at Jo.

'He will have heard the shooting and stayed inside.'

'No, if he heard shooting he'd go and join it, this is what he was waiting for.'

Isaiah had followed the detentions as some people follow sport, the names, the dates and times; Mazrui, Mukaru, Oyugi, Wachira. '*They were accused of having abused their responsibilities, of teaching subversive literature*', his eyes had burned with admiration. His concern had bordered on envy.

'He'd be proud to be arrested,' Jo said.

Jerusa had tied a scarf around her hair and put on earrings and shoes with heels. Jo and the dog walked with her as far as the Church, then they went on up the mountain.

'I'll pray for Isaiah to return here safely,' Jerusa said.

Now that it had happened everything added up: the months of detentions, banning of plays, the repeated closure of university colleges, the legal institution of a one-party state, dismissal of George Githii the newspaper editor. '*Soon this Government will learn what's coming to it,*' Isaiah had said.

She pictured troops firing on a crowd, people falling, Isaiah wounded, staggering against a wall.

A few children tagged along behind Jo for a short distance but they were wary of the dog and hung back and then disappeared. She climbed the steep hillside, following the path that Isaiah had shown her which ran through someone's compound and then up along the terraces of the shambas. Towards the top of the hill where there was no more cultivated land but only boulders and sharp grasses the dog found a pool of water on a muddy ledge and plunged in up to its belly drinking thirstily. She watched indulgently, talking to him. A couple of girls were peering down from the rock above, giggling behind their hands. She waved and greeted them.

'Where are you going?' they called down.

'To the top.'

Jo dragged Bouncer out of the pool and clambered up to join them.

'It's very fierce,' they said, backing away from the dog. They'd been filling gourds from the trickle of water that came from the rocks, the smaller girl stepped back in terror as the dog yawned, and knocked over one of the containers.

'It's alright,' Jo said, 'He's not fierce, he won't hurt you.'

But it was too much for them. They picked up the gourds and ran off down the slope, quickly disappearing behind the tall grasses.

In the weeks before Isaiah had left he and Jo had taken to exploring the highest points of the land around. Few people climbed to these places and they were seldom disturbed. Only once had they been surprised by a boy who was shooting birds with stones from a sling. Isaiah called him over and asked what he had caught.

'Nothing.'

'What's in your pocket?'

There were two dead lizards. Isaiah took one and gave it to Jo. Its limbs were locked rigid, it had a bright white stomach. She gave it back to the boy, who was watching anxiously, standing on one leg with his catapult clenched in his hand.

'I used to do that,' Isaiah said, when the boy had gone, 'We made traps too.'

'Did you eat lizards?'

'Of course, we ate anything we caught. We used to come up here because there were a lot of birds that were good for eating. Then we would go home and steal wood and charcoal to make fires at the bottom of the shambas.' He was less serious when he talked about his childhood. 'We used to collect caterpillars and locusts too and fry them with salt.' He laughed, 'My mother beat me so hard when she found I'd cooked insects in her sufuria.'

Isaiah had taken her to visit his mother. Mama Mutisya was a big woman, taller than Isaiah, with a stocky body and thin legs. Her face was lively, though one eye was clouded blue from cataracts. She had the same habit as Isaiah of drawing her hand over her cheeks as she listened, the same sudden wide smile. She spoke only Kikamba.

'She says you can marry and come and live with her, she'll teach you how to be a good wife.'

'Tell her I wouldn't make a very good wife. I'm not as strong as African women.'

'She's asking where your mother is.'

'In England.'

'She wants to know how you can live without her.'

'I don't know, it's very difficult.'

They ate chapattis with sukuma wiki, sitting outside on low wooden stools in the compound.

'I'm sorry we can't afford meat,' Isaiah said.

'I prefer this.'

Mama Mutisya watched as they folded bits of chapatti over the vegetable and mopped up the juice. She refused to eat until they'd finished, then after she had cleared the plates and brought them tea she sat in the kitchen with the children and shared the last of the food. It was a poorer home than Jerusa's; none of the houses had iron roofs and many were in a poor state of repair. Isaiah was the oldest of the family, he had brothers and sisters who were still quite small. They came and pulled on his arm and asked for sweets. The father was away in Nairobi. They had a small shamba and a few goats and chickens but the cows had been sold to pay for schoolfees.

Jo sat at the top of the mountain beneath the tree with the twisted trunk and reddish leaves where she'd lain with Isaiah. The dog flopped at her feet and she pulled a couple of ticks from its ears; they were swollen and tenacious, suddenly coming away with blood and a matt of hairs, she flicked them into the scrub.

If Isaiah were dead – in a terrible way she almost wanted it to be so – if he were dead, there'd be no point staying here, there'd be no point in anything any more.

A brown kite was soaring in the sky, its tail tilting tiller-like, this way and that. It dived, plummeting into the bush, and rose again. Jo got up and walked over to the opposite edge of the mountain top; from there she could see more mountains, a few houses on the side of the hill below, a river twisting into the distance, eastwards to the Indian Ocean.

The attempted coup had failed – at the airport the red-bereted troops of the General Service Unit stormed the building and the crowd of anxious passengers grounded on the Olympic Airways flight cheered. The leaders of the coup hijacked an air force plane and flew to Dar-es-Salaam, 'haven of peace'.

It wasn't until late afternoon that the President came on the radio, J.K. had returned with batteries and the whole family was now gathered in the small 'table room'. The children, even the smallest, were unusually quiet, sensing that no one had time for them.

The President spoke in Kiswahili – but slowly, she could understand. He thanked the Army, '*They have fulfilled their job and I pray that God bless them and they will continue to defend the lives of the people.*' J.K. cheered and the children started clapping.

'I thought you wanted to join the rebels,' Jo said.

'We don't want Odinga in power,' J.K. replied.

'How do you know he was involved?'

'He's against the government.'

'Still he may not have been involved.'

'He's got many supporters.'

'But why are you against him?'

'He's a Luo, he only wants to make the Luos more powerful.'

Ben Kyalo was sitting forward on his chair with his large flat hands grasped over his knees nodding in agreement with J.K.

'The President is strong in nation building,' he said.

She had a nightmare that night; that a man had entered her house again and put a gun to her head. And then a strange dream; she was sitting with Isaiah in the Hotel Relax, Jerusa was wiping the glass on the picture of the President, but as she put it up on the wall the face moved. The President was drinking Coke through a straw in the gap between his two front teeth. 'I will suck the poison out of this nation,' he said.

The following morning, August 2nd, the President closed the university and ordered all the students to return to their home areas. In Nairobi people walked to work with hands above their heads. The city mortuaries were crowded with people queueing to identify the dead. Another lorry-load of bodies arrived from Kibera. The Army was sent out to track down the last of the rebels; they cordoned off the city, set up armed road blocks, searched the houses.

In Mathare Valley thousands of people were ordered out of their homes and forced to lie with their faces to the ground. Their houses were upturned. The 'loyal' soldiers looted and raped as they went about their duty. The rebel Air Force men discarded their uniforms and fled to the country. Two hid naked beneath the bridge near the Boulevard Hotel, but soldiers found them and shot them dead.

CHAPTER FOURTEEN

When a policeman turned up at Jo's house a few days later her first thought was that it was something to do with Isaiah.

'We've arrested the man who robbed you.'

She couldn't believe it.

'Where?'

'We found him hiding in the forest.' It was the tall policeman with the hanging earlobes who'd taken her statement. 'You are wanted to identify him.'

She went to town in the police truck. The policeman drove fast, skidding round the sandy corners, frightening the goats and children playing football on the track. They crossed the river and climbed up through the forest.

'Are you sure it's the right man?'

'No doubt about it, he fits the description and has admitted to the crime.'

'What about the others?'

'He says he was alone. But we will soon make him speak some more.'

'Who is he? Is he from around here?'

'I can't tell you – first you must identify him.'

When they arrived at the police station she felt a wave of sickness. She could so easily get it wrong, it had been dark, she'd hardly seen him. The young policeman led her through the courtyard and showed her into a small cell.

'Wait here.'

He shut the door. Outside she heard coughing and the policeman shouting. A parade of men was brought into the courtyard. He called her out to face them.

'You must walk along the row, when you see the man put your hand on his shoulder.'

The suspects stood with their heads hung and eyes averted. She recognised the two old men who'd been brought in for cattle rustling. The others were younger, all thin-faced with matted hair.

She walked slowly along the row, forcing herself to look at their faces. One of them stared back, his eyes begging her not to pick on him. She reached the end of the row where the khaki-uniformed officer stood impatiently tapping a stick in the palm of his hand.

'The man isn't here.'

'Are you sure? Look again.'

'No, I'm sure. I don't recognise anyone here.'

'Take this,' he said, giving her the stick, 'You can point to him with this.'

She walked along the row again, the men seemed to be shifting, cowering back as she passed. Her hand was sweating around the stick. They all looked familiar this second time, but he wasn't here, she'd recognised no one.

Just as she reached the end of the row, another police officer came rushing out.

'There's been some mistake, the man is not here, take these ones away.'

Jo was sent back to the cell. It had a small window with bars, but no chair or stool. She leant against the wall by the window and waited. She'd know him when she saw him. A long time seemed to pass, no one came to get her, she went to the door and knocked.

'Hello. Hello!'

She rattled it and banged.

'Can you let me out?' she shouted, but still no one came.

She slid down against the wall and sat on her heels, staring at the bright light through the window. The parade passed before her eyes; the man at the end, it could have been him.

'You can come out.'

'The door's locked.'

There was a rattle of keys, then the policeman with the missing ear opened the door.

'What's going on?' she asked.

'Come this way.'

'What's happening?'

He led her back across the yard and into the room where she'd first made her statement. A senior policeman was sitting behind the desk.

'I am the Chief of Police, Mwangi Njoroge,' he said, 'Sit down.'

A Kikuyu name. She sat opposite him, holding her hands on her lap beneath the table. He had close-shaved hair that was grey at the temples, and brown-stained teeth.

'We have arrested the criminal, but it has been very difficult.'

'Thank you.'

'Very difficult.'

'Yes, thank you. I understand I have to identify the man.'

'In one moment. First, now, maybe you want this case to go to court.'

'Yes.'

He scratched his nose, pulling on the nostril.

'That is not easy – because perhaps we have not got enough evidence.' He stared hard at her. 'You understand?'

'If there's a problem I can ask my Director to come from Nairobi.'

'No problem.'

She was surprised how quickly he backed down – how weak the attempt at intimidation had been. He took her round the back of the building and opened a cell door.

'Just take one look and say if this is the man.'

The Chief of Police shouted in Kiswahili and the man stood up from the curled heap he'd been lying in in the corner of the room.

It was Bhangi, the madman, handcuffed and shivering with fear. When he saw Jo he let out a small animal-like whine.

Day after day Jo waited for Isaiah to return. At lunchtimes she'd walk the five miles home and back from the new river site just in case he'd appeared during the morning, and in the evenings she'd leave the doors open until it was totally dark, pitching her fear against the hope of his return. As night fell every sound became his footstep, the flick of his stick on the bushes, the silhouette of him against the sky on the track above her house before he turned down the path. She imagined his arrival, what she'd say when he walked in, how he'd look. She'd bought a bottle of honey for him in Matundu market, it was dark clear honey in an old Treetop squash bottle and when she put it on the kitchen shelf in the sun she saw that there were bees and bits of wax suspended in it. He liked to eat honey on a spoon or stirred with milk and thought it odd that she should spread it on bread with margarine.

But more than a week after the closure of the university Isaiah still hadn't returned. On Saturday morning Jo went to the hospital with Jerusa and they sat waiting with the other sick and pregnant mothers in the shade of the trees.

'I think I'm going to lose the baby.'

'No you won't. You've just got to take it easy. You haven't tried to get rid of the baby have you?'

'The last time I wanted so much to lose it, but not now.' Jerusa rocked back and forth as she spoke, clasping her stomach. She was sweating, her face darker than usual and eyes dulled with pain. 'Then I was just a girl. My mother took me to a woman at Matundu who was clever in these things. She put sharp sticks inside and made me lie without eating, only drinking hot water with leaves. It was too bitter and made me sick.' She hugged her stomach. 'So I just decided to get up and run away.'

'I'm sorry, I'd no idea.'

A boy came into the hospital compound selling sweets and bottles of soda. Jo bought a Coke for Jerusa and a handful of 'Tropical mints' to take back for the children.

'Where's Museo's father?' she asked.

'I don't know. He's not a man I loved.' She put the empty bottle down on the sand. 'He was a teacher at Kingangi. He liked me too much, always trying to touch me – one day he called me into the classroom after school. I felt so ashamed. And then the baby came.'

She'd probably been like Museo then; tall and bright, in a dress she'd long outgrown and with hair combed and twisted into tight plaits. Only fifteen or sixteen, just a few years older than Museo was now.

'They sent me out of school.' Jerusa said.

'Didn't they get rid of the teacher?'

'How is that possible? He denied everything. Even when I went with my mother to the school to face him he said I was lying. I tell you it was very bad.'

When Jerusa had been taken into the hospital to wait for a doctor, Jo wandered into town and found a newspaper. She sat in a chai shop drinking sweet tea and reading it. Loyal rallies were being held across the country to declare support for the President and condemn the coup plotters, the curfew had been relaxed but arrests continued. Most of the Air Force, two thousand or so men, were in custody, and thousands of civilians, many of them women, had been arrested for looting. It seemed ridiculous to arrest so many people just for taking a bit of food and a few cooking pots and radios. The Air Force men who'd flown to Dar-es-Salaam had been identified but Tanzania was refusing to extradite them. There were letters in praise of the President, photos of cheering crowds, a eulogy on the strength of national unity, just a short paragraph mentioning the first political moves; the dismissal of two senior Luos who'd previously been linked with Oginga Odinga.

A boy wearing shorts and a man's jacket came into the chai shop offering 'shoeshine' but she was wearing flipflops. He went away and returned only a minute or two later with a fistful of biros, she bought one but the boy had vanished before she discovered it didn't work.

Jo flicked through the rest of the paper, scanning each story, convinced that she might find Isaiah's name or see his face in one of the pictures. But there was no mention of students, no official death toll. She wondered how she'd know if he'd been killed, whether the names of those who'd died would be printed in the paper.

Jerusa was given the standard collection of giant green and yellow pills, but the reassurances of a doctor had left her smiling. They got a ride on the back of a lorry across to the other side of town.

J.K. had found himself a job at the garage in town salvaging tyres and parts from crashed and broken-down vehicles. He got the gossip from the drivers who'd come from Nairobi and was more interested in telling his stories than hearing about the visit to the hospital.

'All the shops are boarded up . . . . There's still blood on the pavements . . . . You can buy a radio for sixty shillings, three pounds in Mathare, and a fridge for a thousand shillings, fifty pounds . . . '

'How much is a sewing machine?' Jerusa asked.

'Maybe six hundred shillings.'

J.K. was convinced that Isaiah had been arrested.

'He's got no chance, there are police and army blocks on all the roads out of Nairobi. They're stopping every vehicle that goes through. How can he prove he's not a rebel?'

'Do you think he was involved?' she asked him, 'Do you know?'

'He is too clever,' J.K. said.

Too smart to get involved or too bright not to? All those long conversations she'd had with Isaiah, she'd retracked them many times but he'd been elusive, giving little away. Enigmatic, enjoying it.

'*For my thoughts are not your thoughts, neither are your ways my ways* . . . from the Bible, *Isaiah*,' he'd said. He was probably right, she'd no idea.

Now, listening to J.K. boasting about Nairobi as if he'd been there, she thought, *perhaps I was just a status symbol for Isaiah, a useful provider of money and books and clothes and food, a passing experience for an African man. And I've kidded myself into believing otherwise.*

On August 16th Isaiah turned up, in quite an ordinary way, knocking at Jo's door one evening when she was busy cooking the dogmeal over the jiko. She knew at once that he'd come straight to her house; he was still sweating from the long walk and was carrying his blue tin case and a paper package of books. His clothes were unfamiliar, an oversized jacket with frayed cuffs and dirty grey trousers. He wasn't wearing his hat, nor had he shaved or combed his hair. His face looked darker, bruised and swollen about one eye, a cut across his forehead. He shook her hand, this way and that. She couldn't stop looking at him, wanting to touch his face but hesitant. He seemed so different. They were both awkward, he turned away to get something out of the trunk and she stood back watching as he fiddled with the lock. Those hands; the line that separated the dark from the pale of the palm, the long fingers and strong nails that he cut with a razor blade. He took out a piece of paper and handed it to her. It was the note she'd pushed under his door.

'So you got it?'

'Do you know where I was when you wrote this?'

She shook her head. There was so much to tell, why begin by playing guessing games?

'Just nearby. At a student meeting.'

He moved about the room as he spoke, then paused and looked at Jo. She was thinking of where she'd been that night, her own story running parallel to his; the night after the rape, at Diana and Jeremy's party, standing in the bedroom combing her hair, the scent of moonflowers coming in from the terrace, the hubbub of party chatter, the wine and the arrogant man.

'I found your note when I got back.' He took it back from her, folded it and put it away again. 'I went everywhere looking for you, to all the places where the whites go, the Thorn Tree, the swimming pool, the post office, and then down to the bus station. I hung around there for hours waiting to see if you would come to take a bus back home, but there was no sign.'

'I'd gone to stay with friends.'

'Which friends?'

It pleased her that he sounded jealous.

'Just friends of my family.'

'You weren't sick?'

'No.'

He was suddenly concerned, looking disbelieving, forgetting for a moment his own tale. He came and sat beside her on the blue sofa.

'You were alright?'

'Yes.' The rehearsed account failed her, she wanted to save it to shock him.

He looked at her for a moment longer than was necessary, then he took out a half-smoked cigarette from the pocket of the jacket and got up to light it on the coals of the jiko. He smelt of stale sweat when he moved, not clean as she remembered him.

'What happened during the coup, were you out there?'

'I only heard gunshot, everyone was awake, some of them went out, we tried to stop them, we knew that this was not the one.'

'What do you mean?'

'This attempt, it had happened too soon, it wasn't expected,' he looked ugly, older, with his battered face and matted hair, 'The President was due to leave for the OAU summit on the 3rd of August.'

'So you thought it was going to happen while he was away?'

'I heard rumours.'

The dogmeal was burning on the bottom of the pan and Isaiah, not minding the heat, took it off the jiko with his bare hands and put it on the step outside. Bouncer had been sleeping in the room next door but now came out stretching his legs and curving his back so his belly brushed the floor, growling as he yawned. Isaiah backed away to the door.

'Jo, take it away. It will bite.'

'It's OK,' she couldn't help laughing.

'Take it away.' He'd picked up the broomstick by the door ready to defend himself, but the dog merely sniffed at his shoes as it passed and went to lap at the dish of water in the corner of the room.

'What is it, a guard dog?'

'Not really. I got him in Nairobi, from some people who were leaving.' Isaiah was still watching it nervously. 'Don't worry, it won't hurt you.'

He put down the broomstick. 'Alright, I'm forced to believe you,' and for the first time he smiled, in the familiar sudden self-mocking way, 'But that animal is a lion not a dog.'

She put a pan of milk and water on the fire now the dog food was cooked and made tea. There was no food to offer, she'd picked up the bottle of honey but then felt foolish at the thought of giving it to him and returned it to the shelf.

'Where have you been since the coup?' she asked.

'I left as soon as they shut the university and went to Samson's place in Diego Road.'

'Why didn't you come straight back here?'

'There were roadblocks, I was frightened that someone would pick me up for questioning.'

'So how did you get here?'

'On a beer lorry, hidden under the tarpaulin between the crates – the driver had friends at the Tiptop and they persuaded him to take me.'

She poured the tea.

'What happened to your face?'

He put up a hand to cover it.

'It's an old wound.'

There was silence.

'How's J.K.?' he suddenly asked.

'Fine, he's got a job at the garage in town. He thought you'd been arrested.'

'Where is he? I must see him, we have some good talking to do.'

He got up as if he were going to leave that moment.

'Won't you stay here now?'

'I can come back later.'

She stood up too. 'J.K. will probably come here, he often does. Don't go just yet.'

'Something has happened,' Isaiah said, 'Why have you put bars?'

She'd thought he hadn't noticed the wire mesh on the windows but now he went over to it and pulled to test its strength. He ran his fingers down it, making the metal ring – flip, flip, flip – waiting for her answer.

'Has someone tried to rob you?'

She felt foolish to have kept silent for so long, thinking proudly that for everything he'd endured she too had suffered.

'Tell me what's happened,' he said.

'Some men broke into my house . . . '

She told it all quickly, hardly pausing for breath. No longer wanting to hurt him. When she looked up he was staring through her and seemed diminished, crumpled against the window.

Then he came across the room. She was standing at the door, twisting the handle back and forth, he took her hand away from it and held it in his.

'Sorry, sorry,' he said.

She was glad of his sympathy and wanted only to hug him and be silent. But he went on,

'What did they do to you?'

He questioned her, making her repeat things, forcing her to describe in detail the violence she'd skirted over, conveying in the tightening grip on her hand his growing burden of guilt.

'It was my fault, I should never have stayed in this house with you. I'm the one who led you into danger.' He let go of her hand and put his face in his palms. There was a long silence. 'I let you be hurt.'

'It would have happened anyway.'

He was almost crying. 'If only I hadn't slept here with you.'

'What do you mean?'

'I told people, you know I did.'

He closed his eyes and pressed his hand to his face so it half-covered his mouth, 'Maybe I even boasted.'

'They came to rob the house, not to rape me – it happened afterwards, it was a second thought.'

'Of all the things I never imagined this could happen. It would never happen in England.'

'It does, of course it does, it's no different there.'

'No. People are bad here.'

'That's not true.'

'You should never have come to this place – if you had never known me.'

'It wasn't your fault, how can you think that? It would have happened whether I'd ever known you or not.'

He pulled the door wide open and she thought for a moment that he was going to walk away and leave her.

'Isaiah, it wasn't anything to do with you.'

'Don't cheat me.'

Nothing could be said now that would make him change his mind. She'd already told too much and he was drawing away.

'Have they been caught?' His questioning was distant.

'No, the police aren't interested. Last week they arrested Bhangi and beat him up. Mr Katambo had to go there to get him released.'

'Would you recognise the right man?'

'I think so.'

'How sure are you?'

'I told the police I was certain, but it's hard to know.'

'What about the other men?'

It was awful to be spoken to in this way.

'I only saw one other, I wouldn't recognise him.'

'Who else knows about this?'

'Everyone, I suppose – everyone in Kingangi, Mr Katambo, Geoff – the Field Director. Everyone except you.'

'And what have they done?'

'Geoff came to see the police and bribed them. There's a new watchman.'

'But why are you still here? It's not safe alone. You should be with Jerusa.'

'It's been OK, I wanted to come back, there's the dog now and the bars on the windows . . . '

What was it that stopped her from admitting how terrified she'd been? All these nights living alone.

The rape had curtailed her life, made her sleep with the dog beneath the bed and a panga at her elbow. Tied her to the noises of the night, captured her in her own fear, in the waking dreams of repeating violence. She slept in her clothes, sometimes with shoes on her feet so she could kick and run. Several times before she could rest she'd put out a hand and touch the wooden handle of the knife. Once, hearing sounds in the roof above she'd pushed the bed to the door and jammed the handle with a stool. There was a hatch from the ceiling, she heard them easing back the board, slowly, silently. The dog began to whimper. She sat upright, the knife in her hand, and strained to hear the sounds – questing for the slightest, softest foostep, barefoot, towards her door. She moved behind the door, pressed her back to the wall, waited, the knife tight in both hands, her heart pounding too loudly, deafening her to the men outside the door.

'Go away!' she said, breathless, 'I've got a knife.'

The dog barked once, roughly, and then turned round and round in circles settling once more beneath the bed.

Hours later when nothing had happened she sat down again on the bed with her back to the wall, the cold blade of the panga lying along her leg.

The dog woke before dawn, whining to go out, licking at her arm. She steeled herself to open the front door and he raced away into the darkness. She waited there standing firm on the doorstep, forcing herself not to be afraid, looking into the blackness, pounding with fear at the slightest movement – the interminable minutes while the dog peed and raced around the scrub chasing night animals. It returned panting at her bare feet, she locked the door and it snuffled round and round before slinking beneath the bed again.

She forced herself to leave the bedroom door open, to lie down beneath a blanket and then she slept, exhausted from the terror of the long night vigil – a deep warm sleep, every muscle twitching away from her, knowing that it was now light outside, that dawn had come and people were moving around.

'I will see J.K. tomorrow,' Isaiah said, 'I'll stay here tonight on guard while you sleep.'

'I'm OK.' She smiled and tried to touch his arm but he didn't notice and moved away to organise the room. He pushed the heavy blue sofa up against the wall and put the stool beside it with the hurricane lamp.

'Where's the panga?' he asked.

It was beside her own bed, she went there, found it easily in the dark and pulled a blanket out of the cupboard for him.

'You might need this, it's been quite cold at night.'

Together they folded the blanket across the sofa and as he stood up she touched his shoulder,

'Isaiah, it wasn't your fault.'

He was about to say something, but held it back, she thought she saw a flicker of warmth but he restrained it and drew away.

'Time will tell.'

She went to bed alone, hoping that he would follow – but only the dog joined her, circling beneath the bed as it always did. Isaiah bolted the doors and lay down on the sofa with the hurricane lamp burning low and the panga at his side.

CHAPTER FIFTEEN

There was a cold cup of tea on the stool beside her bed when Jo woke the following morning, it took her a moment to work out how it had come to be there. But Isaiah had already gone; the blanket was folded neatly on the sofa and the tin trunk and package of books had disappeared. The dog sniffed around, nosing at the blanket and then followed Jo into the bathroom and lapped at the pool of water that hadn't yet drained through the hole – Isaiah must have washed before he went, the bucket was upturned with the soap and scrubbing brush on top of it – the way he always left it. And he'd combed his hair, the comb had been put back the other way up on the shelf and there were a few tight circles of black hair on the edge of the basin. She instinctively bent to blow them off but then stopped and left them.

In the front room the hurricane lamp was warm, the glass blackened. She put her hand in the folded blanket and thought that it too was still warm, with the lingering heat of his body. He must have been very silent as he got up, moving barefoot through the house, willing her not to wake, yet tempting fate by bringing her tea. Not even the old dog had stirred.

'Some use you are. What's the point of having you?'

Bouncer looked puzzled and cocked an ear.

'I'm sorry. I didn't mean it.' She rubbed his head. 'It's not your fault. Come on, let's get out.'

It was only just light outside, the ground was still cool underfoot and the scent of the night flowers sweet on the air. Bouncer raced away down the slope and Jo went along the path to the pit latrine. No flies yet in there. She washed her hands and splashed her face with water at the tank. Why did Isaiah leave without waking her . . .

'Jumbo!' Hassan called out to her. He was the new watchman, a warrior-like man who crept through the bushes with his bow and arrows and frightened the children away. He never went home to sleep until he'd greeted Jo in the morning.

She called back to him, 'Jumbo sana. Habari?'

'Nzuri, mama. Fine.'

They seldom exchanged more than smiles and greetings. He came from Mandera in the far north-east of the country and spoke neither English nor Kikamba. His Kiswahili was as poor as hers. She heard that he'd walked south to sell his cattle but they'd died on the way, so he'd taken a lorry to Garissa and then down to Kizui where he'd found work as a watchman in the Government school. Mr Katambo had got him from there.

'He's a very strong watchman,' Mr Katambo told her, 'People will be fearing now he is here.'

Hassan raised a hand and walked away up the hill. It was a solitary life, away from his family, awake all night, waiting for intruders, sleeping all day, talking to no one. She went indoors. Maybe Isaiah had left a note, but opening the pad of paper she found it as it had been for the last few days with a half-written letter to her family. She picked up a pen and began to write angrily:

'I want to come home. I hate it here. I'm frightened. Everything has collapsed.' She drew patterns for a while, angry triangles blackened in with ink. Then wrote, '*Isaiah, Isaiah, ISAIAH,*' going over and over his name with the pen, darkening the letters. 'I still love him. I don't suppose you want to hear any of this – no one does – no one knows what to do. It's easier to pretend it never happened, but I'm sick of pretending. I should have told you before, but I thought it didn't matter, I thought it would go away.'

She stopped abruptly and ripped out the page and threw it on the fire, but the coals were no longer hot and it didn't catch. She got the matches, put one to it and stood waiting for the scorched brown edge to spread and flare.

In Jerusa's compound it was the usual morning commotion; a couple of boys were kicking a football made from tied-up polythene bags against the mango tree and Museo was trying to quieten a screaming baby, flying it up and down above her head. The other children were running around shouting. They came rushing out when Jo arrived. She tied the dog up to one of the small Grevillia trees at the entrance to the compound and went in. Jerusa no longer came to work at the river because of her pregnancy but Jo still stopped on her way to the site and talked for a while. Outside the kitchen hut one of the girls was scratching the sticky ugali from the cooking pots of the night before with a stick and handfuls of earth. Inside the kitchen it was smoky, Jerusa was sitting by the fire on a low stool, her feet planted wide apart, cooking ugi, a thin maizemeal porridge. In the corner of the room Ruth was nursing her newborn baby, a tiny thing with a screwed-up face and soft black hair. She pulled the khanga across her breast and over the baby's head as soon as Jo came in. Jo greeted them.

'Isaiah's back, he came in the night,' Jerusa said.

'I know, he came to my house.'

'He was nearly arrested in Nairobi.'

'He told me.'

Jerusa took the pan off the fire and poured the ugi into an assortment of chipped enamel mugs and bowls.

'Can you take some?' she asked Jo, 'There's no sugar.'

'I've had tea already.'

The children came scrambling into the room and sat uncomfortably, legs on top of each other, to be as close to Jo as possible. Museo's dress was slipping off her shoulder, she pulled it up but it fell again.

'Isaiah came to visit,' she said to Jo.

'When, this morning?'

She nodded, 'He hurt his face,' she looked away and giggled with excitement.

The other children were bursting with the story too, but unable to tell it in English they shouted at her in Kikamba.

'Did he say where he was going?' Jo asked Jerusa.

'He just passed by, looking for J.K. But he'd already left for town. I think Isaiah went on that way.'

'Is he coming back tonight?'

'He didn't say. Come on, eat,' Jerusa said, giving Jo the largest mug of porridge, 'What's wrong?'

'Nothing.'

'Are you sick?'

'No.' Jo took the mug and sipped the porridge. She was aware of the children watching her, eyes looking over the tops of their mugs, now quiet as they drank the hot ugi.

Museo lingered behind after the other children had left for school. She collected her schoolbooks and tin of water and sat beside Jo again, a hand across her knee. Her hair had been plaited into tight twizzles sticking up from her scalp which drew attention to her pretty face.

'You'd better go to school, you'll be late.'

'Go on,' Jerusa said.

But Museo showed no sign of moving. 'Who hurt Isaiah?' she asked.

'I'm not sure.'

'Was it a soldier?'

'You! Get out now,' Jerusa shouted at her in Kikamba.

'Was it?'

'I don't know, I think it was.'

She sprinted off.

'You shouldn't tell her these things, Jo, she knows too much already.'

'I expect she already knew, she just wanted to make sure it was true.'

'It's not good for her. She hangs around all the men, asking questions the whole time.'

There were wild screams at the river. As Jo and the dog arrived in the clearing she saw two of the women running towards them, hurling stones at the ground. Bouncer pulled forward on his chain, barking. One of the women picked up a stick and beat it hard down upon the earth. The other women stood back a short way off.

'What is it?'

'Snake.'

It was about two feet long, they said it was a young one, greeny-grey. Jo squatted down to look; its head was pulverised, but the body fat and firm. The dog patted it and jumped back.

'Careful, it still has poison. Keep the dog away.'

Celiaka, the woman who'd killed it, bent and picked it up on a stick. The snake's belly was white and as she flung it into the bushes it flipped in the air looking as if it were still alive. The dog whined, straining on its lead to chase after it.

'Where did it come from?' Jo asked Celiaka.

'It was sleeping, just on a bag of sand.' They'd filled more sandbags the day before ready to drag into the water to divert a channel. They were lined up on the bank. Celiaka took Jo by the arm and showed her the spot; on the top of the sandbag were the faint marks where the snake had lain. It must have been peaceful in the hot sun, before the shouting and thrashing and the fatal blows to the head. 'We call that one a killer, if it bites a baby they'll die.'

Celiaka was about fifty, maybe older, but with limitless strength and vitality. She was fearless; there were stories of her rescuing a baby from the river flood when she was only a girl and of carrying a wounded calf five miles on her back. She'd been hard to get on with.

'We don't want to learn stories,' Celiaka had told her in the first literacy class when Jo had come with primary school books, 'We want to know how to send letters and write forms for the bank.'

'We've got to start with something easy.'
'Then we don't want these lessons.'
'OK, tell me exactly what you'd like.'
'Reading newspapers.'
She'd tussled constantly with Celiaka, relying on Jerusa to sort things out. Before the long rains came Celiaka threatened to leave the group.
'You promised us water.'
'There will be water.'
'But not for everyone.'
'Anyone can use those standpipes.'
'We were told we would have taps in the home.'
'I never told you that.'
'For some it is still too far.'
'But we're going to set up another pump, near Matundu.'
'And where is all the money?'
'Some is in the bank, some has been spent.'
'How can we trust you?'
But it was Celiaka who'd been the first to come after the rape, bringing Jo a present of medicines and sugar.
They were nervous after finding the snake, but work went well that morning and by the time Jerusa arrived bringing a tin of cold maize and beans for lunch, nearly all the sandbags had been positioned in the river. The other women had gone home to their children and shambas, Jo and Jerusa ate sitting under a tree and then walked on to Matundu market.
'Did you tell Isaiah what happened?'
'Yes.'
'But not everything?'
'Of course.'
Jerusa shook her head, 'Ngai, ngai, ngai! You shouldn't have said. What can he think now?'
'I had to tell him, everyone knows. It was better that I should tell him, rather than hearing from someone else.'
'People don't know.'
'Of course they do.'
'They only think the house was robbed.'
'J.K. knows, he would have told Isaiah.'
'He only thinks that you were beaten.'
'I wanted to tell him.'
'But Jo, you've forgotten he's an African man.'

CHAPTER SIXTEEN

Mr Katambo lived in a stone house about a mile from Kingangi village. It was visible from the road, a large square building with a shining corrugated iron roof and cobalt-blue painted window frames and door. He'd planted a hedge of fir trees which would soon hide it from view and put a barbed wire fence around the compound and ironwork double gates at the entrance with the notice 'Mbwa kali sana' – 'very fierce dog' – although he hadn't yet got a dog.

A young boy, the son of the driver, had been sent to fetch Jo and was waiting for her that afternoon when she got back from Matundu market. He seemed anxious that they should leave at once so she gave the dog some water, tied it up to a tree in the shade behind the raintank, and they set out. The boy was bright and talkative, he bullied her with questions about tractors and boats and aeroplanes and she was relieved when at last he lapsed into thoughtful silence. They walked quickly up the hill behind Kingangi, she had to go fast to keep up with him as he strode ahead with ease. Sweat ran down her back and tickled behind her knees.

At the top they paused to look back in the direction they'd come from.

'Look, you can see your house.'

Her white house with its iron roof stood out clearly from the other thatched homes around.

'Where's your home?' she asked him.

'On the other side, we will pass it on the way.'

They reached it a short while later, just before the turning to Mr Katambo's.

'This is the one,' the boy said. Three round houses in a small compound, surrounded by an untidy hedge of euphorbia and thorns. He whistled to the children who were sitting in the yard.

'Mzungu! Mzungu!' They came rushing out.

'I know my way now,' Jo said. But he insisted on accompanying her up the track and the other kids followed along behind, close on their heels.

The fir trees gave shade on the path and there was a cool fresh smell of sap. Jo pulled off a small branch, and rolled the needles between her fingers. This was the closest she got to England, this sweet smelling enclave on the top of Ngondi hill.

She parted from the boy at the iron gates and he heaved the bolt across behind her.

'I will come to escort you home, ask for Boniface, that is my name.'

She walked up the drive, past the wreck of an ancient car which now housed chickens, past the duck cage and the borders of stout orange canna lillies. On the other side was a square of lawn; it gave her a strange feeling seeing the close cut green grass and the dilapidated garden chair which remained there month after month. At the back of the house a woman was pounding maize and a man scything the long grass, but neither of them noticed her as she came up the front drive and rang the bell.

It was pleasantly cool inside. Mama Katambo, the Assistant Chief's wife, greeted her at the door. She was a plump beaming woman who seemed to carry herself with confidence and show. They had eleven children of which they pretended not to be proud, saying it was far too many.

'Is Mr Katambo here?' Jo asked her.

'He's coming from town. Please sit.'

Jo went into the sitting room and sat on one of the crochet-covered chairs. There was a jug of orange squash covered with a beaded doily and some upturned glasses on the table. Mama Katambo poured her a glass and left the room. There was chatter coming from the kitchen, the smell of meat and onions frying. Jo drank the orange in one and leant back in the chair. The room was spotlessly clean, she could smell the Omo on the crocheted cover behind her head. The red floor was polished and the fluffy rug beaten and brushed. All around were ornaments and decorations; a homemade paper chain and lanterns hanging from the ceiling, some old calendars pinned to the wall, one advertising Maloprim, the other with American pin-up girls. There was also a collection of photographs, some hanging, the others balanced on the picture rail. Mr Katambo had taken them all down the first time she visited, dusted them on the sleeve of his jacket and shown them to her one by one. He'd been handsome as a young man, with short hair and a serious smile, there was a picture of him on graduation from Makerere, another of him laying a foundation stone at Kingangi Harambee School. He'd been the driving force in starting the school and was only thirty when he was elected Chairman of the Board of Governors.

Jo got up to look at the photos again and was reminded of Isaiah, understanding why he admired Gabriel Katambo.

She poured herself a little more orange – the beads on the doily clinked as she draped it over the jug again – then she picked up the newspaper from the table. It was a couple of days out of date, August 16th, someone had tried to do the crossword in biro, there were smudges and a lot of crossing out. She picked up the pen and filled in the remaining clues. Then she read the cartoons.

There was no sign yet of Mr Katambo. Mama Katambo came back in, she'd taken off her khanga and changed into a white nylon dress with a pleated skirt and tight red belt around the waist. She had matching red shoes with heels and crisscross straps. Jo felt dirty and dishevelled.

'Is Mr Katambo bringing visitors?'

'The Chief of Police is coming. Do you know him?'

'I've met him once before.' Her mouth went dry. 'Do people like him?'

Grace Katambo frowned and put a hand to her mouth. 'He's a Kikuyu.'

They were an almost indistinguishable pair; Mr Katambo in a dapper safari suit, the Chief of Police in belted khaki uniform. Both with greying hair, hanging jowls and tight bellies. Jo shook hands with the policeman.

'I think we met once in the police station,' she said.

'No, I have no recollection.'

'Sit. Sit.' Mr Katambo was fussing around in the usual way, he pulled out chairs for Jo and the Chief of Police on either side of the main table and sat down at the head. One of his daughters came in with a bowl of warm water, soap and a towel and they washed their hands. The beers were opened and poured into glasses, Mr Katambo called the girl back to take away the empty bottles and bring some more. His extravagant gestures did little to disguise the fact that they'd already had a few drinks on the way up from town. Mama Katambo laid out the dishes of rice and potatoes and a tray of roast meat with hot chilli peppers, then returned to the kitchen. The two men ate noisily, Mr Katambo only pausing occasionally to take another roast rib from the tray and put it on Jo's plate,

'And potatoes, have more potatoes, they're from my shamba.'

It was hard to eat opposite the Chief of Police, sitting as they'd been in the police station. She eyed him nervously, uncertain of the purpose of this meeting. Grace Katambo was hovering in the doorway watching them eat, Jo took some more potatoes to please her.

After the meat another girl, a younger one in a frilly dress and long white socks and shoes, brought in slices of pineapple on a china plate. The Chief of Police refused,

'I don't take fruit, it's too acid for my stomach.'

'You have an ulcer?' Mr Katambo enquired.

'Not an ulcer, but too much bile.'

Excluded from the conversation Jo took a toothpick out of the green plastic pot in the middle of the table and tried to get the strings of pineapple from between her teeth. The girl returned to clear away the plates and Mr Katambo belched appreciatively.

'I haven't taken meat for two days,' he said.

'Me, for three days,' the Chief of Police replied.

After tea they got up from the table and sat in the comfy chairs. The Chief of Police eased the belt of his trousers. He'd brought with him a brown paper bag which he now picked up and put on the low table. He said something to Mr Katambo who nodded, then he turned to Jo.

'I understand you reported the loss of property arising from robbery.'

'And assault . . . '

'Yes, sir,' Mr Katambo interrupted her, 'The incident was reported on July 21st.'

The Chief of Police continued, 'We believe we have located some of your missing items.' He delved into the paper bag and pulled out an assortment of things, laying them one by one on the table in front of her.

'I would like you to identify whether these belong to you.'

Her thin Indian shirt, crumpled and mud-stained, her sunglasses, her multi-coloured sweater, her camera case and a watch.

'They're all mine, except for the watch.'

How soiled and sordid the evidence of crime, she thought. No longer hers, these sad dirt-covered things.

'Are you sure this isn't yours?' the Chief of Police asked picking up the watch and winding it up.

'Yes, quite sure.'

'I think maybe it is and you have forgotten,' Mr Katambo suggested.

'Maybe.' Perhaps it was important that she should say it was hers.

'Fine. Now I can tell you that we found these items buried in the garden of Mama Munge. We have reason to believe that her son is the man who robbed your house.'

Mr Katambo was nodding.

Mama Munge, Jo couldn't think who she was, which compound it was.

'She said her son hadn't been there for five years, he's an Administration Policeman in Mombasa and doesn't return home. But then she admitted that he'd come in the night some weeks ago.' The Chief of Police swatted at a fly on his arm. 'She led us to your things buried in a bag in the shamba. So you can see we have really been working on this case.'

The things remained on the table in front of them, Mr Katambo was fiddling with the pair of sunglasses. Jo wished she could take them out of his hand and put everything away out of sight.

'Did you find anything else. The radio?'

The Chief of Police laughed, 'That will have been sold straight away.'

'But you'll find the men now?'

'That is the business we must now discuss. I have received this letter from your Director,' he pulled a neatly typewritten letter from his pocket and handed it to Jo.

> Dear Sir, I'm writing in connection with the robbery case involving one of our workers, Ms Josephine Kelly, at her home in Kingangi village on July 20th. Whilst I appreciate that you are dealing with a considerable number of cases I am nevertheless concerned about the pressure under which Ms Kelly is being placed by the delay. As you will know from the details of the case she was subjected to an extremely unpleasant and frightening experience and the stress of continuing to work in the area while the men are at large is considerable. Consequently I have notified the British High Commission in Nairobi and would be grateful if you could put all your efforts into solving this case as soon as possible . . .

He began to speak before she'd finished reading it.

'I don't think it is good to interfere with police work.' He sounded resentful. 'As you can see we have worked very hard on this case and have recovered your property. We are doing our best to catch these criminals. I think you can report that to your Director.'

'Do you think they're still in the area?'

'They are most likely hiding in the forest.'

He took back the letter, looked at his watch and got up to go, then he remembered the stolen things and stuffed them back into the paper bag.

'These must be taken as evidence.'

Mr Katambo accompanied the Chief of Police out of the house and Jo watched through the window as the two of them walked a short way down the drive to the duck cage. Mr Katambo pulled out a fat duck by the scruff of its neck, tied its legs with a bit of string and handed it to the Chief of Police. Then they shook hands.

Mr Katambo was fussing again when he returned indoors.

'I've done my best,' he said.

'Thank you, I can hardly believe it, I just thought the whole case had been dropped.'

'I'm worried that the Field Director will take you away.'

'He can't do that. I think he just wanted to stir up the police. It seems to have worked.'

She felt frightened walking home with Boniface and Julius, another older boy, who'd been sent together to escort her; the dark fir trees seemed menacing, shadows leaping from their trunks. She thought of the men in the forest, hiding, knowing that the police were now on their track. The boys walked fast and didn't talk, she got the feeling they were frightened too, but there was a bright moon illuminating the path and they could see far ahead. A couple of young men came past. Julius stopped and greeted them, there was an exchange of news, Jo and Boniface went on a short distance and waited.

'They are going on G.H.' Boniface said.

'What does that mean?'

'Good Hunting, they're going to find girls.' Boniface laughed, 'But I don't know if they can be lucky.'

When they reached the top of the path that led down to her house she felt nervous again.

'Can you find your way now?' Boniface asked.

The watchman would be out by now, it was quite safe, yet she didn't want to walk it alone.

'Could you just come as far as the hedge?'

The two boys hesitated.

'What is it? The watchman?'

'No, the dog. It can bite us if we come.'

'OK. Don't worry, this is fine. Goodnight, thank you.'

She ran down the stony path, fumbling for the key in her pocket and clasping it tight. The door was already unlocked and swung open. Someone moved in the corner of the room.

Isaiah struck a match.

'You frightened me! How the hell did you get in?' Jo said.

'I took a key this morning.' He struck another match and lit the lamp.

'This is my house, you've got no right to just wander in. Why were you sitting here in the dark?'

'Don't be frightened. I was just waiting for you. I don't need light to think.'

She went to the bedroom to get a jersey and then outside again to untie the dog. Bouncer was excited to see her, leaping up and licking her face and snuffling round her ankles. Isaiah drew in his legs as the dog came up to him. Then he steeled himself to pat its head.

'I was worried,' he said. 'I was expecting you here. No one had seen you since this afternoon.'

'I've been with Mr Katambo and the Chief of Police, they've found out who did it.'

'The Chief of Police has been bribed by the other side.' Isaiah spoke softly.

'That's not possible. They've found some of my things, I identified them. And he told me he knew who it was.'

'They've known who it was for some time. You remember how they arrested Bhangi? They already knew who it was then, they were just trying to confuse you.'

'You're mad. Why would they want to confuse me?'

'Because someone has made it worth their while.'

He leant back in the sofa with his hands behind his head, looking smug.

'I don't think it's as simple as you think, he's had a letter from my Field Director. Geoff's already been in touch with the British High Commission.'

Isaiah laughed. 'So, the poor old Kikuyu is on the horns of a dilemma!'

She smelt beer on his breath.

'You're drunk. Where have you been?'

'In town with J.K. at the Babylon.'

He got up from the sofa and leant against the table facing her.

'I'm not drunk.'

'Well, stoned or something.'

'No. Listen. I'll tell you what I know.' He took a half-smoked cigarette from under the rim of his beret and lit it. 'The criminals have bribed the Chief of Police. Yesterday he came to the garage with his car. He had four new tyres fitted. Brand new tyres. J.K. did the job himself.'

'That's not true; I saw his car just a couple of hours ago, I would have noticed new tyres.'

'Not the pick-up, it was his other car, the white Peugeot.'

'I don't see how new tyres proves he's been bribed.'

'There's a radio repair shop in town. It's run by a man called Mohammed. The same Mohammed owns the garage.' He spoke quietly. 'The criminals do business with the radio repair shop – that's where everything goes, stolen radios, cassette players, cameras, watches – straight to the back of the shop where the serial numbers are taken off or they're broken up for spares.' Isaiah stubbed the cigarette out on the floor, it was only then, as she expected him to flatten it beneath his shoe, that Jo noticed he was barefoot. He had wide feet, the toes splayed out from walking barefoot as a child. 'Are you listening?' he asked. He sounded angry. 'So Mohammed has taken money from the criminals and paid off the Chief of Police with a gift from the garage. That way nothing looks suspicious. Now the police will leave the radio shop alone, Mohammed will be safe and the criminals will keep out of sight until the case is dropped.'

'But this is just based on what J.K. has told you, it doesn't fit with what happened this evening.'

'It does. The Chief of Police has to be seen to be working, that's why he asked to see you so you'll report back to your Director.'

'So you think he's tricked Mr Katambo as well do you?'

'No, Katambo's not stupid, he knows more than you think. He's got a lot of friends in town.'

'Well, he gave the Chief of Police one of his ducks.'

Isaiah laughed and stood up from the table, brushing some dirt from his shirt and straightening his beret, he'd taken to wearing it pulled down on the back of his head.

'Katambo's famous for his ducks! He's a good man, you can trust him.'

Jo was stroking the dog, its tail was thumping appreciatively on the floor.

'So what's going to happen now?'

'We'll have to wait and see, but you're safe here.'

'I don't feel safe.'

'I am sleeping here to guard you. I've brought another blanket, it was too cold last night.'

Isaiah moved around the house, shutting the windows and

checking the bolts on the doors, ignoring her. Not like before when she was always busy and he was so lazy. He used to come down from school in the middle of the day between lessons and stretch out to sleep on her sofa. When he woke he'd lie there watching her as she worked.

'Why are you staring at me?'

'I'm just watching.'

'There's nothing to watch.'

'There's plenty. I've been watching the way you keep pushing your hair back from your face.'

'Why don't you read or something?'

'I'm quite content.'

'I can't concentrate with you staring at me.'

'Then you should stop.'

In bed in the middle of the day, with the curtains closed, the doors bolted and her drawings abandoned on the desk, feeling the thrill of guilt. They slipped against each other in the sweat, she watched his rough hair between her legs. She kissed the pale soles of his feet.

He laid out the two grey blankets, put the panga beneath the sofa and the lamp as before on the stool close by.

'You'll be safe tonight,' he said, 'I'm going out early again tomorrow, I won't wake you.'

CHAPTER SEVENTEEN

A week later Jo was back in Nairobi sitting at the Thorn Tree. It was seven in the morning, no one much around, a few waiters polishing the tables and straightening the chairs, a couple of men across the street setting up their boot polish and newspaper stands and a man in a bundle of dirty clothes still asleep on the pavement. The British Airways flight got in early, another half an hour and Rick would be with her.

She sat down at one of the tables near the trunk of the tree but then moved to another closer to the pavement from where she could look down the road. One year and four months since they'd seen each other – she imagined him striding up, tall and thin, with his swept-back hair, grinning when he caught sight of her, swinging his old blue rucksack off his back. A waiter came hurrying over, 'It's not open yet. You can't order.'

'Can I just wait here, I don't want to order anything?'

'It's not possible.'

'Could I just rest, I'm meeting someone from England?'

Grudgingly he let her stay.

She hadn't slept much the night before in the stuffy room in the Uhuru Hotel. The windows wouldn't open and mosquitoes had whined around her head. She couldn't stop thinking of Rick, on the plane somewhere over Europe, the Mediterranean, North Africa, heading towards her. She got up at half past five, left the hotel and wandered into town. She stopped to look in the windows of clothes shops, and peered through the grilles on the radio stores, still half expecting to see her short-wave radio for sale in one of them. A chai shop was already open on the corner of Latema Road, she went in to drink tea and pass the time. The man behind the counter was slicing betel nuts onto leaves. The 'plane would have landed by now, they'd be disembarking into the heat. The man sprinkled fine red powder onto the leaves and arranged them in the glass counter. Behind him on the shelf were other plastic jars of spices, boxes of Aspro and Maloprim, bars of chocolate and cheap Rooster cigarettes. She bought a bar of Dairy Milk and ate it slowly as she headed towards the Thorn Tree.

Now she sat at the table on the outside terrace looking down the road for the airport bus. The city buses had begun to rumble by and the first smart-dressed office workers were on their way to work. A group of tourists in khaki shorts and floppy hats emerged from the hotel and gathered on the pavement waiting to board their safari van. The waiter, standing idle, was watching them, when they'd gone he came across to Jo.

'What do you want?'

'Nothing yet thank you.'

'You can't sit here without taking something.'

'OK, I'll have a soda.'

The soda still hadn't arrived when she thought she saw Rick stepping off the bus, a tall man dressed in a bright-coloured shirt, for a moment he disappeared from view behind some passing people. She stood up and was about to call out when she realised it was someone quite different.

The waiter brought the soda.

'Still your friend hasn't arrived?'

'No.'

'Then someone else must sit at this chair.'

The terrace was filling up. The person she'd mistaken for Rick came in and joined a long-haired man in shorts who was sitting at a table writing postcards. Jo moved her basket and gave the chair up to an African man in a suit. He tried to make conversation but she ignored him, keeping her eyes on the road; looking for a white face amongst the crowds of people piling off the buses. The man drank a soda quickly and left. Jo got out Rick's letter again and checked the date and time, *I can't wait to see you*, it said. When she'd read it the first time she'd picked it up and kissed it.

She'd waited till the last moment before telling Isaiah that Rick was coming to visit.

'A friend from England is coming to stay.'

'Rick. I know. I read the letter.'

Isaiah was sitting on the doorstep smoking a cigarette and Jo was watering the small pink flowers that grew along the side of the house, she'd wanted to tell him casually, to make it seem quite natural.

'How dare you read my letters. It's none of your business.' She splashed the last of the water on the plants.

'You left it out. I thought you wanted me to.'

'Of course not, I didn't know that you were going to be snooping in my house while I was out.'

'It's OK. I knew you had a man in England. You couldn't hide it from me.'

'I've told you about him before. He's just a friend.'

'Even the first time – remember I came here in the evening from school and you were digging. I brought you your letters and I could tell then.' Isaiah was drawing with a stick in the damp patch of earth, Jo was standing in front of him with the water from the perforated can dripping onto her skirt. 'Because you took one letter and ripped it open and read it very fast. Then you hid it away. Do you remember?'

'It was nothing special.'

'But I knew I had no chance.'

He looked up at her.

'But I've told you about Rick before. He's just a friend now, he's just coming for a holiday, we planned it ages ago. Even if he weren't it doesn't make any difference now does it?'

She went to the tank to fill another bucket of water, Isaiah followed her.

'Jo, you can't deceive me, why did you ask him to come out?'

She began to water the passion fruit tree, 'I didn't, I just told him what happened, he's my friend, I had to tell somebody.'

'You had to tell somebody white.'

'I had to tell someone who'd care.'

He went indoors. When she'd finished watering she found him sitting on the sofa staring into space.

'You always intended to go back to him. You've used me. You've exploited a black man.'

'What the hell do you mean? Who's to say you haven't used me, living off my money, my food, my books. You're the one who's been taking.'

'Josie!'

There was a shout from behind her, she turned and saw Rick, laden with luggage, stepping over the concrete border full of plants. She jumped up and flung her arms around him as he struggled to put down his rucksack. He hugged her hard and kissed her. When they sat down she saw that people were watching them.

'We've just provided a show for everyone!' She was proud of it.

Rick laughed. The waiter had already come over.

'What do you want?'

'Anything, something cool.'

'Soda moja na kahawa moja,' she said.

'You speak a different language – I'm not going to understand a word you say.'

'I only asked for a soda and coffee, you'll soon pick it up.' She took both his hands across the table, pressing his fingers, because she didn't know what to say. 'I'm so pleased to see you, I can't believe you're here.'

'Only nine hours from London, though British Airways design their seating for midgets,' he smiled, 'How are you? You look great, you're so brown.'

He looked older and slightly fatter than she remembered. He was wearing his favourite summer shirt which came out year after year but had a new pair of trousers and a pale cotton jacket. He flicked back his hair and smiled again.

'Well,' he said, flipping the lid of the metal coffee pot.

'How's my family?'

'Fine. I've got a letter from your Mum, written at teatime yesterday. And she's sent you lots of things.'

He turned out his pockets looking for the letter. She put a hand on the passport and wallet that he'd laid on the table.

'You must take care,' she said, 'There are a lot of thieves around, it's easy to get things nicked here.'

'That'd be a bad start.'

He found the letter and gave it to her.

'Can I read it now?'

'Of course, go ahead.'

He couldn't stop smiling at her.

'They sound very well. What's England like at the moment?'

'Same as ever.'

'Are there plums yet?'

She wanted to hear about the country, the trees and plants in the garden, the cool damp mornings.

'I don't think so, I can't remember.'

The waiter came and gave them a bill, Rick got out his wallet and produced a five hundred shilling note.

'That's a bit big. Don't worry I'll pay, I've got change.'

She paid and gave the waiter a generous tip which he pocketed with disregard.

'Well, what now?' Rick asked.

She'd never seen him so enthusiastic at the start of a holiday before, even in France he'd got annoyed when everything was new and he couldn't understand the language or work out the money as fast as her.

'I thought we'd spend tonight in Nairobi and go home tomorrow. We can find a room first, then I've got to go and see Geoff – the Field Director – if that's OK. Then we can just enjoy ourselves.'

Rick fell silent as they headed downtown towards the Uhuru Hotel. The city was dirtier out here with dust and rubbish on the pavements; newspaper, maize cobs, lumps of chewed and spat-out sugar cane. The air was close, thick with exhaust fumes from the slow-moving traffic. At the end of Tom Mboya Street they passed the fire station, crossed the roundabout and went down a steep hill. A couple of mechanics in oil-blackened overalls were working underneath a lorry, further down a man on the pavement was welding a metal bed frame. Jo felt conspicuous with Rick and his bulging rucksack.

'Where the hell are you taking me?'

'It's a cheap hotel, I stayed here last night.'

They had their first argument in front of the man at the desk, Rick stood with his rucksack on one shoulder refusing to put it down.

'We can't stay here, it's filthy. It stinks of urine.'

'It's OK, I promise, I stayed here last night.'

'It's a pit, for Christ's sake Josie.'

They followed the man in the white vest and loose wound kikoi cloth up the back stairs. She bargained with him for a room, only half listening to Rick behind her. The man unlocked the door to the room opposite the one she'd had the night before. There were two beds, one against each wall. Rick pulled back the bedclothes, the mattresses beneath were stained.

'There's absolutely no way I'm staying here, come on Jo.' He took her arm and turned to the man, 'No thanks, it's not clean.'

Out on the pavement she turned to him aggressively.

'What was wrong?'

'I'm sorry, I just couldn't face the thought of spending my first night here in a place like that, with bedbugs and that awful stench. Let's go somewhere else.'

'There isn't really anywhere else, all the cheap hotels are the same, at least that one's safe.'

'What about in the centre of town where we were before?'

'Everything there is about ten times as expensive.'

'Look I'll pay, you don't have to worry about that, just let's go somewhere decent where there's clean sheets and we can wash.'

They walked in silence back towards the centre of town, passing the pavement stalls of secondhand schoolbooks, the piles of newspapers weighted down with chunks of broken glass and the charcoal burners of roasting maize and cassava.

'Don't be angry, you know I'm not as tough as you.'

She took his hand as they crossed the road, it had been unfair to test him so resolutely, she'd known that he wouldn't like the Uhuru Hotel.

'No, you're right, it is an awful place. I've just got used to it.'

'I might have guessed you'd still have this masochistic tendency. You're just the same.'

'I suppose so.' She stopped by one of the charcoal burners, 'Do you fancy a bit of cassava?'

'What is it?'

'Roast cassava with chilli.'

'I suppose if it's cooked it's safe.'

For such a big man he was very timid, she hated herself for thinking it, all his life he'd suffered from looking strong and brave when really he wasn't. Every summer when he was a boy his parents had sent him away on adventure holidays when all he'd wanted to do was stay at home and practise the piano.

They ended up at the 680 Hotel, the room was clean and neat, with thick candlewick bedcovers, starched sheets and a carafe of water with an upturned glass on the table between the beds. When the porter had gone Jo went into the bathroom and ran the taps, she splashed her face with water and bent down to drink, then she flung herself on one of the beds and bounced on the mattress.

Rick was busy unpacking. He'd laid out his hairbrush and suntan cream and malaria pills on the dressing table and put his toothbrush and shaving things in the bathroom. He'd brought a money belt into which he transferred his passport, credit card, travellers cheques and cash. She watched, looking up at him from the bed as he moved around the room, taking a hanger from the cupboard and putting his jacket on it, lifting up his shirt to tie the money belt around his waist.

'You've put on weight!' She stared as he tucked his shirt back into his trousers, his body was too familiar not to comment on.

'And you've lost weight, you're like a rake.'

There'd been a time in London when she'd got quite plump with all his cooking. He'd found her more attactive then, with fuller breasts and tighter clothes, but she preferred to be thin and to feel her hip bones rubbing on her clothes.

'Anyway your Mum has sent you lots of food.' He delved into the side pocket of the rucksack and produced a homemade cake, a carefully wrapped wedge of cheddar cheese and then a huge bar of dark chocolate. There was also a bag of Coxes apples. She sat up and surveyed the store, the familiar shapes and packaging; the cake wrapped round in silver foil, the cheese in a white paper bag, the brown paper bag of apples with the corners flipped and twisted over.

'Fantastic, how did she know what to send?'

'I think she asked her friend out here, Diana is it? She's been in touch with them quite a bit. She hadn't heard from you for months. I think she was worried that you might have got caught up in the attempted coup.'

'I was miles away.'

'That's what Diana told her, but you can understand why she was worried.'

'I did write to tell them I was OK.'

'She still thought you were hiding something.'

Jo had stood up to get an apple from the bag but stopped midway, 'You haven't told her have you?'

'Of course not. I haven't told anyone,' he put down the books he was taking from the bag, 'I'm so sorry about what happened.'

'I was unlucky.'

'It must have been terrible.' He stepped across his bags and hugged her to him, holding her tightly round the shoulders. She pressed her head against him and closed her eyes as he stroked the top of her arm.

'I don't know how you've been so brave.'

'I haven't been that brave.'

'You must have been very frightened.'

'It's hard to believe it really happened now.'

He was so kind and sympathetic, so understanding, but now that he was here she felt distant from him. She made herself hug him and press her head closer to his shoulder.

'But you must still be frightened.'

'Sometimes.' She conjured up her fear, the darkness, alone in the house, noises outside, the repeating nightmare of a knife at her neck, 'Sometimes I feel as if it's going to happen again.' She eased herself away from his embrace and sat on the bed. She took an apple from the bag and twiddled it on its stalk, watching it spin, the green and red blurring, 'Quite often I get the feeling that normal, ordinary people are watching and going to grab me.'

'Poor Josie.'

'Sometimes I feel as if I'm going mad. I walk down the street, or through the villages at home, looking at all the faces, suspicious of everyone, thinking that people want to hurt me. I told you in my letter. It's stupid really, but I can't control it, it's just fear inside, it grows and grows. And at night in my house I hear the slightest sounds and think they're there again.'

'You're not still living alone in that house are you?'

The apple broke from its stalk and rolled across the room, she picked it up and went into the bathroom to wash it, calling back to him.

'I'll tell you everything later. We'd better get to the Field Office before Geoff goes for lunch.'

She ate the apple on the way to the Field Office, it was hard and sour, quite unlike the soft sweet fruit of Africa.

'Do you want a bite?'

'No, I've had plenty, they're all for you.'

'Where did you buy them?'

'In the market.'

'From the same old woman?'

'That's right.'

'Funny to think of people going on doing the same things.'

'Nothing much changes.'

'I know, but I can't help feeling that other lives have stopped.'

They turned off Kenyatta Avenue and walked past a row of stalls selling carvings and baskets and bangles. In an instant a man had spotted Rick and was dancing backwards along the pavement in front of them waving a fistful of bracelets and flywhisks.

'How much you want? Real elephant hair. Ivory.'

'No thanks,' Rick said.

'Bone, real giraffe bone,' he flicked the flywhisk in the air, 'Only twenty shillings. For you, fifteen.'

'Jo, can't you tell him we're not interested?'

'Sitaki, bwana,' Jo said, 'No thanks. Kwaheri.'

They'd almost ground to a standstill with the man blocking the pavement ahead of them.

'I thought they'd stopped selling real animal stuff.'

She was just about to answer when something made her turn, a man behind them was putting his hand into her basket.

Jo swung around at him, shouting in Kiswahili, '*We*! You!'

He turned immediately and ran off down the street.

'What was all that about?'

'That bloke just tried to pick my bag.'

'Which man?'

'He's gone now.'

'Which way?'

'I don't know, he's disappeared.' She could see him loitering a short way down the street but Rick was angry.

'Are you OK?'

'Yes, of course, I should have guessed that the other guy was just distracting us.'

'The bastard, what bloody cheek.'

'I suppose it's fair game, he's not to know I'm not a tourist.'

'Even if you were.'

'Well, I'm not sure, I reckon if I was an unemployed Kenyan I might start nicking things from all these fat rich tourists.'

'You don't mean that do you?'

'In a way – yes. Why not?' How easily shocked he was.

'Come off it Josie, everyone's got a right to their own belongings.'

'I'm not sure about that, some have got more right than others.'

They walked on down Mama Ngina Street and passed some more men with carved giraffes and 'ebony' elephants blackened with boot polish.

'I've worked out what it is Jo, if you don't look these guys in the eye, then they don't hassle you.'

The Field Office was on the tenth floor of an office block with a view across the city. Jo left Rick in the secretary's room and went in to speak to Geoff. He was eating a hamburger and chips at his desk and looked tired and ruffled.

'Sorry about the food, I haven't had time to get out for lunch. Have a seat.' He wiped the ketchup from his beard with the back of his hand and chucked the rest of the food in the bin. 'I'm afraid it's been a bad day.'

'What's happened?'

'We've just lost the accountant.'

'Ernest?'

He nodded, pulling on the hairs of his beard. 'He's been fiddling the books for some time – I called him in yesterday for a chat and this morning he just disappeared, along with all the petty cash and a two hundred pound cheque for the bank.'

'Don't you know where he's gone?'

'God knows. There's only a young girl at his home, the maid, who says the family has gone to Uganda.'

'Is he a Ugandan?'

'Yes, and a very dishonest one at that, I don't know why I ever employed him.' Jo couldn't bear to watch him tugging his beard and looked away. 'Except I suppose he spoke good English and gave me a sob story about his family. Anyway it's not the first time.' He heaved a sigh. 'But how are you? How's that old dog?'

'Fine. The dog's fine.'

'Was that your boyfriend I saw out there?'

'No, just a friend who's come to visit. I've really come to talk about the case.'

She saw his mouth tighten. 'Sure. I hope there's been some action. I wrote to the Chief of Police . . . '

She interrupted him, 'Thanks, he showed me the letter. The thing is he's been bribed by the other side.'

'How do you know that?'

'Someone from the village told me.'

'And can they be trusted?'

He pulled a folder out of the cupboard beside him and flicked through until he reached her section, she saw, upside down, her original application for the job and a reference from the Head of Department. Geoff scribbled something on a sheet of paper and stapled it in.

'OK. This whole business is dragging on far too long, the only thing to do is for me to make another trip to Kizui and sort this chap out. How long's your friend staying?'

'A couple of weeks.'

'So you'll be alright while he's around.'

'I suppose so. Couldn't you come a bit sooner?'

'Not really.' He flicked through the pages of a large desk diary, 'I've a meeting with the heads of the other agencies at the beginning of the week and then a new group of workers is coming out the following Friday. To be honest the earliest I can make it is the 25th.'

'I don't feel very safe at the moment.'

'Listen, if you're not happy about being out there then you should stay in Nairobi or take your friend off to the coast or something – it doesn't matter if you take a bit of time off work.'

'No, it's OK, I think we'll go back, at least for a few days, I want to show him the pumps and everything.'

Jo and Rick went down in the lift. 'Damn him, he doesn't really care what's happening out there,' she said as soon as they were out of the building. 'He doesn't even care about my work, for all he knows I could just be on a two year holiday. And he's been there!

He knows exactly what happened and all he can do is sit in Nairobi writing polite letters to the police.'

'You haven't really told me what's going on.' Rick followed Jo as she dodged out across the road in front of a city bus. 'Cool down Josie, you'll get run over.'

'I don't care, that would serve him right.' She stopped. 'Sorry, I just think he's incompetent, he doesn't understand the way things work here, he still thinks because he's British and has got a nice white face that people are going to respect him and get things done.'

'That must be true to a certain extent.'

'No, it's not like that. There's a minimum of respect – it's every man for himself – and the police aren't going to follow up my case just because some "mzungu", some foreigner, comes along and speaks politely to them.'

Jo headed off towards the swimming pool, longing to get there and plunge into the cool water. 'He's just naive, he's never lived in the bush. He's from an old colonial family, brought up with the notion that when it comes to the crunch the Africans will always fear a white man. It's not his fault, he just shouldn't be doing this job, he should have stuck to being an economist.'

'Well, I'm here now. I'll look after you.'

Jo and Rick raced each other in the swimming pool at the Boulevard Hotel and then lay in the sun on the blue towelling mattresses and ordered cold sodas. There was the usual crowd of Asian men propping up the bar, all in brief black trunks with gold chains nestling in their hairy chests. They stared as she rubbed suntan oil onto her legs.

'Those men like the look of you.'

'They're always here, they usually try to buy me drinks. Just ignore them.'

Rick continued to stare back.

Jo wasn't surprised to find that he'd brought the same pair of faded swimming trunks that he'd worn every year on their holidays to the Norfolk coast. He was very white. He hadn't been anywhere that year but had spent it in London giving extra piano tuition and playing in some concerts himself.

'You'd better put some suntan stuff on.'

'I don't think it's too hot.'

'It is, you just don't notice it because of the breeze. I'll do it for you. Lie down.'

She rubbed the suntan cream into his shoulders and down into the small of his back, taking longer than was necessary.

'That's nice.'

She enjoyed the flirtation, rubbing her fingers down the sides of his stomach as far as she dared.

They dozed for a while then Jo asked him about their friends, what people were doing, who was with who. He answered briefly, with little gossip.

'Have you got anyone else living in the house?'

'No, just me.'

She wanted to hear how much he'd missed her, but life had obviously been little different. Unless he had a new girlfriend, but she didn't ask.

After a while Rick got up to sit in the shade. Jo watched him examining his chest and pulling his trunks a short way down to see if he'd gone brown.

They left the swimming pool towards dusk, the lights were already lit on the fountain in the drive and the taxis drawn up outside the hotel. Opposite was the Voice of Kenya radio station, there were soldiers guarding the entrance and dark green tents pitched within the fence.

'This is the radio station, it looks more like an army camp doesn't it?'

'I thought it was a camp.'

'It's because of the attempted coup, it wasn't like this before.'

'We got stopped twice on the road from the airport. But they look so young, these guys with their guns.'

The soldiers stared as they passed within a few feet of them and Jo stared back. Rick was right; they were just boys like the boys she saw in the village, dressed up with boots and guns.

Jo took Rick to the Minar for dinner, it was an Indian restaurant where, so she'd heard from Diana, the food was extremely good. It turned out to be much smarter than she'd anticipated, with a small bar cut off from the dining area with carved wooden screens, pierced ceramic lights and soft low chairs, the sort of place where you have a drink and look at the menu before sitting at a table. But Rick seemed to like it.

After a gin and tonic they were given a place at the back of the crowded room. The faint smell of incense, the music, loud laughter and conversation livened her up. They drank beer and ate poppadoms until the food came, it could have been anywhere in the world, this spice-smelling room with the slim Indian waiters in neat black trousers and starched white shirts, the polite service.

Rick's face was glowing, he looked brown in the light but there were fine white creases around his eyes where he'd screwed up his face into the sun. She flirted with him, a teasing testing conversation, reminiscing about old times.

'Do you remember that awful Indian place I took you to in Manchester?'

'On our first night out together, when you'd missed the train and were trying to make up for it.'

'We were really ill weren't we?'

'Not as bad as those whelks you made me eat in Norfolk.'

The curry seemed to burn her stomach but she ate a lot, he kept finding the best bits, a piece of chicken, the last prawn, and putting them on her plate.

'More beer?'

'Why not?'

Suddenly he pushed aside his plate and looked serious.

'We've got to talk about it Josie, what has this Field Director chap actually done for you?'

'I'll tell you the whole story. The day after I reported the rape . . . ', Rick winced at the word, 'Geoff came back to Kizui with me. We went to talk to the police and he bribed them with fifty quid. That was a couple of weeks before the attempted coup. Nothing happened, the men weren't found, the police said they'd run off to Nairobi and there was nothing they could do. A few weeks later Geoff wrote to the Chief of Police and got in touch with the British High Commission here in Nairobi. Then last week I met the Chief of Police with Mr Katambo, the Assistant Chief. He'd found some of my things and said the men were hiding in Kizui forest. He assured me that they'd be caught. But the same night I discovered that the Chief of Police had been bribed by the other side, someone had bought him new tyres for his car.'

'So absolutely nothing has been achieved. And Geoff is letting you go on living out there with those men probably still around.'

'I suppose he's tried to get things moving, but everything's very slow here.'

'He sounds totally irresponsible letting you stay there alone.'

'I don't think it's dangerous.'

'I think you're mad Josie, of course it's dangerous if those men are out in the forest.'

'You don't understand, they won't come up to Kingangi again, I've got a dog and a new watchman and a friend comes to sleep in my house.'

'Geoff should have put you up in a hotel in Nairobi until those men were caught.'

'He would have done if I'd wanted it, but I thought it was better to get on with the work.'

'And risk your life?'

'It's not a risk. If I went away from Kingangi then everyone would think I'd given up and gone back to England. The water project would stop, people would lose interest. And those guys would have just got away with it. They'd probably go and rape someone else. I've got to stay there and face up to it.'

'What about a medical check-up?'

'I went to a doctor.'

'But did they examine you properly?'

'Of course.'

'And you're OK?'

'Fine.' She sipped her beer.

'You're hiding something. Were you pregnant?'

'No, not that.'

'Injured?'

'No, I'm fine. It's just the doctor was a real bastard, he seemed to relish the whole thing. He asked me if I'd enjoyed it. You wouldn't believe it, he asked if I'd had an orgasm.' She didn't lower her voice, glad for people to overhear. 'Then he said that African girls consider it a compliment to be raped.'

'You told Geoff about this?'

'No.'

'Why not? That's appalling, he can't send his workers to people like that.'

She pushed the rest of her food to the edge of the plate and screwed up her napkin and put it on the table.

'Can we stop talking about this?'

'Of course, I'm sorry, it must be awful for you. I don't know how you've survived.' He took a long swig of beer and looked up at her again, 'You know I've always admired your bravery.'

'Don't be stupid.'

'It's true, I've always been a bit in awe of you.'

'I didn't think you thought much of me.'

'How can you say that? You know how much I loved you.'

'Did you? I don't know, you never told me that you did. Anyway I was always in awe of you, you're so talented.'

'What, playing a few tunes on the piano? That doesn't count for much.'

'Of course it does, that's why I fancied you in the first place.'

He flicked back his hair and picked at the label on the beer bottle. 'And then you realised you'd made a mistake.'

'No.'

'Why did you leave?'

'You know why.'

'Tell me again.'

'I just wanted to do something worthwhile.'

'So it wasn't me?'

'We can't have this conversation.'

The waiters were hovering around them, the room was almost empty.

'I still love you Jo.'

'I love you too, but we annoy each other too much as well. We must go, they want to shut the place up.'

She insisted on paying the bill and they left. She was slightly unsteady on her feet, wondering if she could walk with composure past the almost-bowing waiters who were waiting to lock the door behind them. Outside on the pavement, half-leaning against the restaurant front they kissed each other.

'Lucky the curfew's been extended, we've got ten minutes to get home.'

The hotel room was cool from the air-conditioning. She flung herself onto the bed again.

'I'm drunk!'

He took off her clothes for her and lifted her under the sheet.

She was almost asleep when he came back from the shower and climbed in beside her. She woke enough to feel aroused and to slide on top of him. He was cold from the water, she pressed down on him, pinning his arms to the pillow. She closed her eyes again, still half-dreaming, hearing his sighs, moving till he vanished. Till the body she was loving wasn't his but Isaiah's.

CHAPTER EIGHTEEN

'How many more hours in this chicken coop?'

Jo and Rick were squashed together in the back of a Nissan van with about twenty other people, it was going at sixty miles an hour down the fast Mombasa road and everyone was quiet. Rick's question cut the silence.

'How much further?' he asked again.

'We're about half-way,' she whispered and looked away from him out of the window. The man in front translated for the rest of the passengers. The woman next to Rick tried to shift to give him more room but she was jammed against the side and couldn't budge.

'We should have hired a car, this is ludicrous.'

'People will get out at Machakos.'

'How far's that?'

'Half an hour or so.'

Rick hadn't slept well, he'd felt hot and sunburnt, and had been struggling all morning to suppress his irritation at the inefficiency of Kenyan transport.

They bumped into the pot-holed bus park a short while later. Three people got out, but four more and a child were squeezed in. The driver went off in search of a cigarette leaving a boy in charge who sat in the driving seat revving the engine.

'That kid's not going to be driving is he?'

'No, he's just trying to keep us interested, making sure no one gets out and finds a faster van.'

'What we need's a slower van.'

The man behind tapped Rick on the shoulder, 'This one is the best, very reliable,' he explained.

It was cooler as soon as they started moving again with the breeze blowing through the windows. They went just as fast, swinging round the sharp downhill corners with the driver occasionally stepping on the brakes to avoid a goat that had strayed from the roadside. But they hadn't gone very much further when they punctured a tyre in a pothole. Everyone had to pile out and stand in the sun while the driver and the turn-boy changed the wheel. Rick watched as they jacked up the van, took off the wheel and put on another with a tyre even more bald than the first.

'This is ridiculous, we should have hired a car.'

'I couldn't turn up at Kingangi in a car.'

'Well, how about a camel?'

'It's always like this, it's OK really.'

'I still think it would have been safer by camel.'

They were separated in the fight to get back on board again. Jo joined the push but Rick stood back waiting for everyone else. He ended up in the front seat between the driver and turn-boy and another woman. Jo was behind him. They were silent for the rest of the journey. She sat looking at the line of pinkish skin on the back of his neck and the familiar pattern of checks on his shirt, hating herself for wishing he hadn't come.

When they arrived in Kizui, Jo took Rick to the Hotel Relax. There were few other people in the room, just a couple of young men eating alone, folding chapatis and dipping them into dishes of goat stew. She took Rick's hand across the table, disturbing the flies from the sticky surface.

'I'm sorry about the journey. It was bloody awful. It's just I'm used to it.'

'That's OK. I might have guessed you'd be into maximum hardship, just so long as you don't expect me to enjoy it too.'

The old man came over with the kettle of tea and a plate of greasy orange dough cakes.

'Here, have your first mandazi,' Jo said.

'What are they?'

'Like doughnuts without the jam.'

The flies were already settling on the dish, she flicked them away.

'Thanks.' He took a large bite. 'They're rather good.'

She laughed. 'You don't have to be brave!'

'Oh, I might as well.'

When they'd finished their tea they set off for Kingangi, stopping at the market to buy bananas and a cabbage. They were heading down the sandy slope towards the river crossing when a car passed them. It hooted and stopped a short way ahead in a cloud of dust. It was Mr Katambo's but he wasn't in it, only the driver with his son Boniface riding in the front seat. The boy leapt out and opened the doors. Jo and Rick got in the back. Boniface took the rucksack, jammed it into the front seat and squeezed himself in beside it.

'That was lucky, this is the Assistant Chief's car, it's about the only vehicle that ever uses this road.' Jo was excited, anxious to explain everything to Rick. 'This is the car I came in when I first arrived here.'

Boniface had twisted around on the front seat and was staring at Rick.

'Where have you come from?'

'England.'

'London?'

'That's right.'

'What is your name?'

'Rick. What's your name?'

'Boniface Wilson Ndeti.'

The driver said something to the boy which made him smile. The man repeated it and Boniface turned round again.

'My father wants to know, is he your husband?'

'No, not my husband.'

Boniface reported back to his father and Jo laughed.

'I think he's told him that you're my brother.'

Jo felt proud of the way Rick got on with the kids. He'd brought a harmonica with him and took it up to Jerusa's home that first evening and played some tunes. Then one of them asked to have a go and he patiently gave it to each in turn, wiping the dribble from it with his handkerchief. Then they sat in Jerusa's room and ate heaped plates of boiled chicken with rice. When Jerusa had gone to make the tea Ben Kyalo came in from the compound. He'd been drinking local beer with some other men and was unusually talkative, trying to speak English to Rick.

'In Kingangi, we were very backward, but now Miss Jo she has come to develop our people. This "mzungu" she is too good.'

Museo was peering through the curtain from the bedroom and giggling at the old man.

'And she is brave. She fought those criminals who came to her house.'

Rick couldn't understand all that he was saying and became embarrassed. He listened with a fixed smile, smoothing his hair with his hand and looking to Jo for help. She tried to interrupt but the old man was enjoying himself.

'I'm afraid I didn't understand much of what that old man was saying to me,' Rick said as soon as they'd left the compound.

'It doesn't matter, he was drunk. He was only asking if you were my husband and if you had another wife in England, but he didn't need any answers.'

'What was all that about developing the people?'

'I think he thought it would impress you.'

'That's not what you tell people is it, that you've come to develop them?'

'You must be joking! It's just because of all the government propaganda about nation building: "*The President today visited a new water pump and praised the people for their efforts in nation building,*" that sort of stuff.'

'I must admit I didn't think it would be quite so primitive.'

'It's not primitive.'

'Well, you know what I mean, basic. Pit latrines and bare mud huts.'

'Houses.'

'You'll have to teach me the OK words.'

He was searching through the pockets of his jacket and trousers.

'Damn, I've lost the harmonica, I thought I'd put it away.'

'You must have left it on the side, don't worry, Jerusa will look after it. The kids really enjoyed it.'

'You don't think one of them stole it do you?'

'Of course not.'

'Well, they'll probably have fun with it.'

They'd reached her home. She went straight in and lit the lamp which she'd left ready with matches on the table.

'There's a bowl of water in the bathroom for washing, but you can get some more from the tank outside if you need it,' she explained. 'And it's best to knock on the door of the latrine before you go in. Just in case there's a snake in there.'

'You're kidding – you mean I have to warn the black mamba when I'm coming for a pee?'

He was being falsely jolly. She too was nervous. It was impossible to ignore the fact that they were now alone together in the house in which she'd been attacked. While he was fetching more water she took his rucksack into her bedroom and checked all the bars on the windows. The dog was still at Mr Katambo's home where she'd left it before she went away. Strange not to have it following close behind her as she went around the house, lighting a candle, getting out a towel for Rick, putting away the book that Isaiah had left behind. She'd asked Jerusa where he was and was told he'd disappeared. Where to? Why?

Rick bolted the door behind him when he came in, he was slightly breathless.

'Jo, I thought I saw someone lurking down the bottom of your garden.'

'It's probably the watchman. Did he have a bow and arrows?'

'I couldn't see, he moved behind a tree.'

'Don't worry, it's only Hassan, he often goes down there to check along the hedge.'

'You're sure?'

'Quite sure.'

'I hope I didn't frighten you.'

'No.'

'I must be over-reacting.'

He took the water into the bathroom.

'You'll need the lamp,' she called after him, 'There's a hook on the wall to hang it from.'

She tried to fight back the fear of being trapped in the house for the night. She lay down on the sofa. Isaiah had taken away his blanket and comb. No one had seen him since the day she went to Nairobi.

'Blimey, there's a frog in here,' Rick suddenly called out.

'It's a toad.'

'Is this one of your little nature reserves?'

She laughed. 'It comes in through the water outflow.'

'Go on froggy . . . out!'

She heard him swishing the water through the hole. Then he came out of the bathroom looking rather pleased with himself.

'I got rid of it.'

In the morning Jo took Rick up to Kingangi to show him the standpipes and storage tanks, and then they walked on down to the pump. To her surprise he was interested, asking how she'd worked out how much water was needed in the village and what would happen if the pump broke down.

'It shouldn't be too much of a problem because it's quite simple. It can be mended in one of the workshops at the village polytechnic.'

'Don't you get sticks and things jammed in it?'

'Not sticks, it's mainly weed that gets tangled up, that's the real problem.'

'And who cleans that out?'

'The woman on duty. We pay someone to inspect it every day for a week. Then someone else takes over.'

'I'd no idea it was such a large-scale thing.'

'It's not really.'

'Still it's pretty amazing to turn a tap on and get water out.'

'I had help from other engineers in Machakos.'

'Don't do yourself down, Josie. It's brilliant.'

That evening the donkeys were in the garden, grazing on the grass around the water tank.

Rick watched Jo lighting the jiko, arranging the odd-shaped pieces of fuel with total concentration, then screwing up a piece of paper, dipping it in paraffin and lighting it. She stepped back as the smoke blew up and he put his arms around her, but with the slightest shrug she moved away.

A couple of children had come up the hill and were peering through the greenery of the hedge. When Jo called out they climbed through, each trying to push the other one first. They'd brought a huge papaya, its skin a blotchy green and yellow and the white sap still oozing from its stalk where it had been snapped from the tree. Jo gave them a mug of milk with sugar to share and they sat in silence watching her and Rick until dusk came and they ran off home.

He watched her winding up the wick of the hurricane lamp, lifting the cooking pot from the fire, spooning the stew of maize and beans into two tin plates.

They sat on the doorstep in front of the smouldering jiko, looking down towards the river and the forest beyond, and ate the githeri. She'd washed and tied up her hair and knotted a khanga around her. Her shoulders were bare; brown and bony. The dog was eating the last of its dogmeal from the battered aluminium pot, pushing it round and round. Then it came and laid its head on her lap and she picked the swollen ticks from its ears. The sun had gone down and the light was fading rapidly.

'What's that noise?'

'I can't hear anything.'

'The humming.'

'Cicadas. And frogs, I think, down at the river, mating calls.'

Jo didn't listen to the night sounds of animals any more, her ears were always tuned for the sound of people. She got up and stacked the dishes into the empty cooking pot, taking it in one hand and the hurricane lamp in the other she went to the kitchen leaving Rick in darkness. He drank the last of the coffee and watched her through the open doorway as she began to wash the plates in a bowl of water on the floor, absorbed in the task as if she were alone, her giant shadow moving on the grey stone wall. He suddenly wanted to grab her and drag her to the sofa. He wanted to hurt her, to force her to love him.

'You can sleep in my bed tonight,' she said, 'And I'll sleep here on the mat, it's just too uncomfortable for both of us.'

'For Christ's sake Josie, I haven't come all this way to sleep on my own. I understand about what happened, we don't have to make love.'

'It's not that, it's just uncomfortable, I can't sleep.'

'Of course you can, it's better if we're together. Why don't you leave the dishes now?'

'I can't leave them, they'll attract the rats.'

Later they went to bed together and lay side by side listening for sounds outside the house. At one point she thought she heard something and shot up on her elbow, but it was just the dog in the room next door chasing cockroaches. She lay down again staring into the darkness.

'Rick, you know I've had another boyfriend out here.'

'I guessed.'

'I just wanted you to know, that's why I was feeling strange.'

There was a long silence, so she thought that he wasn't going to say anything else, then he asked,

'Was he an African?'

'Yes. But it's all over, it didn't work out.'

She tried to kiss him, but he turned his head away,

'Not now Jo.'

She persisted, touching him until he turned towards her.

He felt jealous and inadequate. In the depths of her body he began to taste the black man's sperm – vile, bitter. On her breasts he smelt the African's sweat and found her unclean, no longer beautiful. Again and again he saw a dark body plunging towards her.

CHAPTER NINETEEN

Jo arranged that she would only work in the mornings while Rick was there, so the afternoon literacy and accounting classes were closed for an unofficial holiday. He seemed content to stay at her house until she returned, sleeping for much of the morning and then sitting on the doorstep practising the harmonica or reading the thrillers that he'd bought at the airport. He got in the habit of making lunch for her, conjuring up out of the unvaried food, strange delicious dishes: mango and cabbage salad, chilli bean pancakes, pawpaw with cinnamon. Although it was hot in the afternoons they went out for walks with the dog, climbing the mountains and visiting her friends in distant homes. On Saturday when she didn't have to work they got up early and taking a picnic of bread and honey and bananas walked out to the waterfall.

'How high is this waterfall?'

'About a hundred feet.'

'I hope it's worth it, my feet are really blistered.'

He was wearing a pair of shorts and trainers without socks, his legs were burnt and the skin had rubbed from the back of his heels. When they arrived he pulled off his shirt and plunged into a pool of swirling water. It was shallow and he began to clamber over the rocks in the river approaching the bottom of the fall. He called out to her but she couldn't hear, so he came out back onto the bank flicking back his wet hair and shaking off the drops like a dog.

'I think there's a way up,' he said, 'It looks as if you can climb up the side and then crawl along that ledge and get right behind the waterfall.'

'It'd be too dangerous.'

'Come on, I thought you were a real tomboy.'

'No, it's slippery up there, I can see from here.'

He waded back into the river and made his way to the face of rocks at the side of the waterfall. She watched him as he climbed a short way up. Then he waved and came back down.

'You're right, it is a bit dangerous.'

They stayed on the bank, eating their lunch; cutting chunks of bread with his penknife, spreading on honey, and slicing bananas on top. She told him the story of the thief.

'How did you find this place?'

'One of my friends brought me here.'

They passed through Kingangi on the way home. She'd lent Rick her socks to protect his feet but he was limping a bit and glad to stop.

'How about buying some beer for tonight?' he suggested.

'I don't usually buy beer here, it means going to the bar and I'd rather not be seen in there.'

'You're much too abstemious Josie, some beer would do you good – you might even like me again with some alcohol inside you.'

'I do like you. You go, then.'

'How do I ask?'

'Just say "Tusker *nne*" – four beers.' She gave him her basket, 'Wrap the bottles in the khanga so people won't see them on the way home. I'll wait here.'

'What do I say?'

She told him again and he went into the bar.

Someone whistled from the trees in the middle of the market square, and she heard her name. It was J.K. dressed in unfamiliar clothes with a woollen hat instead of his battered black one.

Rick was standing outside the bar looking lost, she went back to him and picked up the basket from the ground.

'Who was that man you were talking to?'

'Just a friend.'

Rick looked at her. 'Is he the one you slept with?'

'No.'

'You might as well be honest, I know that something's going on that you won't tell me about.'

'He's Jerusa's boyfriend, you've met him before.'

'I don't remember, everyone looks the same to me.' He scuffed his foot in the sand.

She lifted the basket onto her shoulder.

'Let me carry that.' He tried to take it from her.

'No, it's OK, I'm used to it.'

She let him tag along behind, going slowly on his blistered feet, hardly able to keep up with her swift stride and sudden turns down the narrow shamba paths. He was sweating and out of breath, still not accustomed to the altitude.

When they arrived at the house she went straight in and started heaping charcoal into the jiko.

'What can I do?'

'Nothing, just relax.'

She dipped a piece of paper in paraffin, stuck it under the coals and lit it.

'I know you don't want me here,' he said, 'I should never have come.' He'd taken out a handful of matches, lit one and was lighting the others off it, speaking into the sudden bursts of flaring sulphur. It was an old trick, he didn't know that matches were hard to come by.

'I do want you here, of course I do. It's just strange after being alone for so long, I'm not used to having someone else tagging around with me.'

'I don't mean to get in your way, I'm sorry if it feels as if I'm hanging around, but what else can I do? I don't know anyone here. I've come to be with you.' He paused and put the handful of burnt matchsticks into the fire. 'I thought you wanted me.'

'I did.'

'I can see I should never have come, you don't have to make it so obvious. I'm sick of "tagging" after you, you don't think it's much fun for me do you, listening to endless conversations in Kiswahili that I can't understand?'

'Kikamba.'

'Whatever it is. Can you imagine what it's like spending the mornings all alone with no one to talk to – just those bloody kids shouting "Mzungu, mzungu!" every time I so much as step out of the house? And that loony laughing through the hedge. And what about just now, standing in that marketplace wondering where the hell you'd got to?'

She looked at him without speaking, waiting for it all to pour out.

'Listen, Josie, I can't stick another two weeks of this. You've changed, you're not the same person I remember.' He paused, looking at her sadly. 'You used to be so kind to everyone. You were never cruel before.'

'I'm sorry – I don't know what to say – I haven't changed . . . '

'Maybe you don't see it, but you've become selfish living out here.'

She felt herself smile – embarrassed yet strangely pleased that he at last had hurt her too.

'Maybe that's what Africa does to people,' he said.

'Don't blame Africa.'

'What's got into you? All the Africans are so bloody wonderful, but I don't matter any more.'

'That's not true. Of course you matter, I just want you to like it here.'

'Well, I don't much like it, frankly the place stinks.' He unloaded the beers from the basket, slamming them on the table, then turned and faced her, speaking softly. 'What the hell are you doing here? Anyone can see you don't belong. All that smiling, greeting everyone, but it's just a charade isn't it? People are just using you.'

'What for?'

'I don't know – money, prestige, to get their kicks. I saw all those men leering in the marketplace . . . '

'They weren't leering – I know them, they were schoolkids from Kingangi.'

'They were leering at you, watching your breasts as you bent over to buy things, and you grinned.' He drew a breath. 'It's not surprising what happened.'

She put her hands to her ears and turned away.

'I'm sorry, I didn't mean it.' He tried to pull her arms down but she tugged away.

'I don't want to hear it.'

'I'm sorry. Honestly, I don't know why I said that, I didn't mean it, not at all. You can't imagine how it hurts me, thinking about what they did to you.'

While they'd been arguing Museo had arrived at the door with milk and a dish covered over with a tin plate. She was standing, watching, mesmerised.

'What do you want?' Jo asked. She'd never spoken abruptly to her before, the girl put down the dish of food and turned and ran away. Jo went to the door and called out after her 'Museo! Thank you,' but it was too late, she'd already disappeared through the hedge.

Jo took the lid off the plate, it was a dish of goat stew, lukewarm, a strong smell pervaded the room.

'We might as well have some,' she said to Rick, drawing up a couple of stools to the table.

'It looks disgusting.'

It had been a present; she picked out a piece of bone and began to chew it, wiping the juice from her mouth with the back of her hand, enjoying Rick's displeasure.

'I'm going to open a beer.' He got out his penknife and eased the top off a bottle, then he went outside and sat on the doorstep staring at the ground. She remained at the table, fishing pieces of potato from the stew and eating mindlessly as the conversation went round and round in her head. *All Africans are so bloody wonderful. . . .*

Surely all we've shared counts for more than this. Bouncer was waiting at her side. After a while she put the dish down on the floor for him and went out past Rick to wash her hands at the tank. Then she came and sat beside him.

'Maybe I have changed but there's no reason why we can't get on. I think I wanted to make it difficult, I'm sorry, I really am.'

'It's a bit late now isn't it?'

'No, of course not, you've got another two weeks.'

'I'm going to hire a car and go down to the coast for a decent holiday.'

'You can't do that.'

'Why not? You'd be better off without me, I'm only getting in the way up here.'

'You're not serious are you?'

'Of course, I've got the message Jo.'

'Don't go. Please don't leave. I've been longing for you to be here,' she paused, 'You're the only person who really knows me.'

There was silence, he took her hand and squeezed it.

'Things have been pretty tough on you, haven't they?'

'It's my own fault.'

'Have some beer to wash down that old goat.'

'Thanks,' she smiled. 'I only ate the potatoes.'

'Well you need feeding up.'

'Tomorrow will be better. It's Sunday, we can have a lie in, forget we're in Africa. I'll make you breakfast in bed.'

In bed they cuddled close to each other.

'What do you want for breakfast then?'

'Oh, croissants, coffee . . . '

'Orange juice . . . '

'Sunday papers . . . '

'Sex . . . '

They hugged each other hard.

They were woken in the middle of the night by sounds of footsteps coming towards the house. A knock at the door. Jo woke at once. More knocking. Rick was still asleep, she shook his shoulder.

'Rick, there's someone at the door.'

The knock again, this time raised voices.

'Don't open it.'

But she was already out of bed, dragging on a t-shirt and trousers. The dog growled. She went to the door with the torch and panga in her hand.

'Who's there?'

'Open up, Assistant Chief.'

At first glance she thought she'd been tricked; a crowd of men, three or four, invisible faces.

'Don't be frightened.' Isaiah's voice. 'May we come in?'

'Isaiah? What's happened?' Her own voice trembled.

'Who is it?' Rick was beside her, dressed in the flowery khanga hastily twisted round.

'It's OK.'

The men came in and sat squeezed close together on the blue sofa – Mr Katambo, the headmaster of the school, J.K. and another man she didn't know. Isaiah bolted the door behind them.

'What's going on?' She saw they all had sticks, Isaiah had a knife in his belt, he pulled his jacket across to cover it.

Jo lit the hurricane lamp, turned off the torch and sat down on a stool by the table. Rick remained standing beside her with his arms folded across his naked chest.

'We've caught the men,' J.K. said.

'No mistake this time,' Mr Katambo puffed himself up as he spoke, 'Mwambete here was at the Babylon Bar last night,' he indicated the man beside him, who'd taken off his hat and was sitting awkwardly with it on his knees. 'How can I say? . . . . He was relieving himself when he overheard some quiet talk.'

Isaiah had picked a matchstick out of the box and was chewing it, flicking it up and down between his teeth. Jo glanced at him and saw that Rick was also watching. Mr Katambo got out a handkerchief and mopped his brow – it must have been out of habit as the room was cool and he wasn't sweating.

'As soon as I heard a description of these men I knew it was the ones. Even the shirt was the same as you described, a black shirt with a white V.' He got it the wrong way round, it had been a white shirt with a black V, but she didn't interrupt. 'They were planning to break into the bar at Kingangi.'

Rick sat down on the edge of the table, pushing the khanga down between his legs. Isaiah was tapping the floor with his foot.

'When Mwambete told me we went straight to Kingangi. It was four hours before they came – but they weren't expecting an ambush. We caught them red-handed, isn't that right, Mwambete?' The man was fiddling with the band on his hat, he nodded. It was a strange scene; Rick in the thin cotton khanga, the other men dressed warmly in dark clothes, all gathered around the low-burning lamp.

Isaiah was sitting close to her, she uncrossed her legs and moved her foot so it was only an inch or so from his. He was barefoot again, she glanced at his splayed-out hard-nailed toes. He didn't draw his foot away. She looked at the men sitting opposite, low down on the sofa, with their sticks on the floor, and couldn't think what to say.

'How did you catch them?'

'I'm coming to that.' Mr Katambo tucked the handkerchief back in his pocket. 'We waited, just silent, listening. When they came we heard a noise. They took out the panes of glass. One of them climbed in and unbolted the door. We stayed behind the counter, they couldn't see us there. But it was just as Mwambete had heard; that big man went to the bedroom, the others broke open the money drawer. Then we jumped on them and tied their hands and feet with rope.'

The same crime again.

'Was it the same man – the one I described?'

'No doubt. This is the one. A thug.'

'Where are they now?' Rick suddenly asked.

'I'd already alerted the police, one was with us, the other waiting at my home with the car.'

'So they've been taken to the police station?'

'That's right. We will go there tomorrow and Jo will identify them.' Mr Katambo leant forward and lowering his voice said, 'The police may try to confuse you, but this man is wearing that same shirt with USA on the back, you must just point to him.' He looked at Rick, 'Sorry for the disturbance, now I think we can leave you to sleep some more.'

They got up to go, Mr Katambo struggling out of the sofa.

'Thank you,' Jo said.

'I will send the car in the morning.'

They left, each shaking her hand and then Rick's as they stepped out. Isaiah, come and gone in the night without a word.

'Thank you,' she said again as she gripped his hand.

He was unable to suppress a smile.

CHAPTER TWENTY

'Josie, I think you should come home with me now.'

'How can I?'

Jo and Rick were sitting at the back of the Babylon Bar finishing the beers that Mr Katambo had bought them. It was eleven o'clock on Sunday morning and Mr Katambo had left to go to church.

'I've got a Barclaycard,' Rick said. 'I'm sure we could get you a ticket.'

'I don't want to come home.'

'But now they've been caught and everything.'

'There'll be a trial – I'll have to give evidence.'

'Not yet though?'

'On the 23rd.'

She laid the small piece of yellow paper on the table in front of him:

BOND TO ATTEND COURT

I do hereby bind myself to attend before the Resident Magistrate's Court at Kizui at 0900 am o'clock on the 23rd day of October next, or when called upon, and then and there to give evidence in the matter of a charge of ROBBEREY WITH VIOLENCE against one PETER KASINA MALUKI and others . . . A name to that face, Peter Kasina Maluki, *. . . and in case of making default herein, I bind myself to forfeit to the Government of Kenya the sum of Shillings 1,000.*

Rick picked it up. 'They've spelt robbery wrong.'

'I know.' She laughed.

'It's quite soon – two weeks on Thursday. Maybe I could stay another week to be with you for the trial, and then we could go home together.'

'I'm not sure if I'll want to go home then.'

'Just for a rest – you're worn out.'

Jo had slept little after the disturbance of the night before. It got light at six and the dog whined to go out. She left Rick in bed, got dressed and unlocked the front door. Hassan, the watchman, was down by the pawpaw tree, she raised a hand to him and he touched his hat. Then she sat indoors and tried to read but her mind kept wandering. In the end she decided to go outside and slash the grass.

'What the hell are you doing?'

Rick had been watching for several minutes before she noticed him. There was sweat on her forehead and bloody marks on her legs where thorns had leapt up and scratched her.

'I wondered where on earth you'd got to. You're going to be exhausted – you can've only had a couple of hours sleep.'

'I'm OK.'

'How about some breakfast?'

'No thanks.'

She began slashing the grass again.

'Jo. Don't be silly, you've got to eat.'

'I will later, after we've been to the police.'

He made her a piece of bread and honey and poured a mug of milk. She came in and washed.

'I'm worried I'm not going to recognise them.'

'You will. You'll know as soon as you see them.'

She ate the bread and sipped the milk.

'I just can't remember what he looks like.'

'Don't worry. You'll do fine.'

At eight o'clock the driver arrived and they went straight to the police station. Mr Katambo looked spruce, he was wearing his best blue suit and the orange tie he'd had on the first time they met.

'You've remembered what I said? USA.'

She nodded. 'What about the other two? Will I have to identify them as well?'

'I'm not sure. But it's the big man who matters. The others are just boys.'

When they arrived, the Chief of Police directed Jo straight into his office. Mr Katambo tried to follow but was told to wait in the outer room with Rick.

'I think you know the procedure,' the Chief of Police said, 'You will be asked to identify the man you saw in your house. If he is not there you must say and we will bring others for you to see.'

He took her into the courtyard where a line of men was waiting as before.

She recognised her attacker at once, he was looking at her. For a second their eyes met.

She walked along the row, past the slouching bodies in grey-coloured clothes, the sullen faces. He was tall and smartly dressed, in jeans and a white shirt, she stopped.

'This is the man,' she stepped back as she said it. He had his head held upright, looking at her, defying her.

'Which one?' the Chief of Police asked, 'You say it's him?' He dragged an old man out of the line. 'Is it? Is this the "mzee" who beat you?'

A boy in the line sniggered and the policeman swung around and swiped him across the head.

'So you don't know who it is. You've just invented this story to waste our time.'

'No sir, this is the man,' she pointed again, 'The man next to him.'

'You! Step forward.'

He stepped out of the line, slowly, reluctantly, head still upright but turned slightly to the side as if to avoid a blow.

'Have you seen this woman before?'

The question was in Kikamba, but she understood.

'No, never.'

The policeman hit him.

'Tell the truth, have you?'

'I don't know, maybe she's from the Mission, perhaps I've seen her at the church.'

In the lobby of the police station Mr Katambo was standing at the desk anxiously trying to look through to the yard.

'You identified him?'

'Yes.'

'With the letters?' he whispered.

She'd glanced behind her as the men were led away and saw the bold white letters on the back of his shirt.

'Yes.'

'"USA"?' Mr Katambo checked.

She nodded.

'But did you recognise him?' Rick asked.

'As soon as I saw him.'

'Good, good.'

Mr Katambo was still twitchy. He was called to the other end of the desk by the junior policeman and asked to sign a bond to attend court as a witness.

'You're sure it was the right man?' Rick asked.

'Yes, don't go on at me,' she snapped at him, 'I'm quite sure.'

They left the police station and headed straight for the Babylon Bar.

'Mr Katambo, let me buy the drinks,' Rick said.

'No, no, you are the visitor. And please, call me Gabriel.' He grinned at Jo, 'The Angel Gabriel, is it?'

'I think so.'

He chuckled, 'God has been on our side.'

Three Tuskers arrived as soon as they'd sat down, cold ones for Jo and Rick and a warm bottle for Mr Katambo. He felt it before he poured it out.

'Cold beer isn't good for my stomach,' he explained to Rick.

'You must let us pay,' Jo said, 'So we can thank you.'

'No, this should never have happened, it's terrible, terrible.'

The road in front of the bar was busy with groups of people, smartly dressed in scarves and coloured dresses, the men in suits and ties and hats, all making their way to church. Some of the children were already singing and beating drums. Suddenly, Mr Katambo pushed aside his bottle of beer and got up to go.

'Church, church,' he said, 'Can you come?'

'No, I don't think so.'

'She doesn't like Church!' he said to Rick, 'Take one more beer instead.'

He pulled a bundle of notes out of his pocket, paid the bar girl, and hurried off down the road to catch up with a group of friends.

'He seems to know everyone,' Rick said.

'He's a very nice man, I got him all wrong to begin with.'

'I'm sure he'd understand if you wanted to go back to England for a short while.'

'No, I don't think so, if I left after the trial, he'd think I was never coming back.'

'But you've done your bit for them out here.'

'I don't see it like that.'

'Well, that's why you came isn't it? To make a contribution.'

She put her hands on the edge of the table, tipped back her chair and swung on the legs, staring up at the sky.

'It's different now, I've made friends here.'

'Of course, but you've got hundreds of friends at home as well, people who're the same as you. Anyway, you can't live here for ever.'

'Maybe not. But I don't want to come home yet.' She let go of the edge of the table and let the chair fall forward onto four legs again. 'I'm starving, let's go and find something to eat. Unless you want to go to church?'

In one of the small shops at the back of the Babylon she ordered a bowl of githeri and Rick had stew.

After a while he stopped eating and rested the spoon on the edge of the plastic dish, 'Jo, don't you miss lots of things about home?'

'Not really, apart from people.'

'I mean the comforts, don't you long to have a bath and watch telly and sleep in a decent bed?'

'Only when you mention it.'

She pushed the beans around her plate.

'Don't you think it would do you good to come home for a while? Everyone would love to see you.'

'It's not that I wouldn't like to, but it would be too easy wouldn't it, to go home after the trial and never come back? I couldn't just abandon my work.'

'It's not really that is it?'

'Partly.'

'And partly because of that man.'

'Which man?'

'The one in the beret who came last night. He's the one isn't he?'

She tore off a bit of chapati and folded it in her fingers.

'How do you know?'

'If you really want to know, I saw your feet brushing together.'

'Rick, I'm so sorry.'

'It's alright, don't get all uptight, you did warn me.'

He picked up his spoon and went on eating.

'What about you?' she asked after a while, 'Have you got a girlfriend at home?'

It was both her greatest wish and fear that he should fall in love while she was gone.

'Not really, there's someone I was seeing a bit of.'

'Who?'

'An ex-student, she's at the Royal College now.'

'So we're quits, that makes me feel jealous too.'

'You know it's not the same.'

They saw Isaiah several times before Rick left, but never more than to pass the time of day. They met one afternoon in the market at Matundu, shook hands, exchanged greetings and parted.

'He's a good-looking man,' Rick said.

'Yes.'

'I suppose he's waiting till I'm out of the way again.'

'I don't know.'

'Of course you do, anyone can see.'

At the end of the week, Jo and Rick took a bus to Mombasa and found a place to stay in one of the thatched bandas on the edge of the beach. They swam and sunbathed and at low tide walked out to the coral reef and looked at the corals, the fat red starfish and black-spined urchins. In the afternoons they made love in the cool of the house. They bought limes and mangoes from a local store, and fish from the old men who came along the sand selling their catch from baskets on the back of their bicycles. At night coconuts fell from the palms, thudding onto the sand below, and in the morning Rick went out to find one and smashed it open on a rock by the house. They didn't talk about Kingangi, or the trial. Rick played the harmonica, Jo read and wrote letters for him to take to England. At some unspoken point they made peace with each other.

On the last day they walked up the beach to the clean sand in front of the Jadini hotel where the weed had been swept up and buried. They acquired a couple of hotel sunbeds and ordered expensive lime juices to drink. Before long two young men came along with wooden carvings to sell. Jo bought one for her mother.

'I hope she likes it, will you explain I had to buy it?'

'You didn't have to Josie.'

'I feel so guilty lying here sunbathing.'

'They're used to it, anyway they need tourists.' Rick was running his fingers over the smooth black wood, it was the figure of a woman with a baby on her back, 'Anyway, it's not that bad, in fact I think it's rather nice.'

'Maybe you could tell her it came from where I live, and not say we bought it on the beach.'

'Josie, I'm going home loaded with lies already.'

The last thing Jo did before they left the beach was to dig out the jiggers from Rick's feet. She enjoyed it; the skill of tearing a bigger hole in the skin with the point of a needle and then gently levering and squeezing the jigger out, making sure it came out whole, not bursting and leaving the hooked end embedded.

'Keep still.'

'I didn't move.' He bit his lip. 'I think you enjoy this, causing me pain.'

'Of course,' she laughed, 'This is the last one, I've almost got it.'

'I think it deserves to be transported to England.'

They bought bags of salted cashew nuts down by the ferry before crossing back to Mombasa town, then went to Biashara Street to find cloth and khangas for Rick to take home as presents.

It became cooler in the night as the train heaved uphill towards

Nairobi, the tall palms and leafy bananas that were dripping with moisture soon gave way to flat open plains and dry savannah grass. When they woke at dawn and looked out through the windows there were zebra and gazelle chasing on the plains of Nairobi National Park. Rick's last photo was of a crowd of children gathered in the back yard of one of the railway houses waving at the train.

He hurried through Nairobi like an old hand, refusing all offers of a taxi at the station and crossing the street at once when someone bumped into him on the pavement.

'It's OK once you know the tricks isn't it?' he said.

'I can just see you in London, checking behind you whenever someone stops to ask the time!'

'Funny to think I'll be half-way there this time tomorrow. Then getting the tube back home. And it'll probably be raining.'

'At least you've got a good tan, that should last a while.'

They couldn't afford to go out for a meal so they bought a bottle of pawpaw wine and some bread and cheese and after a long hot bath had a candlelit dinner on the double bed in their hotel room.

The taxi came at four in the morning, she watched Rick dressing quickly, then he came and lay on the bed and hugged her to him.

'It's been great, Josie.'

'Thanks for coming.'

She bit back her tears till he'd left the room and then leapt out of bed and stood at the window with tear drops streaming down her face. It seemed a long way down from the sixth floor, but she could see Rick shaking hands with the taxi driver and the two of them pushing his rucksack into the back seat. Then he got in and the battered old car lurched away.

She didn't stir again till ten o'clock when a chambermaid came in to make the beds; Jo heard the door being unlocked and woke not knowing where she was. The woman retreated as soon as she saw her in bed.

'Sorry, sorry, madam,' she said.

Jo got up and searched the room for a note from Rick. She found it in the bathroom scribbled on a sheet of hotel paper and weighted down with his penknife. There were also two ten-pound notes.

'Just in case you think it's been a waste of time it's been the best holiday of my life. Good luck with the trial. Treat yourself to something nice.'

She read it again and pressed it to her.

'OK, come on Jo, action!' Fighting the emptiness of being alone she talked to herself. 'The important thing is to keep busy.' She had a bath, washed her hair and dried the soap to take with her. Then she smoothed the bed, tidied up the rubbish from their picnic, emptied her coins into the ashtray for the chambermaid and put the candle in her bag and left the room.

In the bank she changed one of the ten pound-notes and then went to Woolworths to buy paper and pencils for the kids and face cream for Jerusa. She walked past the Thorn Tree without looking in, not wanting to be reminded of the morning when she'd sat waiting for Rick to arrive.

'How time flies, so your friend's gone already?' Geoff was eating his breakfast of currant scone with butter off a paper plate on his desk. 'You're looking very brown, you must have got down to the coast after all.'

'We spent a week in Mombasa, staying in one of those bandas on the South coast.'

'How are you feeling then?'

'Fine.'

'I think you needed a bit of relaxation.' He picked up the last few crumbs of scone on the end of a finger, pressed them into his mouth and dropped the plate in the bin, 'So what's new from Kingangi?'

'Quite a lot really. The men have been arrested.'

He wrote it all down as she spoke and when she'd finished he looked up and smiled.

'Well this is excellent news. I thought we'd get them in the end.'

'Will you be able to come for the trial?'

'Of course, no problem.'

'It's on the 23rd.' She fiddled with a pen on the edge of his desk, rolling it backwards and forwards. 'What do you think it'll be like? I've never been in court before.'

'The normal sort of thing – there'll be a police prosecutor.'

'Mr Katambo – the Assistant Chief – wants me to lie about the other two men and say I recognise them as well.'

'Well, that's up to you really. But you've got a while to sort out what you're going to say. We can have a chat beforehand, I'll try and get there early.'

Nairobi city made her think of Rick. She phoned Diana and got on a crowded bus going up to Westlands.

When she arrived the house was in a state of upheaval. Fidelis was busy packing crockery into crates of wood shavings, Moses was taking down the pictures from the walls and Diana was supervising. She had her hair knotted up in a scarf, and was wearing an overall over a t-shirt and jeans.

'Excuse the mess. All this is going on ahead – luckily the company's paying – we've got enough to fill a museum.'

'I'd no idea you were leaving.'

'Well, it's happened in rather a rush really, but Jeremy hasn't been very happy for some time, and what with the attempted coup and everything else it just seemed foolish to hang on any longer.' She passed a glass decanter to Fidelis. 'Jeremy's taking early retirement and we're going to move back to the cottage till we find somewhere in London.'

'I didn't think you'd ever leave.'

'Well, I didn't either, but things have changed so much. Jeremy hasn't been getting the contracts any more, all the work is going to Africans.'

'What's he going to do in England?'

'Oh, he'll paint and maybe do a bit of committee work. He's looking forward to it.'

'And you?'

'Goodness knows, I suppose I'll have to learn to cook and dust the furniture.'

Diana had unrolled a huge piece of foam and was folding it around the tall ebony figure that used to stand in the window supporting a plant on its head. 'I'm trying not to think about it.' She stopped and gazed out of the window. 'But I don't feel that England's home any more, we've been away too long.'

Fidelis and Moses had picked up the packing case and were carrying it out to the garage.

'What about Fidelis?'

'He's retiring. He's going back to his family in Murang'a. Jeremy's opened a bank account for him with enough to last for his old age.' She wiped away a tear. 'He's been with us almost thirty years.'

'And Moses?'

'He wants to be a guard, so Jeremy's trying to get him a job in town. But of course he's terribly tribal, he only wants to work with other Luos.' She whispered, 'He and Fidelis never really got on. Moses says Kikuyus only think about money.'

Jo perched on the arm of the leather sofa while Diana continued to pick things off the shelves and put them in piles.

'Do you want anything? We've got far more than we can fit in the cottage. How about this?' She offered Jo a small bronze sculpture, 'We picked it up in Benin years ago, I think it's rather nice.'

'Oh no, you must take it.'

'Go on, you could always sell it and buy something useful. I'll put it in your room.' She went out of the room, then popped her head back in. 'And you must choose what books you want, there must be lots of young people out there who'll make far better use of them than our kids ever will.'

CHAPTER TWENTY-ONE

In the courtroom the young policeman in the dock wet himself with fear, a pool of urine trickled around his foot. He was the last witness to be called, he held up the piece of rope for the magistrate to see.

'We believe this was used to tie up the victim.'

They'd waited all day for her case to come up, crowding at the door of the courtroom with other onlookers, listening as each case was called; an old man who'd been beaten by thugs and had his cattle stolen, a mother whose child had been raped – none of them were believed. The mother was determined, waving her clenched fist, thumping the dock, not afraid of the magistrate looking down on her. He was a well-dressed man in spectacles, sitting high up at the end of the courtroom, surrounded by papers, doodling with a fountain pen as the woman pleaded with him. He leant forward and whispered down to the clerk.

'Enough,' the clerk said, 'We've heard enough, the next case.'

The woman was dragged out of the dock. She turned defiantly as she left and shouted back at them.

The clerk passed another file to the magistrate. Jo's case was called. The three accused came in, one was wearing platform shoes. Jo was summoned to the dock to face them. She swore on the Bible. The magistrate turned to her.

'Which is the man you say you saw in your house?'

'Saw in my house', that man raped me, put a knife to my throat and raped me.

'The one on the right.'

'What about the other men, were they in your house too?'

'I recognise the one in the middle, not the other one.' All along she'd been going to lie, she knew he'd been involved, there was no doubt about it, she'd promised Mr Katambo that she would lie. But now it came to the point she couldn't.

Mr Katambo had arrived with the young policeman early that morning.

'We need some evidence, what about that rope, the one they used to tie you, where is it?'

'I've no idea, they took it with them.'

'But you have some rope?' He picked up the dog's lead. 'What is this?'

'You can't take that.'

'We must have some evidence, something to show in the court.'

'What about my clothes and the sunglasses.'

'They've been mislaid.'

In the end she'd agreed to cut off a piece of the lead, Mr Katambo had tied a knot in one end and frayed the other with the knife, then he'd given it to the policeman who'd put it in his pocket.

Waiting outside the courtroom by the barbed wire fence, she'd smiled at a woman sitting in the shade. Jerusa noticed and pulled on her arm.

'That is the mother,' she said.

Jo moved away.

'I didn't know that was his mother.' It was the woman who sold mangoes in Kingangi.

'You can't have sympathy for her, everyone knows she's dishonest.'

The woman was with two others, close together beneath the tree that was the only patch of shade. They were knitting children's jerseys in brightly coloured wool.

Isaiah returned from the road.

'I couldn't see the Field Director, maybe the landrover has broken down.'

'He said he'd be here before nine. I hope he hasn't had an accident.'

'He'll come soon, don't worry.'

But by midday Geoff still hadn't appeared.

The court was adjourned for lunch and Jo and Jerusa and Isaiah went to the Babylon to get a soda. Mr Katambo hurried off in the other direction. He'd been agitating all morning, calling Jo over to whisper to her.

'Remember to say about the rope; say your hands were tied.'

They'd pushed their way to the front of the crowd at the door when they thought her case was going to be called and saw the clerk shuffling a file to the bottom.

'They're trying to put it off,' Isaiah said, 'They want to run out of time so it'll have to be postponed.'

'I will speak to the magistrate,' Mr Katambo said.

They didn't eat any lunch but went straight back to the court as soon as they'd finished their sodas. The heavy wooden doors were locked and no one was around. Isaiah leaned against the wall and lit a cigarette.

After a while a lorry drew into the yard. The back was let down and a group of men forced off. They were handcuffed in pairs. The policeman shouted at them and they squatted down in a line.

'OK, move!'

They shuffled forward, hopping across the compound, crouched forms indistinguishable from one another.

'That's him, the second pair, the one in those shoes,' Isaiah whispered to Jo.

She looked but couldn't make him out.

'Which one?'

'With the shaved head.'

Now she faced him across the courtroom. With his hair shaved his head looked bigger, the eyes smaller.

'Now the accused may question the witness.'

He spoke in Kikamba but stared at her as if she understood. The clerk translated.

'You say that the man was five foot eleven inches, but I am not that height.'

'You're wearing platform shoes.' Who should she address? She turned to the magistrate. 'He was barefoot, he's now wearing platform shoes.'

'You say there was a knife at your neck, but you weren't hurt were you?' His face seemed to punch at the air across the room as if he were threatening her again. She waited for the clerk to translate, staring back at him, her hands clasped on either side of the rail in front of her.

'I wasn't hurt with the knife,' she turned to the magistrate again, 'But I was raped.'

'Rape is not the charge, we are considering a case of robbery with violence. The accused is asking if you were hurt, can you answer please?'

'Yes, I was hurt, I was kicked and punched, my head was banged against the wall, my hands were tied behind my back.'

'How can you know I was the man, it was dark.'

She waited for the translation although she'd understood what he said. 'It wasn't pitch dark, I saw your face and your shirt.'

He laughed, 'Too many people have this shirt, haven't you seen so many in town?'

'I recognise your face.'

Confident, he turned to the magistrate and spoke in English, 'I have no more questions, this woman is lying.'

'You may leave the dock,' the magistrate said.

She was paralysed for a moment, suddenly aware of the people who'd been watching, faces she recognised from the village, others she didn't know, schoolboys in pink shirts sitting on each other's shoulders to look in from the doorway.

'Tell the mzungu to leave the dock.'

She was shaking as she squeezed onto the end of the bench and waited for Mr Katambo to be called from outside. He entered the dock and put his hand on the Bible. Jerusa took Jo's hand.

The magistrate interrupted Mr Katambo, 'Be brief please, we are considering one case only.'

The mother of the accused was sitting on the bench in front of them, staring up at her son.

The magistrate left the court. The prisoners were led away, she heard the lorry engaging gear. Still no sign of Geoff. She thanked the young policeman.

'It was his first case,' Mr Katambo explained.

'What happens now?' she asked.

'There'll be judgment in some weeks' time.'

'I thought there'd be a verdict today.'

'The magistrate has to consider all the evidence for the case. But it was very good. I'm sure we have won.'

The driver dropped Jo and Isaiah off at the top of the hill and they walked down to her house. Jerusa had gone home to rest; the baby was due in a month's time and she was tired after the long day of waiting.

'Did I do OK?' Jo asked.

'You were so strong.'

'It wasn't what I was expecting, I didn't think they'd ask me questions.'

'That man's clever because he's been in court before. I thought he was going to trick you, but you didn't let him, you frightened him.'

'Do you think he'll be sentenced?'

'He has to.'

'How long?'

'I don't know, maybe two years.'

As they turned from the track onto the path she saw that a land-rover was parked outside her house.

'Just when I thought we were going to be on our own. Typical that he turns up now when he's no longer needed.'

Geoff was leaning against the bonnet smoking his pipe. He shook hands with Jo and then with Isaiah.

'I'm really sorry I didn't make it, I broke down on one of those hills just after Machakos.'

They went indoors. Geoff sat on the sofa and Isaiah on a stool at the desk. Jo fetched cups and a jug of water.

'We were worried that you'd had an accident,' she said as she gave him some water.

'I got stranded in the middle of nowhere. None of the buses would stop. In the end I got a lift with a priest. Then I had to wait hours at the garage for the mechanics to get back from another breakdown. It cost a small fortune too. But I'm terribly sorry. How was it?'

She was reluctant to talk, wanting to block it from her mind and keep at bay the conflicting feelings of victory and guilt.

He prompted her, 'Jo?'

'Pretty tough.'

'But it went OK?'

'I think so.'

'You made it clear you recognised the man?'

She nodded. 'His mother was there too.'

Geoff didn't respond.

'I didn't realise the accused would ask me questions.'

'That's normal, I should've warned you.'

Geoff finished his water and lit his pipe again. 'And the verdict?'

'We've got to wait,' Isaiah said, 'Judgment won't be till next month.'

Jo told no one about the letter that came a week later from Geoff.

Dear Josephine,

I'm writing to tell you that after discussion with the British High Commission in Nairobi and our Head Office in London, I consider it no longer safe for you to remain in Kingangi.

Whilst I appreciate that the men will be held in custody until judgment day and that sentences may be imposed thereafter, it is nevertheless impossible to guarantee your safety in Kingangi, and the organisation can no longer take responsibility for you working there alone.

This is in no way a reflection on your work which has been excellent, nor will it mean that your project collapses, as we are considering sending a male engineer to take over.

However, our assessment is that in the light of what happened to you and the general feeling of unrest in the country as a whole, it would be advisable for you to leave Kingangi before the end of your contract – as soon as possible.

Please would you reply by return of post so that I can make arrangements for your homeward flight.

I will be writing to Mr Katambo as soon as I hear from you and shall put to him the possibility of a replacement worker.

I regret having to take this decision and would like to emphasise that it in no way reflects the efforts you've made there and the courage you've shown. I hope you will understand that it is for the best – both for you and the organisation.

With best wishes,
Geoffrey Gordon.

She walked up to the school late that afternoon, hoping to meet Isaiah. She'd seen little of him in the week since the trial. He was living as before in the cramped room at the back of the school and teaching English to the 'O' level students. Once every week he had to report to the Chief's office in Kizui.

'That's how they're arresting the students now,' he'd told Jo, 'If we don't turn up we get expelled from the university. But then if our name's on the list we're arrested by the police.'

He'd spoken slowly as if to impress upon her the seriousness of the situation.

'Will your name be on the list?'

'Who knows where they get their information from.'

'But is it likely? Why won't you tell me?'

'You know enough about this country.'

He was distant and enigmatic again, as if determined to suppress his feelings and hold only to this formal friendship. He'd thrown himself into his work, talking of little else, refusing to engage in deeper conversation.

'Why are you being so strange?'

'Strange? I don't understand what you mean.'

'Not speaking to me.'

'I am speaking – we're speaking now.'

She let it drop, reluctant to discover the meaning of his resolve; whether it were the sign of the end or some deeper wish for suffering.

There was to be a harambee – a fund-raising celebration – at the school, to raise money to build a science laboratory. The students had whitewashed stones and laid them on the track leading up to the gates. The hedge had been cut, the barbed wire fence taken down and borders of red canna lilies planted outside the classrooms. Bhangi had been employed to clean the compound. He'd slashed the long grass around the football pitch, cleared the cigarette stubs from under the mango trees at the back of the kitchen huts and scrubbed the latrines. That afternoon when Jo arrived he was sweeping the sand of the front yard. Someone had given him a new shirt and trousers and he'd abandoned the tins that used to hang around his waist. The students were washing the classroom floors. They were barefoot; the girls were scrubbing with dirty sacks and the boys throwing in buckets of water, then sweeping it out with branches torn from the trees.

'Where's Mr Mutisya?' she asked a girl who was crossing the yard with a drum of water on her back.

'Performing drama.'

'Whereabouts?'

The girl put down the drum and led Jo round the back of the classrooms. Isaiah was directing a group of students gathered beneath the trees. They were armed with sticks, acting out a conflict. She watched for a while before he noticed her. Then he came over.

'We're producing a play for the harambee.'

'I won't disturb you.'

'No, stay and watch. You can tell me what you think.' He smiled, 'It'll test your Kikamba.'

She leant against a tree and watched Isaiah as the students acted. She'd left the letter in her house, but fragments of the sentences were vivid in her mind: . . . *no longer safe for you to remain . . . advisable to leave as soon as possible . . . arrangements for your homeward flight . . . for the best* . . . . Isaiah moved around, waving the actors on, signalling them to fall to the ground, once clapping when they got it how he wanted. He was wearing the blue shirt she'd bought him in Nairobi, it had darkened from sweat under the arms and hung loose outside his trousers. Suddenly he pulled a knife from his belt and thrust it towards a student. The boy leapt back.

'OK, act like that!' Isaiah said.

The students left, still fighting with each other, pretending to draw knives and staggering to the ground. Isaiah picked up the couple of chairs that had been used as props and came over to Jo.

'Did you like it?' he asked.
'It was good.'
'It's about an Akamba boy who goes to the University. It begins with the mother selling the cow to pay for his clothes and books. Then he gets involved with politics, there's a coup attempt and he's arrested.'
'Is that what the parents will want to see?'
'It's what the students wanted to do.'
'You mean it's what you wanted to do.'
'It's a serious subject.'
'I was only joking.'
'There are university students now who're locked up. Friends of mine. They'll be beaten by the police, they'll have unfair trials and be sentenced to years of imprisonment. People have got to know about it.'
'It's OK, you don't have to preach to me.'
They walked together back to the classroom and put the chairs away.
'Isaiah?' Her voice echoed in the empty classroom. She picked up a stub of chalk from the edge of the blackboard and rolled it in the palm of her hand. 'I've had a letter from the Field Director.'
He didn't respond. A boy rushed in with a rolled-up exercise book in his hand. 'Please, can you mark for me?'
Isaiah took the book. They went out and he locked the classroom padlock behind them.
'I want to talk to you about this letter.'
'Don't talk about anything until after judgment day.'
'But I have to reply.'
'It's better to wait – until after Judgment, after harambee.'
They walked as far as the turning to the teachers' houses where he stopped and turned at the gateway, forbidding her to follow further.
'I'd like to type the script,' he said, 'With carbons so all the actors can see a copy.'
'When?'
'Tomorrow?'

If I go home to England it'll be safe and I'll be wanted she thought. But the reply could wait. There was no hurry.

Isaiah came early in the morning while Jo was still having breakfast. She gave him some tea and offered him bread and margarine.

'No, I'll eat when I've finished.'

He sat at the typewriter, typing with two fingers, working assiduously, only occasionally pausing to try something out loud. Jo swept the house, did her washing, tidied the bookshelf, moving silently around him.

'How's it going?'

'Good, good.' He didn't look up.

'I'm going for a walk with the dog.'

'Can you buy me a cigarette?'

When she got back he'd finished and was sitting on the sofa stapling the scripts together.

'Here's your cigarette.'

He took it and put it behind his ear.

'You owe me ten cents,' she said.

He turned out his pockets.

'Tomorrow?'

'Forget it.'

'I have to go now.'

'Aren't you going to thank me for lending you the typewriter and all that paper?'

'Asante sana.'

'That's OK.'

He was standing at the door, rolling the cigarette in one hand and clasping the bundle of papers in the other.

'Isaiah, there's no point being friends if we hardly talk to each other.'

'Too many things divide us.'

'Like what?'

'I don't know how to speak to you after what has happened.'

'But it's over now.'

'Not until the judgment.'

She shut the lid on the typewriter and hid it away out of sight behind the bookshelf. Isaiah didn't move from the door. She turned and stared at him. He took out a match and lit the cigarette.

'Tell me the truth,' she said, 'Is it that you see me differently now, because I was raped?'

'No.'

'I think it is. You're making excuses to cover up your feelings.'

'What? How can you know my feelings?'

He bent down and flattened the burning end of the cigarette beneath his shoe, then put the stub away behind his ear and came towards her. She backed away to the wall, arms folded across her chest.

'You're always running away. You're frightened. You don't love me any more.'

She almost smiled, feeling strong and excited by her words. She went into the kitchen to get the hurricane lamp, allowing him to leave. He followed.

'You are the most important person to me.' He spoke gently.

'But only as a responsibility, not a passion.'

His eyes were watery. 'There can't be passion until that man is punished and we're safe to be together again.'

'Just leave me alone then.'

It was still hard to sleep at night. Sometimes the dog growled in its sleep and she would be convinced that it had heard a noise. She stirred at the slightest sound and would turn on the torch and shine it around the room. Sometimes she dreamt that men had entered the room; she would wake and open her eyes to see them leaning over her. In the daylight it seemed ridiculous.

On October 10th, the day before the harambee, judgment was passed.

Peter Kasina Maluki was sentenced to twelve months imprisonment and four strokes. The two other men were found not guilty.

Mr Katambo and Isaiah came together late that afternoon to tell her the news. They sat on the sofa discussing the outcome.

'We've won,' Isaiah said.

'But it's not enough,' Mr Katambo said, 'It should have been five years.'

'Even if he can only suffer some short time, it'll mean he's punished.'

'It should have been more, six or seven years.'

'But he'll sweat in that cell.'

'The others should have been sentenced as well.'

'Yes.'

They talked as if it were not to do with her, as if she no longer belonged to the crime. And then they left to drink beer in Kingangi village.

Alone, Jo felt neither relief nor a sense of victory. She took out the letter from Geoff and walked around the room, reading it over again. Maybe it was just pride that kept her hanging on – a 'mzungu' in a strange land where no one knew her well.

She got out Rick's penknife and opened the tin of sardines that she'd bought from the mswahili's shop in Kizui town. The dog liked sardines, he stirred from under the sofa and came licking at her feet. She put two fish in his bowl and ate the others with a fork from the tin, standing looking out through the kitchen window as darkness fell.

'Hi, Rick, I've come home!' The hugs, laughter, tears, excitement – And then what?

Here, it was still possible that the right moment would come again, surprising her, making her certain that she should stay.

In Kingangi all interest had turned to the harambee. Wherever Jo went people were preparing for the day of celebration. She tried to feel enthusiastic but had nothing to do, no part in this grand affair.

Mr Katambo arrived at her house one afternoon in the car. It was loaded with crates of beer and sodas.

'I would like you to store them for me.'

'Sure.'

'I can't trust myself not to drink them before the day.' He patted his belly in mockery of himself.

Jo and Boniface and the driver carried the crates into the house while Mr Katambo supervised their stacking, and counted and re-counted the bottles.

'How many guests are there going to be?' Jo asked.

'So many. We've invited all the important people – from Kizui, Kingangi, Matundu, Ngondi and further. And the local MP has accepted to come – he'll give us a lot of help.' Mr Katambo picked a couple of bottles out of the top crate, 'I think we can take just one now, in anticipation of good harambee.' He drank some beer and wiped his mouth on the back of his hand, 'I've asked the old men in Ngondi to brew strong honey beer,' he laughed, 'When people are happy they're generous, is it?'

Jo's closest companion now was the dog. With the harambee approaching, interest in the Women's Group work had declined. Jerusa had left because of her pregnancy and other women stopped coming to classes and failed to produce the baskets they'd promised. Jo had to take over maintenance of the two pumps. She went down to the river each day with the dog.

She bought some coloured wool in Kizui and sat at home in the evenings knitting a jersey for Jerusa's baby. Bouncer interfered and nosed the ball around the floor. She wasn't good at knitting, nor did she enjoy it, but it was the only creative thing she could find to do. People had no time to visit her, even Museo would forget to come with the milk. Jerusa was sewing costumes for the dancers, her mother, Mutanu, was planning the food, selecting the best peas and beans and green bananas to cook. The grandmother had been mixing ochres and face paints for the dancers. At night the drummers practised on the football pitch up at the school. The girls passed by, singing. The foreign sounds drifted down.

On the morning of harambee, Museo came to fetch her. Jo had dressed carefully in clean clothes, she'd put on earrings and bracelets and the necklace of beads that Museo had strung for her.

'You must come to help the cooking!'

It was a bright day. There was a bird, a lilac-breasted roller on the post of the washing line, glossy blue in the sun. In the kitchen hut a huge earthenware pot was balanced on three stones above the fire. Mutanu was stirring with a wooden pole.

'Can you do it?' Museo asked.

Jo took the pole and tried to stir. The pot rocked. The food was thick and heavy, a mash of peas and beans, potatoes, yams and green bananas.

'No, no don't stir. Like this.'

Jerusa took the pole and thrust and pulled, mashing the food against the side.

'You must taste some.'

Mutanu scooped out a dishful; it was pinky-grey, glutinous, hot and sweet. Jo sat outside and shared it with the children, all eating with their fingers.

At two o'clock Mr Katambo and Samson Mwanza from the New Tip Top turned up in the car and parked in front of the school. The boys had carried logs down from Ngondi hill and built a banda, it was covered over with grasses and dry branches and rows of the school chairs had been arranged beneath it. Mr Katambo took up his seat in the middle, in front of a large table. He was wearing the cream safari suit, red diamond-pattern socks and polished black shoes. Samson Mwanza was in dark trousers and waistcoat, a checked jacket and wide-brimmed brown felt hat. He'd brought Jo a present of 'English' lavender soap from Nairobi. Boniface sat on the roof of the car and watched as the crowds assembled. Other children climbed the trees and scrambled onto the roofs of the classrooms. The headmaster and governors, the Chief in khaki uniform, other dignitaries and important people arrived and took their seats in the shade of the banda. The people gathered round. There was a smell of soap and hair oil. There were greetings and warm handshakes, laughter, joking. The p.a. system was tested, 'One, one . . . imwe, ili, itatu . . . one, two, three.' The children clapped. It was hot, people waited, brushing away the flies. But the MP did not arrive. He was three hours late, no one had seen him on the way. Mr Katambo stood up.

'I think we can start without our guest, he will be arriving shortly.' He got out his handkerchief and mopped his brow. 'Welcome to you all. Muriega?'

'Ii, turiega,' the crowd replied and clapped.

'Or should I say "Good afternoon and how are you?" because we have a mzungu in our midst?'

People laughed and turned to stare at Jo. Jerusa squeezed her hand. Across the crowd Jo saw J.K. and Isaiah grinning at her.

'But I think she can understand Kikamba these days. So this is harambee! Kingangi Harambee Secondary School was built in 1964. That first year we had two teachers and sixteen students. Now how many?'

'One hundred,' someone shouted out.

'Two hundred!'

'I hear you say two hundred,' Mr Katambo continued, 'Not two hundred but twice two hundred. Who can do arithmetic? We have four hundred students and nine teachers.'

She looked over to Isaiah. Their eyes met and flicked away. Around her, coloured scarves, dresses and shirts, babies tied in cloths and blankets on their mothers' backs, old men leaning on sticks, all faces turned towards Mr Katambo. She tried to listen.

'And we've had our successes. This year our first student from Kingangi will graduate from the university. We can be proud of that.'

Some people clapped. Jerusa whispered to Jo, 'Isaiah, he is the one. The first graduate.'

Jo stared across at him; calm, staring back in unsmiling modesty, the beret at a deliberate angle. A hand holding the back of his neck, the only sign of awkwardness.

'But we must not rest on our laurels. We must go from strength to strength. That is why today we are here to build our school. The money we raise will be for a science laboratory.'

Latecomers were arriving. A group of women dressed in coloured khangas top and bottom, with pink scarves tied around their hair were coming up the hill singing and shaking tambourines.

Mr Katambo went on, 'Many of you have never seen a science laboratory – you do not know what science is. But it is about progress. Progress for our children. To improve their education. To invest in the future of our great nation. Harambee!'

'Harambee!' the cry came back from the crowd.

'Harambee!' he called again.

There was clapping and stamping of feet. An old man walked forward from the crowd and handed over a bundle of notes.

'Mr Daniel Mutua!' Mr Katambo shouted, 'One thousand shillings!'

There was a steady clap.

'Mr John Kilonzo – one thousand five hundred shillings!'

It was Kilonzo, the shop-keeper. Jerusa nudged Jo,

'Where did he get that from!'

'Mr Samson Mwanza – six thousand shillings!'

The money poured in, the notes piling into the baskets on the table in front of Mr Katambo. For each gift was a heavy clap.

'Mr Ben Kyalo – two hundred shillings!'

Ben Kyalo; in his purple shirt, stooped as he walked, lifting his hat as he handed over the money. Jerusa and Museo cheered.

When the large sums had been given people came forward with single grubby notes, taken from under hats and from knots in the corners of khangas. Then the gifts to auction; goats and chickens, a woven basket, a stem of bananas. An old woman gave two eggs, a small boy ran forward with a rabbit. Mr Katambo held it up by the ears.

'A fine rabbit! How much?'

'Five shillings,' someone called.

'Six.'

'That's too cheap.'

'Twenty,' Samson said.

'Thirty!'

'Forty,' cried Samson.

'Sixty!' Jo called.

'Sixty shillings.' Mr Katambo banged the table. 'The mzungu has bought the rabbit!'

Jo pushed her way through the crowd and took the frightened creature in her hands.

'Hold it by the ears,' Museo said.

They squeezed back through the crowd and put the rabbit on a clear space of grass. Its black eyes opened wide and it froze motionless.

'Why do you want a rabbit?' Museo asked.

'I don't.'

'Will you eat it?'

'I don't think so.'

'It must get fatter before you can eat it.'

Jo gave the rabbit to a boy to take home to Jerusa's compound.

'And now we will see a performance of drama – a play – by the students of Kingangi Harambee Secondary School.'

The women with tambourines danced and sang while the important guests moved from the banda to sit in chairs on the grass outside. The shelter became the theatre, coloured sheets were hung as curtains, the stage was set. Children and students sat on the grass, women gathered on one side sitting on the ground, men on the other side on makeshift wooden benches and chairs brought from the classrooms.

A girl came through the curtains.

'This play is called "A Serious Form of Hooliganism by Misguided Youth" – the title is taken from the words of our President' – she translated into Kikamba. Faces were blank except for Mr Katambo's. He was smiling.

It was a short play. It ended with the lead actor coming to the front of the stage, thrusting his hands towards the crowd, raising them and shouting.

'What's he saying?'

'"Am I guilty?"' Jerusa said.

'No!' the crowd called back.

The curtain fell, the audience went on cheering and clapping. One of the smaller children started crying.

Mutanu and the other older women, wearing tight-wound khangas and bright headscarves, brought on the steaming food. It was served on dishes, then on leaves when the plates ran out. The girls opened bottles of beer and took them round on trays. The important visitors settled down to enjoy themselves.

Under the trees the drumming had begun.

'Come and join us!' Mr Katambo called.

Jo went over to speak to the gathered visitors.

'The mzungu, the mzungu,' said Mr Katambo, 'Miss Jo.'

She shook hands with his friends.

'Can you take some honey beer?'

He called to the old man with the gourd of beer who poured out a large tin mugful and gave it to Jo.

'Delicious.'

'The best! Is it?'

She shared the beer with Jerusa and Museo, it was sharp and strong. It filled her head – the first sip of honey beer in the yard outside his house, Isaiah buttoning up the clean white shirt.

A ululation – and from a classroom a crowd of dancers burst out. They were students, unrecognisable in tribal dress, khangas and leopard skins, bodies painted red and white, ochred hair, faces marked, rattles round their ankles. They stamped on the ground, thumping, pace, pace, to the beat of the drums. The girls formed a tight circle, the young men surrounded them, surging back and forth. They turned and faced the crowd – already people were jiggling with them, feet moving, shoulders swaying – they leapt in the air, crying out. The beat got faster, heavier – they leapt again. The women sang out, they backed away, a single dancer entered the ring. The music stopped but for a single drum that kept the rhythm. He stood in the middle pounding his feet from side to side, the animal hair about his waist swaying, swishing, the soft ksk-ksk of the rattle around his ankles, shaking his shoulders, knees bending, closer and closer to the ground.

'He has shoulders!' Jerusa said.

He kissed the earth. The drum called out, a singer replied, the drum sounded back. Dusk had come, lamps were lit and hung on the trees. J.K. and Isaiah came to stand close by. Isaiah smiled at Jo. Museo was dancing with her friends. Another man ran on. He was dressed as a woman, gourds tied to his chest as breasts and a beaded skirt about his waist – the children laughed as he jiggled in front of the guests, flirting, darting round them. The music got louder, the other dancers joined in again, women facing men – girls bending backwards, arched feet, arms thrown back, curving to the ground, men leaping, headdresses flying, limbs outstretched. The girls shaking, men thrusting – shoulders spinning, temples touching – parting, tempting, arousing.

Isaiah was beside Jo, he whispered something in her ear.

'I can't hear.'

He took her hand.

'Come.'

She pushed after him through the crowd. The drum beat was loud, the stamping harder, the ululation carried after them as they hurried down the slope, behind the schoolrooms.

He pulled her into his room and bolted the door. She could still hear the music, but distant now, echoing in her head, the bodies leaping, shaking, sweating. Muscles shining. The room smelt musty. A pile of exercise books on the desk and the *History of Africa* that Jo had brought from Diana; a glossy cover, photos of tribesmen and statesmen.

Isaiah took a khanga from the tin trunk and hung it from nails across the window.

She pulled him to her. He was shaking. She took his head in both hands.

'They want me to leave,' she said.

He paused before he answered, 'I know, I read the letter.'

'I've decided to go.'

It was more a sound than words, 'I know.'

He put his arms around her and hugged her to him. The hard beads pressed into her skin.

GLOSSARY

banda	shelter or dwelling made of wooden poles with grass roof
bhangi	marijuana, dagga
chai	tea. Often sweet with milk, sugar, water and tea leaves boiled together and strained
dagga	marijuana, bhangi
dik-dik	very small East African antelope
gecko	lizard
githeri	stew of maize and beans. Very common dish, staple food in many areas
habari gani? / habari?	standard greeting in Kiswahili, meaning What news? / News? To which the reply is Nzuri / Nzuri sana meaning Good / Very good
harambee	community fund-raising event. Meaning 'let's pull together'
jembe	digging implement with forked or spade-like blade at right angles to handle. It is swung from the shoulders
jigger	parasitic insect. Female burrows into skin of feet and beneath toenails and swells painfully as eggs are produced
jiko	cooking stove. Small round jikos fuelled with wood or charcoal are common in rural areas
kahawa	coffee
khanga	patterned cloth worn by women tied around waist or across shoulders. Also used for carrying babies
kikoi	cloth worn around waist by men, mainly in coastal areas
kiondo	woven basket
mabati	corrugated iron roofing sheets
mama	mother or woman of child-bearing age
matatu	small van which serves as taxi. Often overloaded!

mswahili	person from coastal region who speaks Kiswahili
mzee	old man
mzungu	foreigner or white person
ngai	god. A Masai word
nzuri/nzuri sana	good/very good. Response to greeting
panga	large-bladed knife, machete
shamba	garden or plot of land
shetani	devil
sufuria	round handleless cooking pot
sukuma wiki	green leafy vegetable like kale. Name means 'push the week', it's often used to eke out a small amount of maize and beans or maizemeal so that it lasts the week
ugali	stiff maizemeal. Basic foodstuff eaten with vegetable or meat stew
uji	thin maizemeal porridge drunk from cups or gourds. Often fermented
uki	honey beer